WIELDER

GATEBREAKER: BOOK TWO

MICHELLE WILSON

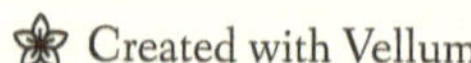 Created with Vellum

For one of my best cheerleaders and biggest inspirations, my Mamaw.

CONTENTS

*C*hills raced along my spine and down each arm as icy wind whipped at my back. I batted at my swirling violet cloak as another gust pummeled me. Only a small expanse of snow-covered ground separated my feet from the winding rows of houses that belonged to members of the Thavellian army. But no matter how small the distance, I couldn't bridge the gap.

"Lady Lydia!" The words carried on a third gust of wind that almost knocked me off my feet. I gritted my teeth and turned back toward the castle. Gabrielle hurried across the courtyard.

"You must come inside, my lady—" Gabrielle's cheeks reddened in the wind and her chest heaved from her rush through the snow. "It's almost time. You're about to be introduced."

I stifled a groan. The past few months, Gabrielle had been invaluable in helping navigate this world I found myself in. Playing soldier in the fall did nothing to prepare me for the noble court of Thavell. Without Gabrielle, I would have been hopelessly lost. She didn't deserve to bear the weight of my bad mood. I let her lead me by the arm back to the castle. It didn't matter; Murphy didn't want to talk to me, anyway.

As we entered the entryway, Gabrielle stripped the cloak from my shoulders. The room provided little warmth, but a respite from the wind was nice. In a flurry of graceful movements, Gabrielle readjusted my hair and ushered me into the line of nobles waiting to descend into the ballroom. After fluffing the giant skirt of my emerald gown, she disappeared into the crowd.

I kept my eyes trained on the couple in front of me. Only two more entrances before my own. I tucked my clammy palms into the folds of my dress. It wasn't the entrance that bothered me. Months of curtsying and dining and dancing with the nobles in Thavell had dulled me to the grandeur of it all.

No, it wasn't the entrance. It was who I had to enter with. The scene I'd had to repeat over and over for each ball of the winter season since the moment King Bleddyn announced me as the Gatebreaker.

Gabrielle explained the decorum to me. I had no family or connections here, but the king wanted to reward my good deeds. So, I became a ward of the crown. But that meant I needed an escort for every social outing.

And only one person had a rank high enough to escort me.

"My lady."

Aidric appeared at my elbow. From his dark hair to his typical dark finery, he looked every bit a fairy-tale prince. His wolf's head pin gleamed on his chest. Evergreen stitching edged the blue jacket that stretched across his shoulders. The same green as my dress. The color of the occasion.

I needed to attempt some sort of cordiality. But just like my feet wouldn't carry me across the snow that separated me from Murphy, my mouth wouldn't form the words I needed to say something nice to Aidric. I was tired of doing what I was supposed to.

Unperturbed as always, Aidric merely bowed and offered his arm. I grazed it with my hand. His arm stiffened beneath my touch. Heat flushed me from head to toe. I lifted my eyes to the ceiling and let Aidric lead us forward into the ballroom.

Swaths of color and fabric cut through the torchlight and glowing mage orbs at the bottom of the staircase.

"Introducing Prince Aidric, the Wolf-Hearted, and Lady Lydia, the Gatebreaker."

A hush fell over the crowd as the herald announced us. Below us, they gathered in a mass of deep red, rich navy, and festive green colors. The Thavellian nobility delighted in their order and customs, I'd learned. The winter was for celebrating and socializing at court. And no holiday was bigger than the Evergreen Celebration at midwinter. And every entrance mattered. Every person entered in the order of their status. The lower-ranking nobility and merchants came first. And unless there was a guest of honor, the king arrived last. Aidric and I earned the spot just before King Bleddyn, so the ballroom was full to bursting. And every eye was on us as we descended.

With each step, my eyes roamed the faces of those waiting at the bottom. The names and ranks that Gabrielle drilled me on each morning marched through my head. As soon as our steps alighted on the green carpet at the bottom of the stairs, the crowd swept into bows. For me. For both of us. It was something I'd never, ever get used to.

But Aidric was born to this life. While the sight of so many bowing made me break a cold sweat, at my side Aidric smiled and waved. The crowd arose and murmurs of conversation erupted again. I let my hand drop from Aidric's arm and he vanished into the crowd as easily as he'd arrived. A chill hit me from the absence of his body next to mine, and it wasn't just physical. I walked in the opposite direction, determined to act like seeing Aidric and his fiancee didn't bother me at all.

At the edge of the long carpet, Annistyn and Maren's faces appeared, pushing through a contingent of rather sour-faced ladies. Without a word, they arranged themselves on either side of me and swept me into the crowd. The knot in my chest loosened as we walked away from the prying eyes and dreamy princes.

"Your gown is gorgeous," Annistyn whispered into my ear.

"You would know, the note said it was a gift from your family and you'd had it specially designed." Annistyn threw a wicked smile my way. Her father was a duke and a distant cousin of the late queen. I squeezed her arm. "Thank you. You didn't have to go through that trouble."

"I enjoyed it." She brushed my thanks away with a wave of her hand. "Besides, my father is in the mood to curry favor this year. He's keeping his eyes open for a proposal."

"There is no 'currying favor' with me. I don't work like that."

Maren gave me a sidelong glance I'd gotten used to receiving these past few months.

"When will you learn?" She whacked me lightly on the arm with her fan. "You don't work like that. But the king does."

The sound of trumpets drowned out my response. The king had arrived. We'd made it to the back edge of the crowd. There we stopped to watch King Bleddyn's appearance. Already Aidric stood at the throne dais in the back of the room. Lady Jaclyn stood off to the side. I ignored the knot that reappeared in my chest.

"King Bleddyn the Mighty, Defender of Thavell."

A cheer rose from the crowd as Thavell's king greeted his nobles. On a different man, the regalia that wrapped the king from head to toe might have overtaken them. But not so King Bleddyn. He looked like he'd stepped out of a dream. Emeralds so dark they were almost black twinkled at the hems and cuffs of his royal mantle. The dark red outfit underneath matched the gems in the crown that sparkled atop his raven's feather hair. He carried a black scepter, using it like a walking stick as he descended the staircase. The black gems wrapped around it looked like they sucked the light into themselves. Each precisely placed jewel and accessory highlighted King Bleddyn's larger-than-life personality. I joined in the applause as the king reached the dais and sat on his throne.

My gaze slid to Aidric as I wondered what he would look like one day. I imagined him decked out in the same finery and sitting on the throne as the leader of his people. Only a few months older than me, Aidric already reached his father in height. They shared their dark hair and friendly dispositions. The wolf represented the Thavellian royal house. But

King Bleddyn was an alpha while Aidric reminded me of a lone wolf. And the king's black eyes didn't compare the gold flecks that sparkled in Aidric's brown ones.

At my side, Maren yanked on my arm like she could see my thoughts leading me to dangerous waters. I bowed along with the rest of the crowd.

"Arise my children." King Bleddyn motioned to us with his scepter. "Tonight, we celebrate the longest night of the year. We will eat and drink and dance to thank the spirits for giving our kingdom with ample harvests and safe borders for another year."

Another roar of cheer rose from the crowd.

"Spirits?" I whispered. Where had I heard that term before?

"It's just a saying." Maren rolled her eyes. "The stories say spirits walked the lands of Adylra before it all became the kingdom of Thavell. There's a spirit of the forest, spirit of the mountains, spirit of the skies, so on and so forth." She waved her fan in dismissal of the rest. "Talking about the spirits came back in fashion once magic returned." She shrugged. "But they're all just legends."

I huffed a noncommittal response. Why would King Bleddyn mention them if they weren't real? I knew at least one legend that was walking around, anyway. But that was another thought for another day.

"I would not be where I am today without you, my beloved nobles." King Bleddyn stood now. He opened his arms like he would embrace the entire room. "You protect the people of this kingdom and carry your humble king on your backs. This past autumn, as I fought the traitors in the Battle of the Forest, you came together and squashed the insurrection here at home. Without you, our country could have fallen."

"As the new year dawns with the morning light, remember, I made a promise to you. I will find those who would rebel and remind them why Thavell is the greatest kingdom Adylra has ever seen!"

The cheer this time made my ears ring. Annistyn, Maren, and I watched the king with rapt attention. I clapped my hands with everyone, but my heart beat against my ribcage. Everyone was so close to me. And screaming. My eyes lost their focus on the king. The sounds of the crowd faded and all I could see were bodies strewn around me on a dark forest floor.

Someone bumped into me, knocking me forward. The lady standing in front of me exclaimed something and yanked her dress out from under my feet. The sound of the crowd rushed back into my ears. I unfurled my fan and ducked my head behind it in apology. Shielding my face from everyone, I took deep breaths in and out to counts of five until my heart settled again.

My magic swelled close to the surface, but I calmed it too. I wasn't in the forest anymore. This wasn't a battle. I heard cheers, not the screams of dying soldiers. The battle was over. My magic had saved them. *I* had saved them.

You didn't save everyone. A betraying thought lingered in my head. *You still don't know where John is.*

From across the ballroom came the sound of music. Annistyn and Maren didn't notice my discomfort. They dragged me toward the dance floor. I thrust my guilt and shame into the furthest corner of my mind. Now was not the time to get dragged back into the memories that still haunted my dreams.

"I hope you've been practicing," Annistyn whispered before she pushed me toward the dance floor.

I whirled to stick my tongue out at her. Instead, she dropped into a curtsy. In response to my arched eyebrow, she glanced over my shoulder. King Bleddyn watched us. My face flushed as I dropped into a curtsy as well.

"Lady Annistyn, how wonderful to see you. Are your mother and father here?"

Annistyn ducked her head politely.

"Of course, Your Majesty. No one would miss the Evergreen Celebration."

"I am glad to hear it! Will you tell them to find me later? I haven't had the chance to greet them properly yet."

Annistyn took the cue and melted into the crowd. Even though the crowd bustled around us, I knew everyone hung on each word and movement of the king. I didn't understand how one person could command so much attention.

"Your Majesty, to what do I owe this pleasure?"

The king offered me his arm. As we walked, everyone parted like water against the bow of a ship.

"Lady Lydia, two of the Scholars' teachers arrived this week. I'd like to introduce you."

Lord Barwick, the Grand Wizard of the Palace Scholars, stood near one of the banquet tables speaking to a middle-aged woman and a younger man. I returned Lord Barwick's kind smile. Both newcomers bowed to me. I dipped my head in response. The lady gripped both my hands in hers and gave them a squeeze.

"It's an honor to meet you, my dear." Crow's feet

appeared in the corner of her eyes as she smiled at me. She had the tanned skin and rough hands of someone who spent most of their time outside. Not typical with the Scholars mages I'd met so far. "I'm Jamine."

"And I'm Simon." The man extended his hand for me to shake. Even though he was a wisp compared to the king, he stood half a head taller and looked down at me from above his arched nose. The king clapped Simon on the shoulder, and I was sure I saw his knees buckle.

"Both Simon and Jamine spent the last two seasons traveling around Thavell, learning from the Scholars in each city. Now they have returned home to share their knowledge with this year's students."

"Will we be seeing you in class, my lady?"

"That would be—"

"Lady Lydia will continue her studies with me," Lord Barwick cut in. I clicked my jaw shut and offered what I hoped looked like a polite smile. "After our discussions, King Bleddyn and I have decided private lessons suit her unique needs best. And we don't want our green Scholars to be intimidated by her presence."

I glanced at my silhouette reflected in the silvery punch bowl. Nothing intimidating there. Simon's eyebrows rose. "In that case, hopefully Jamine and I can take up some of your time. I've heard stories of your arrival and of your exploits this fall. It all sounds *fascinating*."

"Wait until you see her use her magic, Simon. It's amazing what she's learned to do just on instinct. Once Barwick gets done with her, she will be unstoppable."

"We look forward to seeing it," Jamine smiled at me instead of the king. When I met her eyes, she winked.

King Bleddyn surveyed the dancing and dining nobles.

"Why wait? How about a demonstration? The nobles always love to see magic in action. None more than yours."

"Your Highness, Lydia hasn't had time to prepare." Once again, Barwick answered for me. This time I bit my tongue to keep from saying anything. "She should practice a demonstration of this magnitude."

"I've seen Lydia use her magic so many times before, I hadn't considered that." The king scratched his chin. "What do you think, Lydia?"

King Bleddyn's eyes lit up as he addressed me. I smirked.

"I would be honored, Your Majesty."

My magic rose with my confidence, eager for the chance to show Barwick and Simon what I was made of.

Conversations stopped as I marched toward the dais, the king and teachers trailing in my wake. King Bleddyn started asking me to show my magic to Thavell's nobles as soon as I had recovered from the battle. Typically, he had me show a few party tricks to smaller groups. Tonight, almost every noble family in the country watched. The thought didn't make me nervous. In fact, it energized me. My restlessness reached a boiling point, and I was eager for a release.

The room grew eerily silent as word of what was happening spread. Aidric appeared, pushing between a knot of people to make his way to the front of the carpet. Lady Jaclyn stood at his side, their hands clasped.

Darkness fell across the ballroom. Someone close to me gasped. I shoved everything but the grass of my magic away. The power rose to my call and coursed through me.

"During the longest night of the year," I started. My voice echoed, reaching every corner. I waited for a few breaths. To build anticipation. And to figure out where I was going with this. I'd used air to douse the fire and light orbs in the ballroom and to amplify my voice. What next?

I let a strand of ash colored magic extend from the palm of my hand. In my mind's eye, all my magic appeared gold. Earlier this winter, Lord Barwick had shown me how to separate it, and make the strands of color I could see visible to everyone else.

Strands of green, teal, and orange exploded from my hands, joining the ash-colored strand that already twisted and turned over the heads of those gathered.

In my lessons with Barwick, we often focused on one affinity at a time. He taught me how to use them separately, each affinity for its own purpose. But each time I'd needed my magic the most—when I'd first arrived in Adylra and bandits had attacked, and then during the Battle of the Forest —I hadn't used my affinities in isolation. I'd just reacted.

Black, mahogany, yellow, and charcoal joined the other four strands skating through the air. Each individual strand was on its own path. I let them go where they would, circling and twisting and making designs.

I possessed all eight affinities. And they combined in me to create something new.

Maybe that's why my magic appeared gold. I brought my hands together with an echoing clap and let my consciousness sink to my pool of gold within. The strands of color twirled in wild circles until they combined in the center of the room. In the middle of the air, they spun and spun and spun. If I'd used my magic as one entity before, why couldn't I do it now?

"Anything can happen." I clapped my hands again and

the whirling golden strands exploded into millions of gold stars. They twinkled in and out of the darkness, illuminating the rapt attention of everyone. I didn't dare glance to where I knew Aidric watched. Instead, I sunk deeper into my magic. I let it wrap around me like a second skin until it was the only thing I knew. Until it was the only thing I lived for.

Like some beast waiting in hiding, it pounced on the opportunity to escape. Light of red and green and blue danced from my fingertips. I raised my arms and a stream of them joined the gold stars still twinkling.

"In the fields of the tundra." The dancing lights melded together, guided by my thoughts and words. With each swish of my hand, the colored lights created a landscape like a movie playing out in the sky. "In the heights of the sand, in the leaves of the forest. Everywhere, tonight is the night for celebration, merriment, and stories. Tonight, I will share a story."

Now I just needed to think of one. I let my magic determine what I would say. The lights changed into a herd of horses. They galloped through the air and weaved between the people. Laughter and gasps filled the room as the horses neighed and sparked more red and green magic from their hooves. The noises sounded distant, like everyone else occupied a different place than I did.

The horses erupted into a flock of birds. They scattered and then reformed into a massive gold colored tree. All the golden stardust and colored lights descended onto the tree, and with each addition of magic, it became larger and larger.

I lifted myself from the siren song of my magic. I didn't remember thinking about a tree. Even as my mind questioned what was happening, the stream of magic continued to flow through me. The tree grew larger and larger until its crown pressed against the ceiling of the ballroom.

"A story of one spirit who stands above them all." The words came to me like a long-forgotten dream. What was I talking about? The leaves of the tree danced in a phantom wind.

To the side of the ballroom, a unicorn appeared. Even sparkling golden magic made the figure, there was no mistaking the elongated horn that protruded from its head. The unicorn reared, causing multiple people to stumble out of its way. I didn't think it would hurt them, but I couldn't tell them that. The magic had me in its grasp. The unicorn galloped across the ballroom and halted at the foot of the tree. Once the unicorn arrived, the trunk of the tree twisted and out stepped the likeness of a creature with a human body and a massive rack of antlers atop her head.

"The forest watches and the forest waits." I let my voice soften. I had no idea what I was talking about, but the words felt true. They came to me unbidden. "Everyone will remember her power once more."

The doors at the top of the staircase opened with a bang. At the top of the grand staircase stood a girl. Like she wasn't just a creation of my magic. She descended the stairs with the hem of her dress held in one hand. Made of the same stardust illusion as the rest, she walked with an air of seriousness. She arrived next to the unicorn and the creature and placed her hand on the trunk of the tree.

"Even tonight, she is watching and waiting. The realms will open. The Guardians will reunite. And she will take back what was stolen from her."

The crowd grew louder with chatter and clapping. No

one knew this wasn't coming from me. But where did it come from? I clamped down on my magic, willing it to stop. Wind whipped through the crowd, sending hats and fans flying. My hair broke free from its pins and swirled around my face.

The unicorn neighed, the sound ripping through the room. He reared again. As his hooves hit the ground, a shock of green magic traveled through the floor and into me.

Then I was free. I controlled my magic once again. I twisted my wrist and the golden light swirled into a circle. Just before the tree disappeared, a picture flashed before my eyes. Like someone had taken a snapshot, I saw the girl as clearly as if she stood before me. Her face was pale in the moonlight and her dark auburn hair swirled around her. Something twisted in my gut. The tree pulsed with an inner light—a golden light.

The tree shuddered and dissolved. I waved my hands again; the golden lights flew across the ballroom like stardust. They faded as I closed my fist. The torchlight and mage orbs flared back to life.

"Enjoy the Evergreen Celebration. Spin your tales. And may the spirits grant you luck in the year to come."

Cheering filled the room.

CHAPTER TWO

A melodic song filled the air as the crowd enveloped me once more. I tried to keep my shaking hands folded in my dress as the party resumed. Annistyn grabbed my elbow and steered me toward the dance floor again. I let my body drift through the motions of the dances I practiced under my friends' tutelage the past few weeks.

I smiled at each polite young nobleman. Partners changed at each dance. I twirled with the music, little more than a leaf blown by the wind. Magic still captured my mind. The image of the tree, the unicorn, the dryad, and the girl played over and over in my head. Where did it come from? Had I made it up?

At the beginning of the next song, an altogether familiar hand met mine. My eyes drifted from the floor to the owner of the hand. Prince Aidric.

I found myself utterly tongue tied as he pulled me into a small spin. This was the closest we'd been since our kiss in the middle of the battle. Months ago. My cheeks flushed with the memory. As my eyes grazed the set of his jaw and grim line of his mouth, I wondered if the same thought had occurred to him.

Of course, this dance was one of the more intimate court dances. The music started and Aidric tugged me close to his body before I had the chance to excuse myself. We moved onto the dance floor with the other couples, and I decided if there were any spirits watching tonight, they were having fun at my expense.

As our feet found the three-part rhythm, I wracked my brain to think of something that would take my mind off the feel of Aidric's body pressed against me. He leaned in.

"How often do you lose control of your magic like that?"

Problem solved. He might as well have thrown a bucket of cold water over my head. I stiffened and looked away.

"I didn't lose control. I merely gave everyone what they wanted—a display of my power."

Aidric stayed silent as he twirled me again. As the people and finery whipped by me, I noticed more than a few eyes darted our way. This winter I'd learned our short-lived relationship in the fall was the worst kept secret of court. Our dance would be a fodder for gossip. At least we'd given everyone something to talk about. Aidric pulled me in close again.

"I know you better than that."

Something snapped inside me. How dare he act like he knew me! Like what we had was more than just fun. Not after the way he'd disappeared and abandoned me these past few months.

"You don't know me at all."

Aidric scoffed. Actually scoffed.

I saw red. Even in the middle of the dance floor, my feet

stopped moving. Aidric stumbled. The attention of the room shifted to us.

"You can't possibly think that after everything I don't know when you're in over your head? When you're grasping to get your magic back under control?"

His voice was low, and he attempted to pull me back into the fold of dancers. I refused to budge.

"Why do you care?"

The dancers twirled around us, completely unperturbed, though more than a few eyes glanced our way. Aidric ran a hand through his hair, longer than it was this autumn. Long enough for him to put the sides back and tie it with a cord. He remembered the cord at the last minute and let his hand drop. The curls that grazed his shoulders shivered.

"Of course, I care, Lydia."

He touched my hand again; this time I let him pull me back into the dance. I knew as well as he did, we shouldn't draw too much attention to ourselves. But as I stayed silent and let him lead me through the remaining steps of the waltz, my blood heated. My face flushed as my anger refused to abate.

When the song finished, Aidric drew his hands from my side with a wince.

"Lydia?" he asked. His palm shined with a burn.

Not for the first time, I felt like I was going to burn from the inside out.

Maybe I should. Maybe I should just stand right here, surrounded by all the decadence and burst into flames. What a display of magic that would be.

"I need some air."

I weaved in and out of the nobles preparing for another

dance as fast as I could without drawing more attention to myself. Almost of their own accord, my feet found the doorway hidden in the wall. Once out of the sight of the party, I raced through the empty corridors, lit only by flickering torchlight.

I burst out of the castle and into the biting air of the garden. I hugged my body and sank to the ground despite my ballgown. Alone with only the moonlight and trees for company, the fire trickled from my veins.

When I had control of myself again, I leaned against the railing of the balcony. Out in the garden, small glowing flowers lit the pathway. This was a stupid place to come. All I could think about was Aidric bringing me here on our first night in the castle.

How long ago that seemed.

I walked down the stairs of the balcony and knelt next to the flowers. There had only been a small patch this fall, but the little moonbeam flowers—as I liked to think of them—had spread throughout the garden now. They vined between trees and crept up the legs of benches. They didn't seem to damage any of the other plants. In the depths of winter, only the evergreen and the moonbeams flourished. The flowers cast the entire garden in a magical silver glow.

Footsteps on the walkway behind me startled me. I sprang up to spy the king emerging from the sculpture garden. He looked just as startled to see me here. King Bleddyn smiled as I ducked a quick curtsy.

"Oh, none of that, my dear." He smiled warmly. "I don't hold with formality outside of necessity. What brings you to an empty garden when there is such a grand ball going on?"

I never knew what to make of the king in moments like

this. He called me his ward, but my interactions with him were one-sided and witnessed by courtiers and servants. The only time I'd come close to being alone with him was before the Battle of the Forest.

His questions put me off kilter. Part of me felt like everything was a riddle to him. Maybe being responsible for an entire kingdom made you that way.

"I needed a bit of fresh air." As if in response, wind cut through the garden, blowing the skirts of my dress. The king tucked the folds of his jacket tighter around him.

"Well, the air is certainly fresher out here. I feel the same way sometimes. I love to see people celebrating, but even in a room as large as a ballroom, I sometimes feel smothered. Shall we walk somewhere warmer to clear our heads?"

He offered me his arm. I couldn't refuse without being rude, so I walked with him back to the castle. Instead of heading back to the ballroom, we turned down a different hallway. This one even more deserted and shadowy. The king stopped in front of a tapestry so faded, the image was unrecognizable. He pushed it aside, revealing a staircase winding up through the dark.

"After you."

My heart pounded as we began the ascent. I sent a mage light ahead of us to illuminate the stairwell. But after my display, I was tapped out. The light flickered occasionally but did enough to let me see my feet. Round and round we wove until the dark walls and the stone stairs blurred together. I became so used to the movement of climbing, I almost banged into the small wooden door at the top of the staircase. The world continued to spin as I grasped the handle and stepped through.

Large windows decorated the circular room everywhere except for the door we came through. The room was small and held only two chairs and a small table. King Bleddyn beckoned me over to a window.

We overlooked the garden. From this vantage point, we could see everything. The moonbeam flowers illuminated the garden where it extended all the way to the outer wall. We could even see the stretch of the sea on the other side.

"I don't understand." Even my whisper carried through the small room. "Where are we? There's no tower here."

The king smiled, his white teeth shining in the pale light of the stars. "Few people know about this place. After magic seeped into our lands and out of the forest, a friend and I discovered it. No one can see it from the ground. Long ago, the greatest Wielders of their time pulled this castle from the mountain. Now that magic has returned, I bet it has more secrets than we've discovered."

He walked to the wall and lit the lone torch beside the doorway. I stepped closer to the window and pressed my face against the glass. The king returned to my side.

"My friend and I used to come up here and hide away. We were the only two who knew about it. She's been gone a long time, but I passed the secret on to Aidric. Now we are the only three who know."

Grief laced the king's voice at the mention of his friend. I studied the sculpture garden that lay beneath us, unsure of what to say.

"Thank you for trusting me with this secret."

"Being so visible to others is difficult. I thought you might like a spot you can escape to. Unlike the gardens, no one will bother you here."

Again, words failed me. What was I supposed to say? The gesture was friendly, certainly. But did that mean the king knew I was struggling? Would he be upset that I wasn't always grateful for everything he'd done for me?

King Bleddyn sat down in one of the wooden chairs.

"Relax Lydia, I understand what you must be feeling. You've taken on a role you never expected, in more ways than one. It's normal to have a few growing pains."

I sighed. "I didn't realize I was that easy to read."

The king chuckled and some of the tension left my shoulders.

"I've developed a knack for understanding people over the years. It comes in handy in my line of work. You've handled the last few months well. Your friends also seem to be adapting. Well, the two who are here."

The mention of Erin and Murphy startled me. But knowing the king was watching, I attempted to smooth my face.

"We are honored by the king's attention."

King Bleddyn chuckled again.

"And I see you've been a quick study in courtly manners."

I remained silent and continued to study the garden. No one else ventured from the castle out into the cold.

"Tell me, Lydia. How are you adapting? Really?"

I let my breath wash through me and douse the fire that rumbled within me again. The king had no interest in my sixteen-year-old heart, that much I knew. So, what did he want to know?

"It's been difficult. I'm thankful for your support of myself and my friends. Without your kindness, we would not be faring so well. But this is an entirely different world from the one we came from. And learning your customs and what people expect of me can be hard, especially when it feels like all eyes are on me."

"Your arrival was a surprise and a delight to all of us. The Gatebreaker is here. Prophecy is being fulfilled before our very eyes."

It was all I could do not to roll my eyes at my title.

"I might be the Gatebreaker, but the title doesn't help the restlessness I feel. I've been learning more control over my magic with Lord Barwick, but it has done nothing to bring me closer to home."

I turned back to the king. He sat with his arms folded in his lap, his gray eyes watching me.

"You said if I helped you as the Gatebreaker, you would help me find a way home. So use me. I've recovered from battle. My magic is strong. And I've acclimated to your court as well as I'm able, which I'm assuming is the reason you've asked nothing of me these past few months."

The king smirked, confirming my suspicions.

"So use me. If I can't help my friends get home, let me help you. I want a job. I want to pull my weight."

The king stayed silent long enough for me to fear I'd overstepped my bounds. I considered apologizing when he smiled.

"Aidric said you were smart, Lydia. He was right. If you think you're ready, then I do have something for you. How about you come to dinner in my private dining room tomorrow night? I will tell you about it, and you can decide if it's something you want to do."

I bowed my head.

"Thank you, Your Highness."

King Bleddyn stood. He stretched his arms over his head with a groan.

"If I'm not back soon, someone will notice." He waved at the room. "Stay here as long as you like, it's a good place to think."

ater rippled beneath the palm of my hand. It bent and stretched with my magic. I willed it to reflect the image I searched for. The water resisted, and my will wavered. I gritted my teeth and pushed into it again. The pewter bowl vibrated against the table. Then, the surface of the water smoothed. Scrying was like splitting reality. I sat in a musty classroom, and in the bowl was the castle wall. A young man with chestnut hair that grazed his broad shoulders stood behind a parapet, looking out over a city with rainbow-colored rooftops. His hand rested on an axe strapped in his belt. Snow dusted the top of his head and shoulders in a fine white powder.

"That's a neat bit of magic. It's not like you can just walk outside and see the same thing."

My knees hit the bottom of the table when I jumped. The water jerked, and with the smooth surface went the image. I glared at Erin as she smirked.

"It won't take nearly as much energy, either. Especially after you almost wiped yourself out last night."

"It's not as easy without a piece of hair from the person I'm scrying." I hid my shaking hands in my sleeves. "How did you get in here? I didn't hear you."

Erin rubbed her nails on her green tunic.

"I've got skills."

She straddled the bench beside me and rifled through my notes laying on the table.

"Instead of spying on Murphy, why don't you just go talk to him?"

I huffed at her. Instead of answering, I returned the bowl of the water to a place on the shelf next to an assortment of magical objects.

"He doesn't want anything to do with me. He's made that clear."

Erin's face softened. She restocked the papers and laid them down. "Lydia, he was upset. I was too. But if you would just go talk to him, I'm sure you guys can work it out."

I pretended to study the various gemstones and pieces of metal scattered on a shelf. Erin sighed. The wood bench screeched on the stone floor as she stood.

"Fine." She shrugged. "I tried." She waved her hand around the room. "What is this place, anyway?"

"It's one of the workrooms for the Palace Scholars."

"Are you going to be taking lessons with them?"

"No, but I come down here and use the rooms while they're on break."

Erin lifted an eyebrow.

"King Bleddyn and Lord Barwick think having me around will intimidate the other Scholars."

Erin snorted. I kept my eyes trained on the ground.

"Lydia Catherine! You're enjoying this, aren't you?"

I failed to hide my grin. "It's nice to be good at something."

Erin rolled her eyes. "Don't let it go to your head, O Gate-breaker. Your display last night is all anyone can talk about."

She surveyed the room again. I followed her gaze to the bare stone walls and large mahogany tables.

"It's just as well," Erin said. "It's creepy down here."

That was something we could both agree on. I rolled my notes into a bundle and followed Erin into the hall. We walked the long corridor, passing the halls that made up the rooms the Scholars would live in while they studied.

"Apparently, the castle was created by magic, so there are remnants of it in the walls. The further into the mountain you go, the more magical it gets."

I ran a finger down the wall like I could see the magic inside it.

"Do you believe any of that?"

"I don't know." I shrugged. "Magic has been gone for so long. Sometimes I think people are just figuring it out as they go."

And maybe I was one of those people.

Erin shook her head. "You've changed."

"You're one to talk. I don't seem to recall you wearing leather armor back home."

My throat caught on the words. Erin paused for a step. I thought she was going to say something, but she continued on. Now that everyone knew we weren't from Adylra, we could talk about home. And Erin and I had decided we needed to. We needed to keep the memories fresh. But as time passed, it got harder and harder.

No matter how much we tried to hold on to home, the

memories faded a little more each day. We were no closer to getting back home now than we were the day we walked through the gateway. What good was learning about magic if I still couldn't do this one thing? I wondered how much longer it would take for this place to feel more real than home did.

"The other day I had overnight guard duty on the wall—" Erin's voice was thick, but she smiled—"and all I could think about was how much I wished I had my headphones so I could listen to music."

We both laughed.

"Have you found anything else?" I whispered.

"Nothing. I showed you the scroll I found in the library last month. But that's the only mention of the realms I've found. On our next day off, Murphy and I plan to go into the city. Maybe we can find something there. Everyone I've talked to so far just thinks they're a legend. What about you?"

"Do you think prophecies are real?"

"I've never really thought about it." Erin raised an eyebrow. "Why?"

"I've just been thinking..." I hated seeing the hope that painted Erin's face when she thought we were getting close. Did my vision from last night mean anything? I glanced at my friend out of the corner of my eyes. I couldn't get her hopes up for nothing. "Oh, it's nothing. But I'm having dinner with the king tonight, so maybe I can get more information out of him."

Erin bit her lip and tugged on the end of her blonde braid.

"What?" I prodded. She only tugged on her hair when she was nervous.

"I just feel like we're missing something obvious. Getting here was so easy. I wish we could go back to the cliff where we arrived. Maybe we missed something there." She shook her head as if ridding herself of the thoughts. "Do any of the nobles know anything?"

"If they do, they'd never tell me. People are nice to me because they think it will make the king happy. But I may as well be an ornament for as much as anyone ever talks to me. Even Annistyn and Maren. I appreciate their friendship but sometimes I wonder if it's just fun for them to teach the new girl their ways. Everyone wants me to be the Gatebreaker, but I don't even know what that really means."

"What does the king want tonight?" Erin was the only one I'd told about my magic getting out of my control.

"I don't know, really. He says he has a job for me."

"What kind of job?"

"Hopefully it's something useful."

"If they keep putting you to work with your magic, you may not want to take us home."

I stopped in my tracks. Erin bumped against my back. I whirled to face her before she had time to catch her balance.

"What are you talking about?"

"Your magic. When we go home, you won't have it anymore."

"Do you really think I'd do that?" My voice rose, bouncing across the walls. "Do you think I'm that selfish?" I asked, softer this time.

Erin averted her gaze. Heat flushed my cheeks as the silence stretched between us.

"No." Erin hugged her middle with her arms. "No, I don't. I was just teasing."

"But it's something you've thought about before, isn't it?" I'd known Erin longer than anyone but my mom. This wasn't just teasing. "Is this what you and Murphy talk about? That I'd strand you here to keep my magic?"

Something in my chest twisted. Erin tugged the end of her braid again.

"You should've seen yourself that night in the forest. It was amazing, for sure. But also scary. Murphy almost died. And then to see you using magic like that—and then last night—I don't even know what to think. It's like you're a different person."

That tightness in my chest sunk into my gut.

"I'm still me."

Erin pulled me into a hug. I buried my head into her shoulder.

"I just get so worried sometimes. Worried we won't ever get back." Her words faded, but I knew what she didn't say. She worried about John. I did too. We hadn't heard from him since the battle. Even if I did find a way home, how were we going to find him, too?

Erin's body stiffened. Before I had time to say a word, she pushed me behind her. A dagger gleamed in her other hand. Seconds later, footsteps pattered down the hall and Olma emerged from the shadows. Seeing Erin guarding me, he opened his arms in appeasement. The torchlight danced on his bald head.

"Pardon me, ladies. I did not mean to startle you."

Erin sheathed her dagger. She bowed.

"Forgive me, my lord."

"It is good to be cautious in a dark hallway." Olma's lips pulled up in both corners in a small smile. His eyes darted between us. "If I recall, the castle has been cleared. I thought Lady Lydia was no longer in need of a guard within these walls."

"Erin is just visiting with me. She's not on duty."

"Ah, well then..." Olma crossed his head over his rotund belly. "I'm glad to see our lady is fortunate in her friends." His words sounded like a compliment, but his oily voice sent goosebumps down my arms. I preferred to keep my distance from the king's steward. I moved to stand beside Erin.

"How can I be of service to you, Steward Olma?"

"The king sent me to extend his formal invitation for dinner tonight." He reached into the fold of his faded brown robes and handed me a red envelope. With his bald crown and frumpy clothing, I often thought Olma resembled a potato with a head.

I broke the wax seal on the envelope and read the script detailing my invitation to join the king in his private dining room at twilight.

"Please tell the king I am honored by his attention and will join him." A sliver of hope skittered in my bones. If it was just the king and me at dinner, maybe he would have answers for me. And if I accomplished whatever job he wanted me to do, maybe I could get something from him.

"I will take my leave." Olma bowed. Erin copied the motion, and I followed half a beat behind her, already lost in thought about tonight. "Prince Aidric will arrive to escort you to dinner. Good evening, ladies."

He swept back up the hall. Once he was out of sight, I sneezed three times in a row. Erin stared down the hall after the steward.

"Is it just me or was that strange?"

"It's not just you," I told her, pulling out a cloth to wipe my nose. "He's always that strange."

Erin and I parted ways at my rooms after she made me promise to find her the next morning to tell her about dinner. Afternoon quickly descended into evening. I perched on the window seat to gaze out over the city and the bay. A fresh powder of new snow blanketed the castle grounds. In these brief moments before a footprint had even touched the pristine surface, everything felt new and pure.

I waited for the snow to fall again, but the clouds hung onto their flakes. Walking past the couches and tables in my sitting area, I entered my bedroom and unceremoniously threw my white robe onto the bench at the foot of my bed.

Gabrielle found me an hour later attempting to lace a powder blue dinner gown.

"My lady, let me help you." Her practiced fingers laced both sides of the bodice in record time. "You should have called for me earlier," she scolded.

"I'm sure you have better things to do than wait on me. I didn't want to bother you."

I sat in front of the mirror. Gabrielle gave a long-suffering sigh.

"My job is to serve you, my lady." She undid my braid, and the red locks cascaded over my shoulders and down my back. With the rate it was growing, it'd be hanging to my knees by the time we made it back home.

"No, and I wish you'd quit calling me my lady. My name is Lydia."

"And I am my lady's maid. So, my lady it shall be."

I scoffed, but quit arguing. I didn't want to interrupt as Gabrielle pinned my hair into an elaborate updo. Satisfied, she gave it one last pat and let me stand. She stood me in front of the full-length mirror and studied the full effect.

"Well, you're learning, you actually chose an appropriate gown for this occasion." The matter-of-fact words were the highest praise I would get from her. "Are you worried about your dinner tonight?"

Gabrielle's question made me consider.

"The king had been kind to me these past few months. I suppose I'd be embarrassed if there's some piece of etiquette I don't know, but I've messed up before and no one seems to mind." It was certainly less stressful than when my friends and I had been trying to hide where we came from. At least now I had an excuse.

"I just wondered if my lady might be concerned about everyone who is attending the dinner tonight."

I paused, one hand in the middle of fastening an earring. Olma's words about someone escorting me came flooding back.

"I have no reason to be nervous." The stiff words didn't match the now rabid beating of my heart. From Gabrielle's glance, I knew she saw right through me.

"Of course, my lady." Her lips twitched, but she'd been around nobles too long for me to tell if she'd wanted to smile before she smoothed her features. I scowled and opened my mouth to assure her I had no feelings for the prince when a knock at the door caused my heart to drop to my knees.

CHAPTER FOUR

I entered my sitting room in time to see Gabrielle pulling open the door. My powder blue dress crinkled as I curtsied to the crown prince standing at my door. Aidric bowed in return. Once again, we stood facing one another. And, once again, no words came to me.

Aidric cleared his throat and offered me his arm.

"My lady, may I escort you to dinner?"

Gabrielle nudged me from behind when I remained frozen.

"That would be nice, thank you."

I walked out of the door, not bothering to take Aidric's arm. I needed the court ladies to give me lessons on how they remained so collected. The stronger my magic, the more my emotions simmered just below the surface. I'd become a tempest blowing around the stalwart mountains of the nobles.

Aidric let his arm drop as I passed by. The oak door to my chambers slammed shut behind us. Only the echo of our feet and the twirling structure of the spiral staircase kept us company. I glanced sideways at the prince. I wondered if he realized this was the first time we'd been alone together since the night of the battle.

Over the winter, Aidric had let his facial hair grow. He now sported a coating of dark hair down the sides of his face and across his chin. My fingers flinched as an image of me running my hand along his cheek came to mind. I hid my hands in my skirt to fight the urge. My anger at our argument last night was still fresh. So why did walking next to him make me feel as ungainly as a newborn foal?

Aidric glanced over and I diverted my eyes.

"You look nice tonight."

"Thank you."

"Is that dress new?"

"Yes, it's new. Maren gave it to me last week. Although your father has made sure I have more than I need. I'm thankful for your family's kindness." I glanced back over at Aidric, but he faced forward.

We fell into silence again. The words that escaped my lips so fast and loose last night were nowhere to be found now. Aidric ran his hand along the hilt of the sword he wore strapped to his side. Memories of the times I'd seen him use that sword coursed through me. Like him driving through another person to save me. I hadn't known how to use my magic during that first ambush. I'd reacted on instinct. My magic had saved me and Aidric. But I killed a man.

And then Aidric had used his sword in the forest. He'd saved me again. And later, I'd saved him when my power exploded around me. I didn't know how many people I'd killed then. I'd learned later that if it hadn't been for the other

Wielders in our company protecting our soldiers, I might have killed some of them too.

I bit the inside of my lip as the flickering torchlight in the hall swam before me.

"Lydia, are you okay?"

Aidric's deep voice grounded me. I'd stopped walking. One hand gripped the stone wall next to me. The dizziness faded. The chill in the hallway sunk through the sheer sleeves of my dress. I focused on the scratchy material of my shift against my skin. Each detail pulled me back into reality.

"Yes, I'm fine." I brushed my face and found it wet.

"You know, sometimes memories sneak up on me. Here and now fades. I feel like I'm reliving some of the worst times of my life."

"I said I'm fine." There was that bite in my words again. Anger rose to the surface like an old friend. I straightened up and smoothed the skirt of my dress. Aidric's eyes bore into me, but I kept my gaze down.

"Of course," he finally said.

"Will Lady Jaclyn be joining us tonight?" I tried to keep my voice light as we resumed walking. Easy conversation is what this was. I didn't care one way or the other. Really.

"No, not tonight. My father wanted a more intimate setting."

I didn't have time to think about what that meant as we arrived at a massive expanse of room in the tallest tower of the castle—the king's chambers.

DURING THE WINTER SOCIAL SEASON, the castle hosted banquets parties and balls afterward almost nightly. Occasionally, King Bleddyn would invite a few people to dine with him. He reserved this honor for people he favored. My conversation with King Bleddyn last night felt like a distant memory. I wasn't so sure of myself anymore.

I wiped my sweaty palms on my underskirt as we arrived at an enormous set of doors. Aidric knocked once. A valet met us at the door. He ushered us in and through a small sitting room. Through a giant archway, we entered the dining room with an ornate table large enough to hold twenty people.

"Lady Lydia!" King Bleddyn stood from his seat at the head of the table. He kissed me on both cheeks and offered his arm to guide me to my seat right next to his own. Aidric sat directly across from me, his brow set in a frown. Unperturbed by his son's surliness, King Bleddyn beamed at me.

"I am delighted you joined me this evening."

"Thank you for the honor, Your Majesty. I'm looking forward to dinner."

With just three of us seated, the table seemed huge. Unicorns, dragons, wolves, and stags all danced across the table and chairs in intricate carvings. Trees, vines, and flowers wrapped their way up the legs and along the backs of the chairs. I wondered about the story behind the work. The table looked ancient.

I started to ask—when doors at the side of the room opened, admitting the valet and another servant. Like the throne room, the doors to the king's private dining room appeared as part of the wall until they opened.

The two served us each a bowl of cool green soup. I'd

grown used to most of the differences at court, but sitting for someone else to serve me all my meals still felt odd. I'd stopped jumping up to help after Maren informed me the valets would punish the other servants if they shirked their duties.

King Bleddyn and Price Aidric picked up a conversation about a noble from Orsa. I tuned them out as I sipped my soup. I tasted spinach, broccoli, and hints of lime. Food was a great tool for making friends and enemies. So I never hesitated to eat in social settings, even if cold soup wasn't something I was used to.

"So, Lydia," King Bleddyn began once our soup bowls were empty, and the next course arrived. "How much have you learned about the customs of Thavell? Has anyone taught you about our history of banquets and why we serve our courses the way we do?"

"No, Your Majesty," I admitted.

"What do you think of our food compared to your home?" I poked at the oyster and broth appetizer before answering.

"Some things are familiar, mostly the breads and meats. Some ingredients. But you combine everything in new ways here, and there's a greater variety. The food served in the castle is way fancier than what I'm used to. I didn't realize there was a custom in how everything is served."

My answer gave King Bleddyn the opening he was looking for. Without further encouragement, he regaled me with the history of food and the landscape of Thavell. Each of our courses highlighted a different region of the country. As he talked, I realized they organized the nightly banquets the same way. Each meal was like a tour across the country.

The soup we ate had vegetables harvested just outside Alvale. They made our appetizer with oysters harvested from Half-Moon Harbor, just outside the castle. After that was an exquisite vegetable dish with tomatoes, basil, goat cheese, and vinaigrette dressing from Orsa. The king mentioned Orsa grew the finest tomatoes in the entire country.

Throughout the main dish of roasted duck in a rich sauce, King Bleddyn told us about his father, King Lewis, teaching him to hunt ducks. When he told the story about his dog retrieving a duck for him, but then running away with it and King Bleddyn falling into a lake and coming out covered in mud, even Aidric laughed.

By the time the dessert of pear sorbet and pound cake came out, I'd forgotten to be nervous. Even with King Bleddyn's larger-than-life presence, I relaxed and enjoyed his stories about Thavell and his boyhood as he talked about the customs of the kingdom. He speared half a pear on his fork and held it up.

"Pears to remind us of the sweetness of our capital city, Windburn. These pears come from my favorite grove at western edge of the city. When I was young, it was a favorite place for my friends and I to sneak over the wall."

"Who did you sneak out of the city with?" Aidric propped his head on his arm. I wondered how often Aidric and his dad sat together and shared stories.

"Oh, some old friends of mine." King Bleddyn cleared his throat and turned his gaze to me. "Food has a way of reflecting our culture, don't you think?"

I nodded. With my mouth full of cake, I couldn't speak.

"Describe a dish for us from your home, Lydia. And we will guess what it means about your home."

"That's an interesting idea, Your Majesty." I tapped my finger on the table. What could I describe? "Have you ever heard of apple pie?"

"No! Please, tell us about it." King Bleddyn's eyes sparkled with eagerness.

Dutifully, I walked them through the traditional steps of making a perfect, from scratch apple pie. While I talked, our plates were cleared away, and we sipped steaming mugs of tea.

"One Saturday every month my mom and I used to get up and make a bunch of apple pies."

"Your mom, you say? What's her name?"

"Lyn."

"Is that short for anything?"

"No, she's always been just Lyn."

"What a melodic name. What did you do with the pies you baked?"

"We'd take them all over town to friends and people Mom thought *just needed a little slice of love.*"

The lump in my throat cut the words off. I glanced down at my hands, blurry with the tears that suddenly welled up in my eyes. I'd been in Thavell for five months now. That was five Saturdays I'd missed baking pies with Mom. Was she still baking them? Had anyone brought her a pie when I'd disappeared?

Aidric reached out. For a flash of a second, I thought he'd grab my hand. But he only reached for a sugar cube for his tea. I brushed my eyes with the back of my hand and cleared my throat.

"I'm sorry, Your Majesty. I didn't mean to get choked up like that. It's just hard to talk about home, sometimes."

"Please, don't apologize," King Bleddyn said. "I can't imagine what it must be like for you, to be stuck in a different place like this. You must be homesick."

"It comes in waves." I offered a smile at his kindness. "Erin and I talk about home, to keep the memories fresh."

"Well met." The king sat back and laced his fingers over his belly.

"So, Aidric. Lydia told us about food from her home. What do you think it represents?"

Aidric's finger tapped the side of his mug in a rhythm.

"Comfort. Apple pies bring comfort to you and to others in your community."

I ducked my head at Aidric's smile.

"You're right. But I'm trying to focus on now. If I learn everything I can about magic, I can get us back home."

"And we are here to help you do that," King Bleddyn assured me. "You have to admit, travel from a different world is astounding." He stroked his beard as he talked. "If it's ever happened before, surely someone recorded it. We are going through our library here and have sent messengers to our other cities for any records from before magic disappeared."

King Bleddyn acted like his ancestor trapping magic in the Golden Forest was some strange accident. But we all had skeletons in our closet. I couldn't help but think of my mom again. Her parents had died when she was a baby, and her early life was so rough she never talked about it.

"Thank you, Your Majesty. I appreciate what you're doing for us."

A knock on the door interrupted whatever King Bleddyn was going to say next. The valet appeared at the king's side and whispered in his ear. Something crossed the king's expression, but it vanished in an instant. He stood.

"I'm sorry. Will you excuse me for a moment? There's something I need to attend to."

"Do you need my help?" Aidric made to rise from his chair, but King Bleddyn motioned him back down.

"No, please stay and keep Lydia company. I'll return soon."

The heavy footsteps of the king leaving echoed through the spacious dining chamber. Once again, Aidric and I were alone. He sighed and sat back in his chair, holding his cup of tea. The flickering light of the torches danced across the silver circlet that sat on top of his curls. Realizing I was staring, I glanced back at the table.

"Do you have any plans for tomorrow?" His voice startled me. I looked back up to see the edges of his mouth curling into a smile. I blushed. He'd caught me watching him.

"Not really. Maren and Annistyn have invited me for lunch in the gardens. It should be pretty with the snow."

"You've been spending time with them a lot lately."

"I have." I shrugged, not sure how to respond to that statement. "They invite me, and they're kind when I say or do something weird. You Thavellians have too many traditions and rules."

"You're right, we do." Aidric chuckled, and I smiled in return. The tightness in the room eased a bit. I motioned to the torches.

"There are so many Wielders here. Why don't you all use the orbs the light affinities can conjure?"

"It makes some of our less progressive nobles unhappy to

see magic used so casually." Aidric sighed. "As much as they don't want to admit it, the magic scares them."

"But," I countered, "since magic used to be everywhere, wouldn't magic be the traditional thing?"

Aidric laughed again. His voice reminded me of bells. My heart fired at the sound. Easy conversation. We could do this.

"That's an excellent point. Care if I use it next time someone complains?"

"Not at all."

Silence fell again, more comfortable this time. Aidric cleared his throat.

"I'm glad you enjoy Maren's and Annistyn's company. They are nice. Not everyone here is like that, though. You're watching your back, right?"

I raised an eyebrow. Watching my back for what?

Before I could ask, King Bleddyn returned.

"Lydia, last night you told me you were ready to do something tangible."

Aidric's eyes darted my way. I ignored him and gripped my skirts underneath the table, my nerves from last night returning. The king returned to his seat and faced me.

"We haven't had the chance to discuss what being the Gatebreaker truly means. Or what the Gatebreaker can do for us in Thavell. Do you remember the prophecy?"

"Of course." I recited it from memory.

"When the red star is seen anew
Magic will restore,
The balance will renew,
Her magic of gold will beam evermore,
When the Gatebreaker arrives
So will the time for war
For her the affinities will revive.
The wolf will be at her back
And the Realms will arise
Beware, the time is drawing near
If she is defeated by fear
The Darkness will forever be revered."

How could I not remember? I repeated it to myself almost every night, wondering what it all meant.

"Excellent." Something simmered in the king's gaze at the words of the prophecy.

"Lydia, are you aware of how magic Wielders were treated in my father's day?"

One of the first things I'd learned at court was not to speak about the reign of King Lewis—King Bleddyn's father—anywhere near the king. From what I'd gathered about that period, King Bleddyn didn't like to be reminded of those times. But he'd asked me a question, and I didn't see any reason to lie.

"Magic Wielders were persecuted. They were required to get a brand revealing they were a Wielder and what affinity they possessed. Even as the number of Wielders grew, the use of magic was forbidden."

Aidric coughed, but I ignored him. King Bleddyn had my full attention.

"The Wielders weren't just required to get the brand—they were forced. It was an *unsavory* period in our history. And it culminated in a noble born Wielder assassinating my father. I never wanted to earn my crown through bloodshed. So, when I became king, I decided to do better for the Wielders. All of our citizens have abilities to help our kingdom, and none of them should be shamed for that." He continued talking, his hand combing his rough beard again.

"However, good intentions don't get you anywhere. It wasn't just my father who had a problem with magic and Wielders. Now many common born Wielders are reluctant to trust the crown. I don't blame them. I would be too if I was in their shoes."

"Things have come far in the decades I've been king. We've established the Palace Scholars. We know more about magic than we have for hundreds of years. Did you know new students for this year petition to join the Scholars next week?"

"Yes, Lord Barwick told me."

"Each year more people want to study with the Scholars. However, we don't have unlimited resources to train everyone. Starting this year, we are taking the strongest Wielders into our school—whether they are noble or common born."

A school for magic everyone could access. This was no small thing King Bleddyn was proposing. But denying noble students a spot in the Scholars would risk making families angry. The idea didn't seem to bother the king, though. He plowed on.

"I've also been doing some research on the red star that is mentioned in the prophecy. The last time it was seen was when magic was released from the Golden Forest."

"Oh—wow." As much as I thought about the prophecy, it still felt ephemeral to me. I wondered if the Gatebreaker prophecy had anything to do with my vision at the banquet.

"My advisors have been brainstorming, and they think the star could make magic stronger, somehow. And with the mention of war, we want to make sure we train our strongest Wielders."

"This all sounds great, Your Majesty. But Lord Barwick has already told me I won't be studying with the Scholars. So, what does this have to do with what I need to do?"

"Barwick keeps me updated on your progress." King Bleddyn leaned in, lacing his fingers together in front of his face. His dark gaze settled on me. Underneath the table, my hands balled into fists. "You have been learning faster than any student he's ever had. During the battle you mentioned you could see each different affinity of magic around you. Is that correct?"

My mouth went dry at the mention of the battle. I swallowed, willing moisture back into my mouth so I could answer.

"Yes. The colors of each affinity laced through everything they touched. It's how I knew Reynard used air magic."

The eager glint returned to the king's eye.

"Fascinating. I've heard of those who can sense magic, but I've never heard of someone who can see it. Can you see magic anytime you want to?"

"I haven't tried it since the battle." I tried to remember how I did it during the battle. But opening those memories without getting lost in the horror was difficult. I twisted the edge of the lace on my skirt. I was too deep now; I couldn't disappoint the king. "But I can do it again. Is that what you want me to do?" That didn't seem like too hard of a job.

"How about an experiment, then?" Aidric shifted in his seat. The king shot him a glance, and he stilled. "I want to test a theory of mine before I tell you my idea."

I gave a shrug, then realized that might be rude. "An experiment sounds fun, Your Majesty." A nervous laugh escaped me.

The king didn't seem to notice. His attention has already shifted. He rang a bell sitting to his left. The valet reappeared from the side doorway and came to stand between me and the king.

"Lydia, see if you can tell me if Falir here is a Wielder, what type he is, and how much latent magic he possesses?"

"Father, is this really necessary?" Aidric sat back in his chair, arms crossed over his chest. He looked so much like the king when he sat that way, with that stern expression on his face. The king's face clouded over.

"No—it's fine," I jumped into the conversation. "I want to try."

Here was something I could accomplish. I smiled, hoping Aidric and the king would see my confidence. King Bleddyn called this an experiment, but I knew what it was. He was testing me. I wanted to make sure I passed.

Letting all thoughts of Aidric and the king out of my mind, I inhaled and exhaled in counts of five. I let my mind drift closer to the wall I kept shielded most of the time. My heart hammered against my rib cage as the scent of blood filled my nose. Phantom screams played in my ears. Despite trying to lock the emotions of the battle away, I was right back on the battlefield. Aidric was dying. My friends were dying. There was nothing I could do.

The lace I twirled in my fingers snapped, burning my hand with the friction.

I wasn't on the battlefield. Aidric and King Bleddyn were here. I was safe. Everyone was safe.

I cleared my throat as the rest of the memories faded. Then, my find fell into the golden well of power within. This time when I thought back to the battle, I used my magic to shield the memories. It guided me through the steps like a specter, showing me how I used it to see magic that day. When I understood, I pulled forth a strand of aether and opened my eyes.

The magic of the world almost blinded me. Gold strands of magic ran through my hands, shimmering just under my skin. King Bleddyn still watched me in the same position. A glance at the clock told me it had only taken me a few seconds to call the magic I needed. I was getting faster.

Neither the king nor the prince glowed with any sort of magic. I turned my attention to Falir. Faint green streaks coated his neck and hands.

"You're an earth Wielder," I told him, as the colors faded from my vision.

He bowed his head in my direction.

"You are correct!" King Bleddyn grinned. He patted Falir on the shoulder. "Now, can you tell how much magic he possesses?"

"Well, the glow of his magic is faint. So, I think that means his magic isn't that strong?" I winced at my choice of words. Nothing about them sounded technical, and maybe people wouldn't like to hear their magic wasn't strong. I glanced at Falir, but he continued smiling at me.

"You are absolutely right." King Bleddyn clapped his hands in delight. "Falir here is an earth Wielder, but just barely. He typically uses his magic to enhance the plants in the garden."

The king waved his hand. Falir understood the dismissal. The valet bowed and disappeared into the wall as silently as he arrived.

"How do you feel after that?" King Bleddyn's full attention returned to me once again. His excitement was infectious. I smiled in return.

"Great." My veins hummed with the energy that came from using my magic. I loved the power that flowed through me. Erin was right, this feeling would be hard to give up. "I never grow tired of using magic."

"That is music to my ears, Lydia."

Aidric stayed silent through our exchange. He still leaned back in his chair, doing his best to glower at us. I didn't understand what was troubling him. But it wasn't my concern. Maybe now King Bleddyn would finally tell me what he had in store for me.

"Lydia, do you understand that as the Gatebreaker, you're a symbol of hope for magic Wielders across the country?"

I shook my head. I barely knew what I was doing. And I wasn't sure how I liked the thought of being a symbol.

"The Gatebreaker prophecy has been around for a generation. And now here you stand. If the Gatebreaker and the crown come together, we can work toward a common goal: magic Wielders who aren't afraid to use their magic."

"I like the sound of that," I admitted. "What do I need to do?"

"I have lots of plans for you, my girl. But to start, we need to build up trust in the crown. Like I said before, we need only the strongest Wielders in the Scholars this year. As people come forward for acceptance, I need your skill set to tell me who those strongest Wielders are. You get to decide who is accepted into the Scholars."

My heart dropped a beat. The king trusted my abilities that much? He was leaving acceptance to the Scholars in my hands.

"This is a great honor, Your Majesty." I couldn't help but voice my doubt. "Are you sure you trust me to determine this? How do we know that the amount of power someone has is most important? I don't know how to tell how skilled someone is with their magic."

"You have an excellent mind. That is true, we don't know for sure if the amount of magic someone has means they will be a great Wielder. But the only thing we can do is try. Those who have the most power have the most potential. One day I hope all Wielders learn at our school."

I nodded my head in agreement. That made sense.

"Do you accept this job?"

I opened my mouth to agree, then snapped it shut again. My conversation with Erin came to mind.

"I meant it when I said I wanted to help, Your Majesty. But, respectfully, Sire—there are things I need too."

Aidric's eyebrow rose so fast I thought they might fly off his face. I bit my lip but didn't back down. This was my chance to show the king I was serious about getting myself and my friends home.

"Fair enough, let's hear them." But for a slight tensing of his shoulders, King Bleddyn looked unbothered.

"First, I want John found. It's been three months. I want him found and safe."

King Bleddyn remained silent. I plowed on.

"I know I'm asking for more manpower when you have a kingdom to consider. But from what you've told us, the aftermath of the battle has been handled. Surely you can devote a few more people to the search."

"I can tell you've thought about this." King Bleddyn paused; his eyes lost their focus like he was imagining something else. "You are right. Now that we've secured the castle, we can dedicate more people to searching for John." He held up a finger. "However, I can't guarantee we will find him. Even with more manpower, this country is large, and Reynard is not without his own resources we have to contend with. Is that acceptable?"

"Yes, thank you." One knot in my chest loosened. I launched into my next idea before the king could stop me. "My other consideration is this: You told me that Steward Olma, Lord Barwick, and others are searching for the way for my friends and I to get home. I want to be part of the search. I want to know everything. And be included in any meetings about it. The more I learn, the better I can help."

"Done." The king tapped his hand against the table, reminding me of a judge dismissing the court.

"Then I am at your service, King Bleddyn." I bowed my head.

"I am glad to hear it, my dear. I know you won't disappoint me."

"Don't forget about the other part of the prophecy." I'd

almost forgotten Aidric was still here. King Bleddyn gave him a questioning look, but Aidric's eyes were on mine. His smile was a grim thing. "'The wolf will be at her back.' Our royal house is the house of the wolf. We will always have your back."

He tipped his empty cup of tea at me in a toast. It clattered against the saucer when he set it back down.

"Yes, Lydia," the king chimed in. He gave his son a sidelong glance before turning back to me, "a king's greatest duty is to serve his people. If there is any other way I can serve you, you only have to ask."

CHAPTER FIVE

Silence followed Aidric and me back down the hallway after dinner. Starlight and cold wind met us at each small window we passed. My rooms were on the opposite side of the castle. This was going to be a long walk.

"You don't have to escort me the whole way," I told him. "We've already passed your rooms, and it's late."

"I don't mind."

No one was in the halls. It was like the entire palace had conspired to make this the most awkward walk of my life. I started to ask Aidric about his weird tangent at the end of dinner, but as the silence stretched, it became harder and harder to break it.

Finally, we arrived at my chambers. I didn't bother saying anything as I walked inside. With a flick of my wrist, I ignited the fire.

"You use your magic all the time these days." Aidric watched flames dance higher in the hearth. "Almost like an instinct."

"It's easier when I don't have to hide it." I reached to grip the necklace he'd given me, but let my hand drop when I remembered I didn't wear it anymore. I turned my back and took the pins out of the woven hairstyle Gabrielle gave me. My hair fell down my back, releasing the tension in my head and neck.

To my surprise, Aidric hadn't left yet. He stood by the fire, his eyes on the flames.

"That was an interesting dinner," he finally offered.

"It was."

"You know I didn't have any clue why my father invited you for dinner so suddenly." He looked back up at me.

"Maybe he just likes my company." I leaned against a bookcase and stumbled when it shifted. Aidric hid a smile with his hand. I shrugged with a grin and wrapped my arms around myself. So much for being smooth.

Aidric crossed his own arms and leaned back against the wall. Show off.

"When did you tell my father you wanted to do more?"

"I left the ball for some air and ran into him."

"Why did you think that was a good idea?"

"It wasn't like I went looking for him, it just happened."

My words came more easily with Aidric than they did with his father. I ran my hand along the top of the fireplace while he glared at me. Something fell to the ground at my feet and squeaked.

"Oh no!"

"Wait—it could bite you." Aidric grabbed my arm before I could reach out. I shook him off with a glare and cupped the little being in my hands. A tiny person stared back at me. She had charcoal skin and long black hair. Translucent gray wings fluttered at her back.

"Well, hello there," I told her. "What are you doing in my fireplace?"

When the sprite spoke, her words sounded like the popping of logs in a fire.

"I'm sorry, I don't understand you."

"What is it?" Aidric tried to poke her, but the sprite swatted his hand away with a huff. I giggled.

"She's an ash sprite. And I think you've offended her."

Gently, I placed her on the table where I'd been reading a book about magical creatures. I flipped the pages open to an illustration that looked very similar to the sprite in my room. She jumped onto the book and ran her small hand across the illustration. "Let's see," I read. "They're very smart and can understand humans just fine. But we have trouble understanding their language. Maybe I can try to translate with my magic."

Aidric bowed to the little creature.

"I apologize, miss. I didn't mean to upset you."

The ash sprite looked over one shoulder at the prince and wound a strand of hair around her finger.

"Very charming." I rolled my eyes. The sprite returned to my offered hand. I carried her back to the fireplace and knelt so she could climb among the coals. "I don't know how you got here, but you're welcome as long as you'd like." The sprite patted my hand and disappeared into the flames.

"We will have to report her to my father." Aidric watched the fire again.

"Why?"

"She's a magical creature outside of the Golden Forest.

There have been more sightings across the country. He needs to know they're here in the castle too."

"She's not hurting anyone." I didn't like the idea of King Bleddyn knowing about my visitor. "She's probably just lost."

"Okay, I'll let it go." He held up his hands and walked away. "You know, you don't have to do everything my father wants, either."

I stood and dusted my hands on my skirt.

"What are you talking about?"

"This whole identifying people with magic thing. It sounds innocent enough, but my father never has just one reason for doing something. I'm just saying—it's okay to tell him no."

"That's easy for you to say. You're the prince."

"And you're the Gatebreaker. Noble of Thavell. Ward of the king. You have just as much power as I do." He yanked the circlet off his head and ran a hand through his curls.

"Don't act like you care, Aidric." My words snapped through the air.

Aidric looked away, a muscle in his jaw twitching. I turned back to the fire. My words were angry, but they weren't untrue. Aidric's footsteps scuffed across the carpet. My shoulder stiffened, anticipating the moment the door shut behind Aidric as he left. Instead, a warm hand gripped my shoulder and turned me around.

Aidric stood next to me, close enough I felt the heat radiating from his skin. Memories transported me back to the bay. How many nights had we spent sneaking out and practicing magic? And stealing kisses? I remembered the taste of the kisses we stole underneath the stars. I could practically taste the salt water. From the shudder in Aidric's breath, I knew he remembered too.

Aidric's fingertips skimmed my chin. Gentle pressure lifted my head until I met his gaze. The emotion in his eyes threatened to pull me under. My cheeks flushed under his attention.

"Of course I care, Lydia." His whisper boomed in the space between us. I gripped his wrist in my hand. My magic flared to life. Suddenly more than touch connected us. I *felt* the truth behind his words. His emotions flooded my veins as clear as my own.

Aidric let go of my chin like I'd shocked him. Breaking contact made the strength of his emotions fade, but they still swam under the current of my own. Aidric's eyes widened. He felt it too.

"If you care so much, then why do you only talk to me when you have something to scold me about?"

I spoke with more than words. Aidric flinched and gripped his chest like I'd driven a knife through his heart. I didn't know how, but as my anger flared—Aidric felt it too.

"I'm with Jaclyn, now. You know—" His hands flexed at his side as he searched for words, the golden flecks in brown eyes dim. His voice softened. "You were leaving."

"I don't understand." We stood on the edge of something. Something I wasn't sure we had the strength to confront.

"You were supposed to find a way home. You came into my life like a sunburst, exploding everything I know." Aidric's eyes tracked across the mantle, onto the bookcase, to the window. Anywhere but me. "The closer we became, the harder it was for me. And then my father announced my betrothal. That was it. But I couldn't—still—can't stop thinking about you."

"What are you saying?" The undercurrent of his feelings pulsed under my skin. My heartbeat sped up in response. Aidric finally looked at me again. And even if I'd wanted to, I couldn't look away.

"You're going to go back home. And I'm going to have to forget about you. It's hard—hard for me to be around you for too long." Aidric's shame at his confession flooded me. The words circled my brain. My own emotions laced with his until everything inside of me was a swirling mess of chaos and magic. The fire behind us flared to life.

"Too hard for you?" That was his excuse for avoiding me all this time? Confusion, pain, sadness, everything I felt was too fleeting and too intense to hold on to for very long. They morphed into a single ball of rage.

"Did you stop to think that maybe it's hard for me, too? I've stranded my friends in a new world. They hate me. One of them might be dead. Meanwhile, I'm expected to prance around and do magic like your father's favorite show pony without embarrassing myself. Did you ever stop to think that maybe—just maybe I could've used a friend?"

Shame and pain laced through my rage. The tension dropped out of Aidric's shoulders. A tendon twitched in his jaw. But my rage broke the dam of my emotions and words cascaded out of me. I couldn't stop now.

"When I needed you the most—you dropped me for another girl! Sneaking around in the dark was fine—but when things got hard for the crown prince, you bailed and left me to fend for myself."

Aidric raised his hands against my onslaught. A sliver of

anger burned through me. Good. Let him be angry. I wanted it. I needed something to kindle the fire burning inside. If I didn't unleash it, it would burn me up.

"This is not what I came here to do!" Aidric opened his arms to the room, his cheeks flushed, and his voice raised. "I came to help you. I will not have your jealousy—"

"My jealousy?!" The entire castle could probably hear us by now. "I am not jealous of Jaclyn, Aidric. You're the one who's been avoiding me."

Every cruel and spiteful thing inside came spewing out.

"You know what I think? Now that I'm not some lost girl, you're not interested anymore. Maybe you're threatened that I have as much power as you. Or maybe you never cared about me at all. Maybe you just like being the hero."

My chest heaved; my breath came in ragged gasps. Aidric's anger simmered against my bones.

"That's all I was to you, wasn't it? Someone to save. Don't come in here pretending to help and crying about regrets when you hung me out to dry. I don't need saving."

Aidric's arms dropped to his side. His head dropped to his chest. My magic sputtered out, breaking the link that tethered our emotions. The wave of rage crested, leaving hollowness in its wake.

Aidric didn't respond. I wanted him to apologize—or yell —or something. Anything but standing there with that vacant expression. Seconds ticked by. I glanced away, unable to look at him.

The door creaked. Aidric stood halfway out of my room. I took a step forward, then hesitated. If Aidric crossed the threshold, that would be it. The words we said would hang between us forever. Maybe they needed to. Yet, I still couldn't let go.

"Did I really mean that little to you? I'm not even worth a reply?"

He paused, his hand on the door, on foot poised to leave. I leaned in to hear him speak.

"It's hard for me because I fell in love with you."

Before I could respond, he was gone.

The explosion of my temper deserted me, leaving me empty and exhausted.

It's hard for me because I fell in love with you.

His words burned a place into my soul.

I remained standing in the middle of my sitting room, staring at the closed door. Like if I watched it long enough Aidric would come back and admit the whole thing was a joke. Because it was a joke. It had to be. I needed it to be a lie.

Because if he really meant what he said—no, I wouldn't let myself go down that road. The sound of crackling drew my attention away from the door and to the fire. The indignant ash sprite stood on the mantle. When my temper deserted me, so did the fire. The hearth was cold, like flames hadn't been there in ages. The ash sprite flew to my shoulder and buried herself in my hair.

"Sorry, little one. My magic sometimes gets away from me."

She huffed, startling a laugh out of me.

"I know, I know. I need to work on it."

I carried her to the fire in my bedroom. The coals still burned. I didn't have enough magic or focus left to build the fire up, so I grabbed some wood and a poker and did it the old-fashioned way. Once the flames danced again, the sprite patted me on the nose and flew into the flames.

"You're welcome to stay the night," I told her as she buried herself in the ashes at the bottom of the fire and settled in to sleep. "I don't care how long you stay. But be careful. I don't know what King Bleddyn will do if he finds out you're here. And I don't think I sowed much goodwill tonight."

I went through the motions of getting ready for bed. Crawling into the bed with a shiver, I sunk into the warmth that awaited me, grateful Gabrielle had left a warmer at my feet. After tossing and turning, I settled on my back and stared at the ceiling. My body was exhausted, but my mind wouldn't stop.

It's hard for me because I fell in love with you.

Alone in the dark, Aidric's words played over and over in my head. Thoughts I'd resisted early taunted me as they strolled through my memories. He didn't know what he was talking about. He couldn't love me.

But he had saved me. More than once. He'd put himself in danger to protect me. He'd kept my secret even though he knew his father would be angry.

But none of that was love. Was it?

Unbidden memories of our times together came to me. The way I'd felt when I first saw him stuck in that ridiculous trap. How he saved me that first night in the camp. The way he held me when we kissed. How it felt to sit next to him and watch the tide come in. How easy it was to talk to him.

It's hard for me because I fell in love with you.

I'd never forget how it felt to see him on the ground, the air stolen from his lungs. Even then, he'd tried to get to me.

And I'd been so scared. Yes, I'd been scared for Erin and Murphy. I'd been scared for everyone else. But the thought of Aidric dying was more than I could handle. And then it was his voice that had brought me back, away from my magic.

Aidric had been right. It wasn't supposed to happen this way. Walking down this road would only lead to heartbreak. It didn't matter how we felt about each other.

I was going home.

CHAPTER SIX

"Did you hear Kalman ran off with some soldier?"

"I'm sorry—what?" I tore my eyes from the snow-covered plants along the path as Annistyn's voice broke through the fog I'd been in all morning. Sleep never came, and I was little more than a zombie as Annistyn, Maren, and I strolled through the gardens.

"Kalman, Lord Barwick's assistant? He took off with some guard. They disappeared last night! The only thing left in his room was a note to Lord Barwick."

"Who was the soldier?"

"Who discovered them missing?"

"Why did they run away?"

Our questions crashed into each other as we settled on a bench in a circle of giant rhododendrons. Annistyn lifted an eyebrow at Maren, and I leaned in to hear her.

"I don't know who the soldier is. Some commoner. Ray? Whatever. Apparently, they met when Kalman taught the new soldiers magic last fall."

"Rose?"

We'd trained together for the army. I hadn't seen her since moving into the castle. She wasn't much older than me.

"Yeah, sure—" Annistyn rubbed her hands together, eager to get to the juicy bits of the story. "Apparently Kalman and—uh—Rose have been seeing each other for months but hiding it. No one suspected a thing."

"Why would they hide it?"

"You tell me, Lydia. Why would two people want to hide a relationship?" Maren quipped. I'd never mentioned anything that happened last fall, but there was enough knowledge in her and Annistyn's side eye glances to tell me they knew about my clandestine relationship. I smoothed my skirt to hide the flush in my cheeks.

"Never mind. You were saying?"

Annistyn hid a smile as she continued her story.

"Last week, Kalman asked his family's permission to marry Rose. He confessed to the relationship and wanted his betrothal to Valeria dissolved."

"He didn't!" Maren grabbed the side of my arm with emphasis.

"He did!" Annistyn's cheeks bloomed with color despite the cool air. She thrived on court gossip. "He said he loved Rose and marriage to anyone else would be a sham."

"I can't believe it. What an insult to Valeria's family. Her father will not be happy. What's Kalman's family going to do now that he's gone?" Maren took off with the conversation. I stayed quiet. Valeria was from a newer noble house. All I remembered from my lessons with Gabrielle is they were crazy rich.

"Rumors are they'll have to pay Valeria's father for the broken engagement."

"Valeria's father will never shut up about this!"

"I heard Kalman's parents are going to leave and return to Orsa. I'll be surprised if they ever come to court again. It's going to be impossible for Kalman's sister to get a betrothal now. I bet they won't even present her—"

"Wait—I don't understand." Kalman helped Barwick during my magic lessons. I talked to him at least once a week. All of this had been going on and I'd never noticed. "Kalman didn't want to marry Valeria, so he broke off the engagement. Sure, it sucks, but what's the big deal? Why should his parent's leave? Or his little sister be bothered? Neither Kalman nor Rose are nobles, so why does it matter?"

The glance that flitted between Annistyn and Maren told me all I needed to know. My friends had been patient with me as they taught me the social graces that helped me succeed among the nobles. So, I usually overlooked it when they treated me like a child playing 'got your nose.' But right now, sleeplessness and frustration had stolen any patience I once possessed.

"Just tell me, already," I huffed.

Annistyn unfurled her fan with a snap. Maren patted me on the shoulder and suppressed an impatient sigh.

"You're correct. Kalman isn't a noble. But he is Lord Barwick's cousin. And despite not having a noble title, Kalman's family is still very wealthy and connected."

"Okay..." I prompted when they acted like that explained everything. "What does that have to do with Kalman and Rose?"

There was that glance again. It was my turn to suppress a sigh.

"Rose is just a soldier."

"What does that have to do with anything?"

"The army is only for people with no wealth or connections. Anyone can join an army. If you're wealthy and have fighting skills, you go for your knighthood or train to be in the personal service of a noble.

"Besides, it doesn't matter what Rose does. Kalman was already betrothed to Valeria. They've been engaged for years."

"But he said he loves Rose."

This time, Maren snorted in disbelief.

"Love doesn't matter Lydia. Marriage isn't about love. It's about helping your family. And once you sign the contract..." She grimaced at the mere thought. "Because Kalman ran off, his parents are going to have to deal with the consequences."

"Well, I'm glad they ran away. Good for them."

I walked off, knowing if my friends exchanged one more pity glance, I'd bite their heads off. Soon we strolled through the statue pavilion. I ignored the memories of the last time I was there. After last night, it wasn't something I wanted to revisit. We came to the last statue in the garden. It depicted a lovely young woman. In her outstretched hands, someone had draped a single red rose.

"Who are all these people?"

"Thavellian royalty," Maren answered. She stopped beside me. "This is the late Queen Lasha."

"Aidric's mom?" I fingered the red rose. The leaves were wilting, so it had been there for a couple of days at least. "Do you think the king left this?"

"No." Maren shook her emphatically. "My parents say King Bleddyn and Queen Lasha often visited the garden.

They even held courts and banquets out here. The king hasn't set foot in the gardens since she died."

Maren and Annistyn both bowed their heads in respect as we passed the statue. Swallowing the lump that formed in my throat, I followed their example. I didn't mention seeing the king leaving the gardens the other night. If he wanted privacy to visit his late wife and leave roses, I would let him have it.

After a lunch in my rooms while Maren and Annistyn went through my clothes for the next week's dinner, I convinced them to find a tide pool to skate on down by the bay. Annistyn led us to a shortcut through the indoor practice courts for members of the palace guard, knights, and squires.

"For the warmth," Annistyn claimed. As she directed us toward the courts where the young men our age sparred, I realized what kind of warmth Annistyn was looking for. But no one was sparring today.

Another activity greeted us instead. A crown of men gathered outside the far court. They parted and let us through so we could see what was going on. Tristan, the squire who caught Annistyn's eye, stood in the nearest corner. He held a rounded stick over one shoulder. Someone in the middle tossed a leather ball. He swung, hitting the ball with a loud *thunk*. It sailed across the court. I laughed when I realized what was going on. Tristan took off straight down the middle of the court, making the pitcher jump out of his way.

"No, no, no," a voice at the rail called. "You're supposed to run to the base. Where I left the shield. Run there!"

Tristan waved and reversed his course, sliding to touch the base as another player dove to tag him.

"He made it!" Nadine stood in the middle, watching the proceedings like a hawk.

"The word is safe," the instructing voice intoned. "But I'll take it."

I'd been so focused on the game, I realized too late I recognized the voice giving everyone instructions. Then guards and squires parted, revealing Murphy. I slowed, dropping behind Annistyn and Maren. It was too late to turn back.

"Well, good afternoon." Tristan strolled over, slinging his bat over his shoulder. He gave us a bow with a flourish of the bat. "What brings you fine ladies out to our humble fighting courts."

"We were on our way to skate, but this looks like much more fun," Annistyn leaned against the rail. "I've never seen a game like this."

"It's this guy's idea." Tristan pointed at Murphy. He waved sheepishly. "He claims it's a game from back home. But I think he just made it all up. Though I must admit, it gets the blood pumping."

"Tell us, Lydia"—Maren grabbed my arm and tugged me forward—"is this truly a game or did Guardsman Murphy make it up?"

I blushed as all eyes—including Murphy's—turned to me. "It's real. A very popular one, in fact. Murphy would know, he's one of the best players at our school." Even though everyone gathered looked in my direction, it didn't matter. It was Murphy's attention that made me blush. I glanced up at him and offered a small smile. To my surprise, he returned it.

"Well, for all we know, you two could conspire together to trick us poor Thavellians," Tristan said. "Murphy keeps telling us it's called baseball. But clearly the best part is the bat. So, I'm calling it batball." He nodded as if solidifying his decision.

"Stay for a while, ladies. Watch my team beat Murphy at his own game. Annistyn, you can keep score for us." He winked and returned to his base.

Oblivious to my objections, Annistyn and Maren arranged their skirts across the benches. I rolled my eyes but stopped myself when I realized how much attention they were getting already. I chose a spot where the girls shielded me from view.

As the impromptu baseball game progressed, it turned out everyone wasn't as familiar with the rules as they thought. There was a lot of hitting and running and arguing, but not a lot of actual playing. And at the end when they asked Annistyn the score, she claimed it was "Forty-two."

Evening closed in as the game wrapped up. The nobles made their exits. It was time to prepare for yet another banquet. I sighed in resignation as Annistyn and Maren ushered me away.

"Can't I just stay in my rooms?"

"I won't let you," Annistyn insisted. "I've seen what happens when you spend too much time alone. You get melancholy and start feeling sorry for yourself about everything you can't get done."

"Thanks for reminding me," I muttered.

"That's what I'm here for," she said brightly.

"Besides," Maren added, "you promised to demonstrate water pinwheels for us."

I waved my hand in concession and let them drag me along. Wet, heavy snow fell outside, dulling the surrounding sounds. I didn't hear someone calling my name until Maren poked me on the shoulder and tossed her head to the side.

Murphy followed us. He paused and rubbed the back of his neck when we all turned to look at him.

"Lydia, can I uh—can I talk to you for a minute?" Even though his words were soft, he looked like he might run away if I moved too fast.

"You two go on ahead," I told the girls. "I'll catch up. I promise," I insisted as Maren lifted an eyebrow in my direction. Once they were out of earshot, I turned to the castle. He rubbed the back of his neck again and remained silent. I considered following Annistyn and Maren when he finally spoke.

"Um—how are you?"

"I'm okay." I let the syllables slip through my teeth. Murphy shifted his weight back and forth.

"That's good to hear. Erin told me you were okay—but it's nice to hear it from you." He paused.

My shoulders relaxed a bit. This wasn't an ambush. Instead of being grateful Murphy wasn't angry, I bristled. From his darting glances and shifting weight, Murphy clearly had something to say. I bit my tongue to quell my rising temper.

"Erin told me you had dinner with the king last night. She said you were hoping to hear something about John."

My temper fizzled. Murphy watched me still and the hope in his eyes sputtered out. I rubbed my arms, unable to give Murphy more bad news.

"Nothing, then?" Murphy blew out his breath. He leaned his head back, letting the cold snow hit his face. "I thought by now we'd have word of him. Or at least he'd try to reach out to us."

"I made the king a deal to make finding John a priority. He promised he'd send more people to look for him. I'm doing all I can."

Murphy shifted again.

"I've tried scrying him and using a locator spell. Everyone seems to forget that Reynard is a Wielder, too. And a far more powerful mage. I've only been doing this for a couple of months." I'd had it with defending myself to everyone. Again, the words rushed from me like they had a mind of their own. "If I thought it would help, I would saddle a horse and go searching for him right now. John is my friend, too."

Tears stung my cheeks, already cold from the snow. At the sight of them, Murphy grabbed me in a bear hug. I buried my face in his chest. His warmth radiated into me. All my anxiety caught up with me as the tears continued to flow. Murphy held me as I cried, resting his head on top of mine. Homesickness cut deep into my heart.

"I know you would. I know." As I poured out my emotions, Murphy's own thoughts came unplugged. "I'm sorry, Lydia. My temper got the best of me in the forest. I should've come and found you before now. I just never found the courage. Erin told me I was being stupid, and she's right. Seeing you use that kind of power—and losing John. I'm scared. And too stubborn for my own good. None of that excuses how I've been acting."

"I know this isn't your fault." He pulled back and looked down at me. "I know you're trying your best to get us home. I'm a terrible friend. Can you ever forgive me?"

"There's nothing to forgive, Murphy." My voice was still

thick with emotions, but my tears had dried. "If I'd been honest from the start, maybe none of this would've happened."

"You can't blame yourself. None of us know what we're doing here right now. You're smart, Lydia. And you've got good instincts. You need to remember that. And I'll be here to remind you when you forget. We started this together, we will finish it together, too."

"Together," I repeated with a nod.

Murphy's words gave me the surge of confidence I needed. He returned my smile, relief in every inch of his body. Silently, I vowed to see us through that promise. No matter what.

CHAPTER SEVEN

This first night I spent in the castle as the Gatebreaker, I'd told myself I'd never miss the grueling and dirty work of being an army recruit. I kept my word until I stared at the monstrosity of a dress King Bleddyn sent me for my first day of work.

"I'm not wearing that," I declared. I'd trade ten years of early mornings and beating people with wooden practice swords to get out of wearing it.

"My lady, the king sent it special," Gabrielle chided.

"Well, tell him to send it back." I cringed as she fluffed the stiff lace collar.

"I'm not going to do that." A small smile tugged at one side of her mouth.

"I'm glad you're enjoying my distress."

Gabrielle continued fluffing and tweaking the dress, immune to my protests.

"This is even more outrageous than my ballgowns. When do I get to pick what to wear?" My lady's maid answered with a single raised eyebrow. The answer was obvious. Never.

With a long-suffering sigh, I accepted my fate. It had been two weeks since the dinner with King Bleddyn and Prince Aidric. Now I had to make good on my word, no matter how ridiculous I looked doing it.

After more time than it should take any respectable person to get dressed, I was fully ensconced in the costume. The gilded dress stood out amongst the dark red and purple decorations in my room.

"Am I supposed to move in this?" A cardboard cutout wrapped in shades of green and gold fabric would do just as well. The stiff corset cut into my ribs and hips and the golden lace color reached all the way to my chin, making it almost impossible to turn my head. I'd seen some gaudy dresses on the richer nobles during balls, but there was no comparison to the one I wore.

"I expect not." Gabrielle covered a laugh masquerading as a cough. I glared at her, but she ignored me. "I doubt you will move much. This is more about the message it sends."

"And what message is that?" I growled. The rounded sage skirts fitted over the bodice caught in the bedroom doorway. I growled again. Gabrielle fluffed the train straight behind me before I yanked it through.

"As Gatebreaker, you've only been presented to the nobles here in Windburn. Most people know of your arrival, of course, but this will be the first time people get to see you. It's not my place to guess the workings of royalty, but I imagine the king wants everyone to see the wealth and power of the crown on display."

"I guess that includes me now?"

Gabrielle dipped her head. It was answer enough. She helped me pull on the last piece of my ensemble, an emerald surcoat covered in overlapping gold filigree designs. From afar, they looked like swirls of lacy metal. I studied one of the hanging sleeves up close. Eight-pointed stars blanketed the short jacket. At the end of each point was a solid triangle.

I gulped. A glance at Gabrielle's pale complexion told me she noticed too. She rubbed her right wrist where I knew her wielder brand scarred her skin. Somehow, we navigated the spiral staircase from my rooms and the narrow passageways to the throne room without falling and drowning in the folds of fabric that encased me. By the time we'd arrived, I'd calmed my racing heart. I wasn't sure how I felt about flaunting an outfit with a design that haunted so many other people. Maybe this was part of King Bleddyn's plan to change the perception of wielders. It didn't help the unease in the pit of my stomach.

As usual during the day, large dividers blocked the view of the banquet halls as those in the throne room conducted the business of the kingdom. The amount of manpower used in setting up the throne room every day and night during the winter astounded me.

Both King Bleddyn and Aidric sat on the dais at the end of the long room. The king occupied the chair in the middle, and the prince sat in the smaller chair to his right. With trepidation I realized there was a third chair—not throne, I told myself repeatedly—on the dais next to Aidric. I'd entered from the side, so no one had noticed my arrival yet. Just as I considered bolting for my rooms, Commander Nadine spotted me. She offered me a warm smile from her place at a table surrounded by members of her Palace Guard and maps. I smiled back and straightened my shoulders. I could do this.

Steward Olma spotted me next. He looked almost giddy

as he cleared his throat to interrupt the royals' intense conversation.

"Your Majesty, the Gatebreaker has arrived," he whispered. Olma swept over to me with a grace that didn't match his appearance. I resisted cringing as he took my hand and led me to the front of the dais. I curtsied to the king and the prince. Aidric's eyes trailed up my dress, the heat rising in my cheeks with each inch upward. I looked away before he could catch my eye.

"Lydia," King Bleddyn beamed at me. The warm welcome helped calm my nerves. "You look lovely. But something's missing."

My brow furrowed as I looked down at my dress. Gabrielle had placed every piece. What could be missing? The king chuckled and clapped his hands. A servant appeared at his elbow. The pillow she held displayed a delicate gold circlet. Ornate leaves wrapped around the sides and a huge emerald jewel dangled in the front. I blanched at the sight.

"Oh no, Your Majesty—I can't." I stepped back, genuine panic threatening to engulf me.

"No need to be modest, Lydia." Misreading my hesitation, King Bleddyn stepped forward and plopped the circlet on my head. "No expense spared for our Gatebreaker."

Gabrielle appeared at my elbow and pinned the crown to my head. I suppressed a sigh. No taking it off now. She disappeared to wherever she went off to when I was in the throne room. King Bleddyn waved me onto the dais.

"Today, everyone will see you have the love and might of the crown behind you."

The task set before me felt more like a performance than

a job. I glanced toward Aidric, but he had left the platform and was engaged in conversation with Nadine, oblivious to my uncertainty. I'd thought I'd be working in the background. In some room doing interviews with potential students. Not paraded in the open, dressed up and painted like I belonged in a museum.

"Now come, Lydia," the king insisted when I still didn't move. "Take your seat and let me see the full picture."

I stepped onto the dais. But no amount of willpower could make me sit in the chair next to the king's throne. It was one thing for everyone in the castle to know who I was. But standing up in front of the entire kingdom was a different story. Cold sweat coated my back under the layers and layers of fabric.

The king stepped up next to me. He hooked his hands in his waistband and surveyed the people working at the tables behind the throne.

"I was born a prince, so the pageantry has always been part of my life. Aidric's too. But I see how it could be a lot to take in." He offered me his arm. We were only two steps away, but having his confident presence broke me from my indecision and I moved forward. I swept my skirts around me before I sat in a move Annistyn and Maren spent hours teaching me. Too bad they'd never taught me how to breathe in a corset. The emerald jewel bounced against my forehead. King Bleddyn crouched beside me.

"Thavell is energized like I haven't seen her in years. Everyone wants to see the Gatebreaker. You, my dear, are going to usher this country into its next Golden Age."

"I don't know if I can do that." I forced my fear out of my now dry mouth.

"You don't have to, Lydia." The king patted my hand and stood again, his knees cracking with the effort. "You are the symbol that will carry us forward. But the work isn't yours, alone. Today, your status here will be solidified. Everyone will see the support you have from us, and together we will inspire them for the future."

He stepped back and surveyed me. I offered a smile, and he beamed.

"Isn't she lovely?"

"The loveliest." I jumped when Aidric appeared at the side of my chair. He smiled at his father, but avoided looking at me once again.

"Oh—I'm sorry, Your Majesty." A quiet voice chirped from somewhere behind me. "I didn't realize there was an audience today. I was just meeting Aidric."

I froze. It didn't matter that I couldn't turn around in this dress. I knew who that voice belonged to. Lady Jaclyn turned the corner. She was all smiles and dressed for riding in pants and a long burgundy coat. If only I could use my magic to turn invisible. But it wasn't to be as Jaclyn greeted the king and spotted me.

Her eyes traveled from the hem of my gown all the way to the small crown on my head. While the smile never left her face, I expected ice to grow in the air between us. When I'd become part of the nobility, I'd fostered a small hope Lady Jaclyn and I could be friends. Even though she never said an unkind word, her affable personality switched to rigid formality any time I was around. Every interaction with her screamed: *I know.*

And now here I was dressed in finery with a crown on my head, sitting on the throne next to her boyfriend.

Unable to hold Jaclyn's gaze any longer, I watched my finger run long lines down the wide mahogany arm of the throne. I liked Jaclyn, as crazy as it was. And even though Aidric broke things off when Jaclyn came into the picture, I still carried guilt that our relationship bothered her. Unfounded guilt. Or so I'd thought until the other night.

"Jaclyn." Aidric stepped off the dais and kissed his betrothed on both cheeks. I continued running my finger up and down, wishing I was anywhere but here. "Give me one moment and we can go."

"Go?" King Bleddyn broke off a conversation with Olma to stare at his son. "Go where? I thought we'd discussed you staying for the audience?"

"We discussed it," Aidric ground out through clenched teeth. "And I made myself clear about what I thought about this—spectacle."

I decided it would be a nice time for the earth to open and swallow me whole. How much magic would it take to make that happen? I continued to study the arm of the throne like it was the most amazing thing I'd ever seen.

"You're staying." If King's Bleddyn's faced turned any redder, he'd spit flame.

"I've already promised to take Jaclyn riding. I can't back out of my commitment." Aidric's apathy toward his father toed the line between brilliant and idiotic. Poking the beast didn't seem like the best idea. Beside me, the king looked ready to explode. No matter how often the prince and king butted heads, I'd never seen him so close to losing his temper.

Jaclyn spotted the danger, too. She watched the volley of words between father and son with keen attention. She laid a petite hand on Aidric's arm and tugged him further from the dais, away from the look of murder in his father's eyes.

"You know, I'd like to stay." She laced her fingers through Aidric's and gave an upturned look through her eyelashes. Oh, she was good. "I've never watched an audience in Windburn."

"You sure you don't mind?" Aidric still glowered. He tugged his hand out of her grasp and twirled it on the hilt of a dagger at his side. There was no way he didn't recognize the out Jaclyn offered him. Part of me wondered if he'd intended to rile his father.

"With your permission—of course, Your Majesty." Jaclyn curtsied low and gave the king the same look she'd plied Aidric with. She'd diffused the heated argument with ease. Clearly, there were more skills I needed to learn if I was going to keep up with the other court ladies.

"Very well," King Bleddyn nodded beatifically. With his scepter, he motioned to seats to the left of the dais. "Any nobility who wishes to watch is welcome, as always."

Lady Jaclyn curtsied again and slipped into a seat. Great, now someone else was here to witness the *spectacle*, as Aidric had lovingly referred to it. Something burned my hand. I bit back a yelp and stuck my finger in my mouth. There on the arm of the chair were two burnt spots. Oops. I took a deep breath and released the tension in my shoulders and arms. Setting the throne on fire might be a good way to get out of this audience, but I had a feeling the king wouldn't be very impressed.

Aidric returned to the dais and slumped down on the throne next to mine. I yanked my finger out of my mouth and folded it in my dress. For a split second, Aidric's attention caught on the burn marks on my chair and then to my hands hidden in the fabric of my dress.

King Bleddyn called for the doors to be opened, and every other thought eddied out of my mind. The great doors at the top of the staircase creaked as the valets pushed them to the side. The chairs beside the dais filled as everyone working behind us paused their work to see the audience. I straightened in my chair. This was it.

"Lady Roberta and Lord Tristan of Stormguard."

Lady Roberta's angled face was a mirror to Tristan's. While Tristan's expression often looked aloof, his mother's leaned toward severe. She'd pulled her frosted gray hair back into a tight bun, and her stiff silver dress reminded me of the statues in the garden.

"Welcome, Lady Roberta." King Bleddyn acknowledged them with a point of his scepter. Olma appeared next to the king's elbow, ready to retrieve anything he might need. "You're here to present Tristan as a potential student?"

"By your leave, Your Grace." Lady Roberta's voice was devoid of the warmth that Tristan had. "Although I must ask why this youngster must evaluate my youngest son when, at the mere presence of magic you accepted my oldest?"

Bold. King Bleddyn's face smoldered. Instead of responding, he motioned to me. I stopped myself from sinking down into the throne.

"Please assess Lord Tristan for us, Gatebreaker Lydia."

A hush fell over the crowd. Annoyance rippled through me at the king's booming voice. I pushed aside my unease and the heat of everyone's attention. My magic responded as soon as I called. Pulling the thread of aether and bending it to my will was easier this time. I opened my eyes after only a blink. Colorful threads of magic wove their way through everything in the throne room.

Faint flaxen light magic rippled in the beams of sunlight that shone down on us from the tall windows lining the room. Charcoal lines of metal magic veined through the floor. Magic the color of ash ran underneath both Roberta's and Tristan's skin. Air mages.

Tristan's magic paled compared to his mother's. I blinked again, and the colors disappeared. The world seemed dull once the colorful threads had faded.

"Tristan, you're an air Wielder." I didn't know exactly what the king expected of me now, so I just talked to Tristan like I would any time I ran into him. "But your magic isn't strong."

I stuttered over my words when Roberta shot me a glare. On the other hand, Tristan grinned.

"I told you, Mother." He spoke low, but the words were still audible. Roberta switched her glare from me to her son.

"Tristan, you've heard the assessment of the Gatebreaker. We won't be able to accept you into the Palace Scholars this year." King Bleddyn's announcement sounded more official than mine.

Tristan bowed. He turned to leave, but his mother grabbed his elbow.

"But he just turned sixteen, won't the magic strengthen as he gets older?"

"No," King Bleddyn responded. He looked amiable enough, but an edge crept into his voice. "Natural power stays the same. How much you are born with is how much you will possess your entire life."

"How do we even know the girl is telling the truth?" Roberta's eyes flashed to me again.

I dropped my gaze to the ground. This was going to be harder than I thought. In my peripheral vision, King Bleddyn tensed. But it was Prince Aidric who responded.

"Enough." Aidric's voice was far removed from the booming one of his father. But his words held a different sort of power. The energy in the room flexed when he spoke. "You will not insult Lydia's honor. She is a ward of the crown and has our full trust behind her."

Before Roberta could respond, Aidric was out of his throne and standing in front of Tristan and his mother. "You know the best interest of the kingdom is to find our strongest wielders and train them as fast as we can." Aidric spoke softer now. "You can always hire a private tutor for Tristan. I've seen him use his magic. He has a good handle on his abilities already." Aidric glanced at Tristan for confirmation, and he nodded.

"This way my squire training won't be interrupted." Tristan spoke to his mother now. "If I can keep up, I will be a knight within a year."

"A worthy and ambitious goal." King Bleddyn hadn't moved from his rigid position on his throne. But that didn't stop him from taking part in the conversation.

Roberta glanced from the prince to the king, and to the sizeable crowd of nobles now watching. She pressed her lips into a hard line and nodded.

She curtsied again to the king as Aidric returned to his throne.

"Forgive my outburst, Sire. You know I only want the best for my children."

King Bleddyn nodded in acquiescence. I sighed and leaned my head against the high back of the chair as Tristan and Roberta exited through a side door. If the whole day was going to be this hard, I wasn't sure I was up to the task.

Heat warmed my shoulder as someone gripped it. Standing at my side, Aidric gave me a half grin.

"Don't worry about it," he whispered as another group began making their way down the stairs. "Roberta has always been outspoken. Her family's lands produce most of our wheat crop, so she's not afraid to be uh—vocal. Her attitude has nothing to do with you."

I offered him a tight-lipped grin, still too nervous to say anything. With a start, I remembered Jaclyn was still here. As King Bleddyn introduced another mother and son duo standing before us, I risked a glance at her. She wasn't looking at me, but was staring at Aidric as he greeted the newcomers. And her face held such a powerful look of admiration, I had to look away.

I squared my shoulders and focused on the task at hand, ignoring the sinking sensation in my gut and my shoulder that still tingled from Aidric's touch.

CHAPTER EIGHT

The rest of the morning passed uneventfully. Nobles came in one family at a time. One by one, I examined teenagers who had recently turned sixteen and discovered their powers. Occasionally, an older noble came forward, finally ready to seek training for their magic. Seeing the magic became easier each time I tried. Before long, I only had to blink to change my sight back and forth. The nobles' eagerness to be assessed calmed my nerves. I got into the rhythm of the day, announcing the amount of magic to the king who decided who moved onto the Scholars or not.

To dissuade any more bad feelings like Roberta's, Aidric offered those who didn't make it into the Scholars private tutoring under the tutelage of Lord Barwick.

"It's better this way," Aidric confided in me during a brief break. "Keeping the nobles happy feels like a full-time job, some days."

Nobles drifted in and out of the audience as the day wore on. Anyone in the castle had the right to view the king's audiences. Annistyn and Maren stopped by with their families. Many of them were drawn by the novelty.

Instead of ending the day at lunch like I hoped, Gabrielle appeared to serve me lunch in my chair. I sighed, watching Aidric and Jaclyn sneak out a side door. The high back of the throne was uncomfortable and changing my vision so much meant dots of magic continued to show up in my vision.

For once, Olma approaching me wasn't unwelcome.

"You are doing a fine job, Lady Lydia."

I dipped my head in thanks, saving my voice for the afternoon.

"I've noticed you can visualize the magic easier than you were this morning."

"Yes, I am. Some skills come easier. I caught on to this one quickly."

"Why do you think that is? Can you tell the various affinities apart, or is your magic just one pool of force you access?"

"Sometimes I can tell the affinities apart." I shrugged, sending an arrow of pain through my stiff shoulders. "If I'm doing something very specific. But most of the time I don't think about the affinities, just consider what I want to do and go for it."

Typically, I was more interested in using my magic than learning about it. But like Barwick, Olma frequently wanted to chat about thorn. Since there wasn't anyone else like me, no one really knew how my magic worked.

"Fascinating—" Olma stared off into the distance. I scratched my head, easing the tingling that came with repeated use of magic. Before Olma could complete his thoughts, King Bleddyn called the audience back to order.

Aidric reappeared just in time to take his seat next to me. Gabrielle settled my crown and skirts before disappearing once again. I took a deep breath and readied myself for an afternoon of being the Gatebreaker.

"Let them in!"

The doors on both sides of the staircase opened and a large group of people ushered through, escorted by members of the Palace Guard. I glanced at faces, but neither Erin nor Murphy were with them. Nadine left her table and took a position beside the king. At some point she'd donned her official surcoat with the insignia of the royal house, a gray field with a black band and the head of a black wolf. A crossed sword and dagger sat under the insignia, indicating Nadine as the commander. She'd tied a bandana over her close-cropped brown hair. Between that and the weapons clinking on her belt, she made an intimidating picture. More members of the guard had materialized on either side of the nobles' galley.

The group clustered together before the throne. A quick head count told me there were almost fifty people gathered.

King Bleddyn stood. Aidric and I rose from our seats as well.

"Welcome, my loyal subjects. I am honored that each of you are interested in joining the Palace Scholars."

I surveyed the people as King Bleddyn spoke. People of all ages and looks stared back at me. Thavell might be only one country, but the differences in appearance of the people here was unlike any place back home. I wondered if the larger guard presence was just another show of the king's, because I couldn't spot a single weapon among them.

The differences in classes were something that seemed to stay no matter how different our lands were. Standing in the front of the group were those dressed in fine fabrics and clothing like the nobles, clearly members of the upper merchant class.

Behind them stood people more modestly dressed. Many women in simple dresses and head coverings, most of the men in only tunics and pants. Mostly likely tradesmen, hunters, possibly farmers if they lived outside of Windburn city. My cheeks flushed with shame when I noticed the few people that hung in the back with clothing so tattered it could barely be patched. My gaudy outfit had enough fabric to make at least ten different outfits. And what about all the other excessive dresses in my closet?

"I invited you here today because of your magic. You have been tested and determined to be the strongest Wielders from across Thavell. Now the Gatebreaker will examine you and decide who is worthy to be a Scholar."

A murmur rippled through the crowd. I resisted the urge to duck my head, instead keeping my eyes focused on the back of the room. King Bleddyn told me a symbol was what I needed to be. So I would. I was the Gatebreaker. And I was powerful. There was no need for me to hide it anymore.

"Gatebreaker Lydia, when you are ready. Please identify those who are strong enough for the Scholars."

A clerk appeared at my elbow and the guard members shifted people to the front one at a time. My legs wobbled with relief. The strain of using magic all day was wearing on me, but I needed to show my strength now.

The individuals before me blended as I focused only on their magic. I called out each person's affinities and natural strength. It was clear King Bleddyn would not be giving these people the personal conversation he'd offered the nobles.

Once the clerk wrote the information I gave them, someone immediately escorted the person to the back of the throne room.

Even with the expedited process, it was slow work getting through everyone. Every person in this group possessed potent magic. The colors burned bright in my vision. I had to record everyone's affinities, and sometimes it took me a moment to decide whether their magic was strong enough for the Scholars. But I couldn't shake the feeling that I wasn't the person who should make this decision.

Halfway through, the guards moved a girl about my age to the front. She wore a simple yellow dress and a gray head wrap, but something about her straight back and the stern glint in her brown eyes caught me off guard.

For a moment too long, I stared at her instead of looking at her magic. When I called for my magic, we locked eyes. My vision clouded with the strength of magic coming from her. Then a rush of emotions overtook me. They caught me up in a cacophony, almost like everyone in the room threw their feelings at my heart. I reached back to steady myself with the arms of my chair as the cloud of thoughts and emotions whipped through me like a storm.

I was afraid. Afraid of the king, of being exposed. I was excited. A place in the Scholars meant I could prove myself. I wanted to run for the side door. The anxiety welling up inside me was almost too much. But the guards would see me. They would know I had something to hide. I'd never get past them. Pride. Pride in my people. In this place. The people admired me, and when my plan came together, I'd be stronger than ever. Protection. These people standing here didn't know me. They didn't trust me. I needed them to know I was on their side.

I wrenched my eyes away from the crowd and stumbled. Aidric grabbed my arm to steady me. Emptiness washed through me like someone had thrown a bucket of water over my head.

"Lydia, are you okay?" Aidric whispered. Empathy. Just like weeks ago with Aidric, I'd connected myself with other people's emotions. It wasn't the first time it had happened, but I never expected it when it did. And I'd never heard anyone's thoughts before.

I realized Aidric wasn't the only one concerned. The king, Nadine, Jaclyn—and everyone in the crowd—stared at me. I cleared my throat and steadied myself. Aidric let his hand drop from my arm, but he stayed at my side like he thought I might fall over if left to my own devices. He wasn't entirely wrong. My legs certainly felt shakier than they had a moment ago.

"I apologize, Your Majesty." I dipped into a curtsy to the king. A blush colored my cheeks. "My magic got away from me a bit, there." I spoke quietly so the crowd couldn't hear me.

The king smiled and nodded at me. "You may continue when you feel up to it."

I straightened and faced the crowd again. A bitter taste coated the back of my throat. There was excitement among them. But also fear. But now all of their faces blended together, and I felt nothing. I had no way of knowing who among the crowd didn't want to be here or why.

I focused on the girl still standing in front of me. Was it her? She regarded me with her strange stone-colored eyes.

No fear lingered there. In fact, she looked more confident than I felt. I blinked and the threads of magic appeared around her. I had to squint against the glare. Yellow, black, and teal threads intertwined around her body and hands so tightly it was difficult to tell them apart.

"Affinities for light, aether, and water," I called out. The king shifted and his gaze bore into the girl. She didn't blink.

"Three affinities?" the clerk asked.

"Yes."

The clerk stared at me for another moment, but finally wrote it down.

"You, girl, what's your name?" the king called.

"Dana." The guard to her left nudged her. She narrowed her eyes. "Your Majesty," she added as she dropped into a reluctant curtsy.

"Well, Dana, with three affinities it is my honor to welcome you immediately into the Palace Scholars. No need to wait for the start of class. Lord Barwick will instruct you until they start. You can move into the dormitories this very evening."

Applause broke out from the crowd, engulfing the throne room in claps and cheers. Dana dropped into a curtsy again, her cheeks rosy from the attention. As a guard appeared at her side to escort her from the room, I noticed her impassive expression hadn't changed. Watching her go, I wondered if she was thrilled with the announcement at all.

CHAPTER NINE

An hour later, I identified a scrawny teenage boy as being a strong metal Wielder and finished. I dropped back into my seat, and let my head fall back to stare at the high ceiling. A headache pounded at my temples.

"That was excellent work," the king said. On my other side, Aidric had already disappeared. I pulled myself back to reality to pay attention.

"Thank you, Your Majesty."

"We will have three audiences each week for the next two weeks. After that, everyone will move into the dormitories and await lessons."

I flexed my hands to release the tension in my shoulders and neck.

"I am at Your Majesty's service." I offered the best smile I could manage. It must have been enough because King Bleddyn patted me on the shoulder before joining a group of nobles standing nearby. With no one to stop me, I headed for the door.

And ran right into the group of people joining the Scholars. They stood in the antechamber to the throne room with Lord Barwick lecturing them on returning to the castle in a few weeks. I attempted to duck back into the throne room, but a whisper of excited voices worked through the crowd. All eyes turned toward me.

"It's the Gatebreaker!"

"Lady Lydia!"

The group crowded around me. I pressed back into the wall, swallowed up in a flurry of faces and hands and names as everyone tried to get close and touch my hands or bow before me. One man old enough to be my father had tears in his eyes. He gripped both of my hands in his own.

"Thank you, Lady Lydia. Hearing the stories about you using your magic in battle to protect the king and the prince gave me the courage to come forward. I've always been scared to use my magic, but now I can be a part of the Scholars and use it for something useful."

Before I could say anything, a dark-skinned girl my age replaced him.

"Is it true you can use all eight affinities?" I nodded. She squealed. "How exciting. Will you show us?"

Again, I couldn't respond as more people surged in. Barwick made his way to my side. He held his staff out to give me space, but even that didn't stop everyone from jostling to get a spot near me. Shock froze my tongue. I softened as I realized all these people were just happy to meet me. Suddenly, I felt shy before all of this attention. I didn't know what to say.

"I am glad you all could be here," I finally said. "I can't wait to see what you can do once lessons begin."

That earned another excited uproar.

"Will you be teaching us?" someone shouted.

"No," I paused, unsure how many people outside the castle knew about my powers, or my control of them. "But the teachers are wonderful."

Then the dark-skinned girl was back, tugging Dana behind her. She shoved the severe girl in front of me. I offered her my hand, and she gave it a quick shake before hiding her hands back inside the sleeves of her dress.

"I'm Arete. I told Dana that having three affinities meant she was strong. Can you believe she didn't even want to come today? I was the one who convinced her."

"Well, Arete, I'm glad you brought her." I hoped Dana would smile, but she continued to stare with that untenable look in her eyes. "I'm looking forward to seeing you use your magic."

There was a shout at the back of the crowd. Aidric and Nadine waded through everyone to my side.

"Thank you all for coming," he called as everyone dropped into a bow or curtsy at his appearance. "Lydia has another engagement she must attend to now."

He linked his arm through mine and drew me away. Nadine stayed to focus the crowd back on Barwick. Everyone kept their eyes on me until Aidric and I moved out of sight down a side hallway.

As we turned the corner, Aidric moved away. I hugged my arms around myself and started in the direction of my rooms. I thought I was alone until footsteps behind me caused me to turn and see Aidric catching up to me again. He fell into step beside me.

"You're not even going to thank me for saving you?"

I snorted.

"I didn't know I needed to be rescued." His mouth twitched as he suppressed a smile. "They just wanted to meet me and talk to me."

"Did you enjoy that?"

I glanced at him again. He looked curious, not judgmental.

"A little." I shrugged. "It's nice to do something that people are excited about."

"Not letting your magical powers go to your head, are you?" I shot him a side-eyed glare, but the twitch in his jaw gave his teasing away.

"I guess having people fawn over you is nothing since you're such a heartthrob prince."

We reached the spiral staircase that lead to my rooms. Aidric followed me up.

"What's a heartthrob?"

"Nothing," I blurted. *Bad choice of words, Lydia.* The glint in Aidric's eye said enough about his idea of what a heartthrob was. I turned my head to hide my blush.

Late afternoon sunlight flooded my sitting room. At the sight of my comfy home-away-from-home, exhaustion hit me in full force. All I wanted was to get out of this massive dress. I yanked the offensive surcoat off and threw it in a nearby chair. Aidric picked it up and smoothed it out. Reaching the laces of the dress and corset behind my back wasn't as easy.

"How do you think today went?" Aidric asked.

"Fine." I suppressed a yawn and tried to get to the laces again. "Using my magic all day has worn me out, though."

"You can tell my father if—"

"If you're going to stand there and lecture me again," I

cut him off, "the least you can do is come and help me get this dress off."

"I—uh—what," Aidric blushed crimson from the collar of his shirt to the roots of his curls. I giggled.

"Easy there, Prince. I'm wearing basically a whole other dress under this one. It's totally appropriate." I lifted an eyebrow and stared at him. He cleared his throat and came over. I brushed my hair out of his way as his fingers tugged on the laces.

"I was just saying my father gets enthusiastic about his new projects. He forgets not everyone has his stamina. If you need to rest, just tell him."

Aidric's fingers slowly untied each knot and unlaced the strings, working his way down my back. I closed my eyes and leaned into his gentle touch, almost forgetting to respond to him.

"I'm okay. Usually, I use my magic in big bursts, using a little all day like that takes different energy." I covered another yawn. "But it's like any muscle. I'll get used to it."

"You said you lost control of your magic."

I cringed. I should've known he'd heard that. "Only for a second. My magic caught on to everyone's emotions. Mostly excitement, but some people were scared too." I didn't mention hearing the thoughts. None of them made sense, anyway.

"Hmm." Aidric scratched his chin while he thought. "It's probably just because it's their first time in the castle. Most likely their first time meeting the king."

First time seeing you, too, I wanted to add. But then again, Aidric could say the same about me. It was weird to think of myself as someone people were scared to meet. I wasn't sure how I felt about it.

Aidric finished unlacing my dress and stepped back. I let the beaded monstrosity fall to the floor. Reaching around, I yanked the rest of the corset off. I stopped myself from throwing it directly into the fire. The cream linen dress I wore underneath the ensemble was still perfectly appropriate. Still, I looked up to see that Aidric had turned his back to me. I smiled.

"Aidric, why did you follow me up here? It wasn't just to check on me."

Aidric rubbed the back of his neck. He took a tentative peek over his shoulder. Satisfied I had enough clothes on, he turned back to face me.

"I just needed to tell you..." He looked down and hit his knuckles against the chair. "About the other night..." My exhaustion vanished. Every nerve focused on Aidric. "You were right."

I let out a small breath. Aidric looked back up at me. Conflict warred in his eyes.

"Not about me wanting to save you. I've never thought you were lost, or that you needed saving." He paused again. I bit the inside of my cheek to stop myself from saying anything.

"But you were right about me being selfish. You just took everything in stride. I never thought beyond my own feelings. I should have done better. Will you forgive me?"

I waited, but he didn't add anything. The last few months had been painful, and his actions had been a big part of that. Part of me wanted to tell him to get lost, just to give him a piece of his own medicine. But I remembered his last words to me in this room. Words I remembered every night when I drifted off to sleep. I pressed my hand to my chest.

"Of course, I forgive you, Aidric."

He reached out and for a moment I thought he was going to pull me into a hug, but stopped himself at the last moment. His bright smile was enough.

"Thank you, Lydia. I'll be a better friend this time, I promise."

"Good." I smoothed a nearby blanket, fighting to keep my voice steady. I offered him a smile in return.

"I have to go now." To his credit, Aidric looked disappointed. I smoothed the blanket again, unsure of what to say now. He paused and looked over his shoulder before he left. "Oh, tomorrow Jaclyn and I are planning a ride into the city with some other friends. Would you like to go? Annistyn and Maren too, if they'd like."

I ignored the stabbing pain at the mention of Jaclyn's name. "I'd love to. And Annistyn and Maren always enjoy a ride into the city." Aidric grinned again before disappearing down the staircase.

Usually I enjoyed solitude, but my rooms felt lonely after Aidric left. Not wanting to leave the work to Gabrielle, I dragged the Gatebreaker gown to my closet and set it up on the holder the best I could. All the while, the conversation with Aidric turned over in my mind. For the first time in months, we were good. We could move on and be friends. Happiness is what I should be feeling. But somehow, I couldn't let go of the bitterness that tugged at my heart.

My exhaustion meant sleep came easily that night. But it was filled with terrors. Only this time, it wasn't my memories that kept me from resting. It wasn't even a dream.

Thieves invaded my home. These men dressed in all black with hoods over their faces. They yanked me and my sisters from the bed and pushed us out into the frosty night. My father grabbed his axe from beside the woodpile. One man disarmed him with a twist of the wrist and knocked him in the head. He crumpled to the ground. I tried to call out, but someone stuffed my mouth with a gag and tied my hands and feet together.

They threw me on the ground next to my sisters. My mother screamed for help, pleaded for the men to leave. They gagged her too and dragged her to a separate room. I closed my eyes and tried to call on my magic. My parents told me to hide it, told me to keep it a secret. But now I needed it to save my family. I felt the earth beneath our house respond to my call. Roots jumped up from the dormant ground. They twined around the men's weapons, around their throats. The gag had come loose from my sister's mouth, and she screamed as more and more roots shot through the ground.

I was all the plants at once as they grabbed the men. I felt the life drain from them as I willed the roots to go tighter and tighter. My mother was free. She ran to me. Before she made it, a dark shadow crossed my vision, and everything went black.

Leaves crunched beneath my feet. Golden leaves. I groaned, the sound swallowed up in the forest. Was I still sleeping? Or had the forest called me home this time? I stood facing the same tree I'd seen so many times before. Twelve men couldn't wrap all the way around her trunk. Her roots intertwined with each other as they plunged deep into the ground. Branches filled with leaves in every shade of gold crowned her.

I drew in a breath. The smell of the wet leaves and rain hit my senses. A breeze tickled my cheek. It certainly felt like a real forest. But the air was too heavy for this to be true.

"Why am I here again?"

The tree didn't answer. Did I really expect her to? But there was that moment during battle. Thinking about this was making my headache return.

"If you won't give me answers, I'm leaving."

I stepped away from the tree.

And ran straight into a stone wall.

"Ouch!" My voice echoed in a dark corridor. Where was I? A shaft of moonlight from a thin window illuminated a castle hallway. I glanced down at my bare feet and night-gown. How did I get here? I studied the tapestries on the wall. None of them looked familiar. Months I'd been here, and I still didn't know the entire layout of the castle. I wasn't sure anyone did.

I shivered, the cold from the stone floor made its way up my spine. Footsteps sounded in the corridor behind me. No one could find me wandering the castle like this. I tugged on the door handle closest to me. It turned soundlessly. I yanked open the door. My heart leaped into my throat at the group of soldiers staring back at me. It took me two heartbeats to realize I was staring into a closet full of suits of armor. I squeezed in, trying my best not to bump the metal.

The footsteps came closer. I peeked through the crack of the closet door.

"Is it done?" I tensed at the king's voice.

"Yes, Your Majesty." Olma's slippery form moved into view. King Bleddyn stopped at the window across from me. He tapped his foot. Olma paused inches from my door.

"I don't like this," King Bleddyn murmured. "I'm asking these people to trust me. Yet here I am..." he growled to himself. "It feels too much like something my father would have done."

"You cannot let your noble ideals impede your mission, my king." Olma's voice snaked through the dark. I tucked myself further into the closet. "These people trust you to protect them. That's exactly what you're doing."

"You're sure this will work?" King Bleddyn rubbed the back of his neck, reminding me of his son. "Opening one realm won't let them all loose?"

Olma remained silent for a moment. I held my breath, afraid to give myself away. This wasn't a conversation the king wanted me to hear.

"As sure as I can be, Your Highness." Olma ran a finger down the stone wall as he spoke. A spark flared beneath his finger. "It's magic, there's always a risk. Especially when so much knowledge has been lost. But, with the right stones in place, it should be enough to counter any—uh—unwanted effects. You know what I risk by this route, I would not bring it to you if I didn't think it would work."

King Bleddyn nodded, but the tension didn't leave his shoulders.

"The alternative is Reynard or Katalia stumbling upon this knowledge first and putting it to their own use. Then where would we be?"

King Bleddyn whirled and slammed his fist against the wall. The armor behind me rattled. I bit my lip to keep from crying out. The king's face was inches from Olma's.

"Do not speak her name again, do you understand?"

Olma didn't back down from the king's stare. He leaned

forward. To my surprise, it was the king who backed up a step.

"Don't forget our arrangement, Sire." Olma kept his eyes locked onto the king. His robes quivered. "Even if you will not admit it, she is a threat. If she gets her hands on the Gate-breaker, we are through."

I gasped. Olma whirled to look in my direction, his eyes black as void. I clamped a hand over my mouth and sunk to the floor, scooting away from the door, and hiding behind a suit of armor. The handle to the closet door rattled. My heart thumped wildly against my ribcage.

I glanced around, trying to find somewhere to hide. From my vantage point, a shiny metal of a trapdoor caught my eye. The hinges to the door of the closet squeaked. Without a second thought, I lowered myself to the ground below and let the trapdoor shut soundlessly above me.

There was no time to explore the small room I found myself in. I peeked out of it into a deserted hallway. Not risking the king and Olma finding the trapdoor, I fled. Pausing at each corner to check for anyone, I ran down hallway after hallway until I found one I recognized.

Somehow, I'd traveled it to the other side of the castle. Without running into anyone else, I made it back to my rooms. My fear caught up with me, and I careened for the bathroom and vomited until it felt like my insides were completely wrung out. The details of my dreams and the overheard conversation slipped in and out of my exhausted mind.

The family, the forest, the tree. Were they real? Or were they just dreams? What were the king and Olma up to? From their conversation, it sounded like Reynard was still after me.

Who was Katalia? It didn't matter that I was the Gatebreaker. Coming here felt like I'd dropped into the middle of the story already happening. No matter how much I learned, I was still playing catch up. Something bigger than me was going on in Thavell, and I needed to figure out what it was.

Completely spent, I collapsed back in my bed, but the image of Olma's black eyes chased me from sleep until dawn.

CHAPTER TEN

"Lydia, what are we looking for again?" Murphy asked through a yawn.

"I don't know. Visions. Weird dreams—or about out-of-body experiences. Or astral projection. Or stones. Or realms." Attempting to grab a decrepit book, I balanced on a ladder. The book remained just out of reach. I pulled it toward me on a magic wind. My magic sputtered out and the book slipped from my fingers, clunking on the floor.

"Uh—heads up." Both Erin and Murphy looked up from their table and shook their heads. After my sleepless night and using it all day yesterday, my magic was being temperamental.

"Dreams? Stones? Realms? That's a broad range of topics," Erin pointed out.

"I know." I sighed and hopped down the last few rungs on the ladder.

"Are you going to tell us what this is about?" Murphy prodded.

I heaved the tome from the floor to the table. Erin and Murphy exchanged a glance.

"You promised you wouldn't keep anything else from us," Erin pointed out.

"It's not that I'm keeping it from you—really!" I insisted when Erin raised her eyebrows at me. "I had some weird dreams last night. At least I think they were just dreams. But with all the weird magic stuff going on right now, I want to make sure. But I also don't want to make a big deal out of it if it was just dreams."

"Just tell us, Lydia," Erin insisted. "At least that way we can keep up with you when you're being crazy."

I relented and filled them in on my dreams, waking up on the other side of the castle, and the conversation I overheard between King Bleddyn and Olma.

"I know he heard me. He turned and looked right at me. His eyes were just bottomless pits of nothing." I shivered, the image of Olma locked in my memories.

"Has that ever happened before?" Murphy asked.

"No." I scratched my head. "Unless you count the night of the Evergreen Celebration when my magic created that image of the tree. Maybe that was a vision, too."

"Lydia!" Erin slammed her hand down on the table, causing a candle to rattle. "You're just telling us this now."

"I kind of forgot about it," I mumbled.

"How do you forget something like that?" She pressed.

"I don't know." I threw myself in the nearest chair. My hands grabbed strands of my hair and braided it, pulling it out of my face. "Everything's happening so fast. My magic does new things all the time. It's part of me, but so often it feels like it taps into my subconscious or something. I never know what's normal and what's not." I rubbed the spot on my forehead that ached.

"Well"—Murphy pulled a book over and flipped it open—"let's see what we can find and go from there. If anything like this has happened before, we'll find it. Let's start with the realms."

Leave it to Murphy to find the logical solution.

"Thanks, guys. I appreciate your help." I pulled out a piece of parchment and wrote the names of the realms as I remembered them.

Eidoran, the phantom realm
Ziaria, the elven realm
Abrexar, the dragon realm
Selmala, the mermaid realm
Raederion, the faerie realm
Thavell, the human realm

Erin and Murphy gathered next to me and read the names.

"I've been able to find the names of six, but that's all I really know. The king said something about accidentally letting them all loose. Which means they must be real, right?"

"Yes, they're real. But that's about all we know."

The three of us whirled around. Lady Jaclyn stood framed by the library door. My breath caught in my chest when she strode towards us. She was alone. I cleared my throat.

"Lady Jaclyn, it's nice to see you."

She gave me a curt nod. "We both know it's not. But I want to thank you, Lydia. Since you and I researched the realms here last autumn, before um—everything, I've been looking for more details of them. Since the fall of Galan, Fenwood is the fief with jurisdiction over the Golden Forest. And most of the tales about magic seem to end up there. I thought it was in my best interest to understand what the realms meant."

My mouth opened and closed, but no words came out. I didn't know what to do with Jaclyn's arrival or the information she threw at me.

"We haven't met." Jaclyn turned her attention to Erin and Murphy, who both stared at us. When I still said nothing, Murphy stood and bowed.

"I'm Murphy, and this is Erin. We're Lydia's friends."

"Ah, the ones who came over with her?"

"Yes," Murphy said.

"And the fourth one was the rebel who attempted the coup?"

Both Erin and Murphy tensed.

"John is our friend, yes." I finally found my voice. "And we don't think of him as a rebel."

Lady Jaclyn regarded all of us. The first time I'd met her, she'd been open and friendly. But it seemed all the nobles could hide behind masks of indifference and disdain when they needed to. I sighed. Learning how to do that would come in handy. Jaclyn studied each of our faces.

"Loyalty is important," she stated, leaving me more confused than before. "I'm here to return a book and I overheard you discussing the realms."

She held up the book in her hands and shoved it onto a nearby shelf. I exchanged a glance with Erin. If she heard us talking about the realms, what else did she hear? If Jaclyn had heard about me spying on the king, it didn't seem to bother her. She came back to our table.

"If you'd like, I can tell you what I know."

My fingers itched to get inside her head and figure out to see what her angle was. If I did it by accident, maybe I could read people's thoughts on purpose. Jaclyn had made it clear she didn't want to be around me. So why would she offer to help now? Maybe being around the nobles for so long had made me paranoid, but I didn't enjoy accepting help when I didn't know the price. And there was always a price.

But combing through every book in this library was an impossible task. Especially since I didn't have the freedom to fly under the radar now that I was the Gatebreaker. I motioned to our table.

"We would appreciate that."

Erin shoved books out of the way so Jaclyn could sit down. She looked at our stack and pulled one out. A seed of pride bloomed in my chest, knowing we'd grabbed at least one book that was helpful. It wilted when Jaclyn opened the book to only blank pages. She grabbed a quill and drew as she talked.

"Not much is known about the phantom realm. That's Eidoran. I've searched much of this library and the one back home, but information on the realms is scarce. There are some references to Eidoran being a land of many rivers, or being the place where our spirits go when we die, and phantoms being the beings that ferry us to other shores."

"Like the underworld?" Murphy cut in. Jaclyn glanced at him.

"I haven't heard that term before."

"Back home, the underworld is a myth," Murphy continued. "There are legends about it. Some good, some bad. But a lot of legends from home are real here."

"There might be something to it, then." Jaclyn smoothed out a piece of the parchment where she still drew. "We don't know what happened to any of the realms when King Alec closed them off. Most of what we knew has fallen into children's stories. This is what I've learned about phantoms."

She stepped back to reveal the drawing. On it was a being in the shape of a human, but there were no features, just shadows.

"Phantoms are beings whose existence depends on aether. From what I've learned, they have no proper shape of their own, but they still live. They have thoughts and feelings and can speak telepathically. To the naked eye, they are invisible. Only those who wield aether can see them when they don't have a form."

"So, how do they exist if they don't have form?" Erin pulled the parchment over and studied it. Jaclyn scratched her chin as she thought.

"I don't know. Some legends talk about animals with two spirits."

"But if the realms are locked, no phantoms exist here, right?" I glanced over my shoulder like one of them stared from the shadows.

"Theoretically, no. It's been so long since the realms were open. But what about all the beings that were here before the realms closed? And things slip through sometimes, you three are proof of that."

"Do you know anything about the other realms?"

Before she spoke, Jaclyn took the parchment where I'd

written the names of the realms. She studied them for a moment.

"We have stories in Fenwood about the creation of this world. It's said under the light of the red star, eight spirits arrived on our shores. First, they created the Golden Forest, and from there all life came forth. They created magic, they created life, they created the realms. Do you ever wonder if the spirits are connected to all of this somehow?"

"I've never really thought about it," I told her honestly.

Jaclyn smirked, and I spied the fiery girl I'd met the first time in the library.

"I think we don't even know half of what exists in each of the realms."

She stood and dusted off her pants.

"Lydia, would you walk with me for a moment?"

With a glance back at Erin and Murphy, I followed Jaclyn. She stayed silent until we'd left the library and were alone in the hall.

"You know this is my first winter season at court?"

"I didn't." I also didn't know where she was going with this.

"My father is the duke of a powerful territory, one of the largest in the country. But he hates court. Hates the power dynamics, dislikes the proximity to the king. He kept me at home in Fenwood for most of my life—"

Jaclyn stopped and faced a tapestry of a field of wildflowers. I followed her lead. To anyone passing by, it would look like we were discussing the artwork.

"So, it surprised him when the king wrote and wanted to visit with his son, Aidric. We welcomed them, of course. And despite his misgivings, my father accepted the offer of marriage from King Bleddyn. As it stands, one day Aidric and I will marry. And we will be king and queen."

Goosebumps flared on my arms. King Aidric and Queen Jaclyn.

"I can see from your reaction you've not considered that before."

I remained silent; it wasn't like Jaclyn expected me to answer, anyway.

"That brings me to my point, Lydia. Gatebreaker or not, your arrival here has... changed how things are progressing. But here's the thing Lydia, you've only been here a few months. I imagine it's hard being so far away from home, and I'm glad you are doing well. You saved the king and the prince last fall, and I am grateful for that. But please remember this: everything you do here affects this place. Affects our lives. One day soon you will go home. You will leave Thavell and Adylra to its fate, never seeing the consequences of the actions you are setting in motion."

"Why are you telling me this?"

"Last night, Aidric told me about his relationship with you. I know about it already, of course. Everyone does. It's why I need to keep my distance from you. If not—well, that's not important. What I didn't know about were the depths of the feelings he has for you."

"Had," I protested. "The feelings he had for me."

Jaclyn gave me a look that was too close to pity for my liking.

"Regardless, you and I both know he's an honorable man. And I think that you're honorable, too. But rumors can be an awful thing. I'm not as kind or lovable as Queen Lasha was, and I don't think I can ignore the things she looked past. I don't have to tell you that things here are reaching a tipping point."

"What are you asking me?"

"I'm asking—" Jaclyn turned to face me. "I'm asking for you to remember the people you are leaving behind. Do whatever you need to as the Gatebreaker. But, as the future queen of this land, I'm asking you to remember those who will be here cleaning up the mess our fathers and grandfathers have left for us, long after you go home."

I studied her soft features, set with determination. She pleaded with me for her home. And to my shame, she was right. I'd never thought about her as the future queen or Aidric as the future king. I hadn't considered anything past getting home. With a bitter swallow, I realized Lady Jaclyn would make a great queen.

"I'll remember." But there was something else I needed to know. "Do you love him?"

Jaclyn froze. She spread the fingers of her hand along the edge of her skirt.

"I care a great deal about Aidric. And I know he's fond of me. I think we will make a great team."

Two servants burst from a side door and bustled past us carrying armfuls of fabric, startling both of us.

"Think about our conversation, Lydia. And if there's anything I can do to help you with your journey home, please let me know." She moved toward the servants. "I'll see you today during our ride into the city."

CHAPTER ELEVEN

The smell of hay and the quiet whickering of horses greeted me in the stables. We weren't leaving for the city for another couple of hours, but after my conversation with Jaclyn, I needed some time alone. A groom appeared to help me, but I waved him away and let myself into Willow's stall. When I'd become the Gatebreaker, I'd asked for my army horse to be moved to the nobles' stable for me. I leaned my head against his bay neck and breathed in the smell of the stables. This was the only place where I felt close to home.

Eventually, I grabbed a basket and curried Willow's coat. He leaned into my touch.

Sorry I haven't visited in a couple of weeks. I sent the words to Willow through our bond. *King Bleddyn has been keeping me busy.*

This stable is much nicer than my last one. Willow's voice sounded inside my head, and I smiled. There was something thrilling about being able to talk to my horse. *I enjoy the rest. I see you brought your fancy saddle. Are we going somewhere today?*

To the city with some other nobles. We'll both have to be on our best behavior.

There's a heaviness about you today.

Oh. I glanced down at my clothes, just a typical riding outfit with tall boots and a coat. *Do I need to change?*

Willow snorted and bumped me with his head.

Not that kind of heaviness. There's a heaviness in your heart.

I leaned my head back into Willow's neck.

Things have been complicated *lately. And I'm wondering if I'm doing the right thing.*

This heaviness does not suit you. You have a warm heart. My dam always told me to be kind and follow your instincts. Neither will lead you astray.

That's good advice, thank you.

Taking advice from a horse wasn't the strangest thing I'd done in the past few months.

"Lydia!"

The brush I held fell to the floor as Maren's voice startled me out of my conversation with Willow. Her face appeared above the stall door.

"What are you doing? I've been calling you for you." She didn't wait for an answer. "Everyone is ready, let's go."

She disappeared again, leaving me to finish readying Willow. Once I was finished, I threw his reins over his head and led him to the courtyard. Maren was right, everyone waited outside the stable. The group turned towards me when I appeared. I hid my embarrassment behind Willow's saddle. But even after I arrived, no one mounted.

"What are we waiting on?" I whispered to Annistyn.

"King Bleddyn found out both you and the prince are going. So, we are waiting on members of the Palace Guard to escort us." She rolled her eyes. "It's apparently one of the king's new rules."

Hoofbeats sounded on the cobblestones behind us. Murphy and three more people in guardsman uniforms appeared. Once they'd joined us, Prince Aidric mounted his black stallion, Midnight. The rest of us followed.

I relaxed into the saddle, happy to be riding again. On horseback was one of the few places in the world I felt truly comfortable. Willow pranced below me. In the cool weather, he acted like a young colt again. I giggled as he tossed his head and pranced again.

"Think you can handle that horse there, ma'am?"

My biting response died in my mouth when I saw who teased me.

"You know how well I ride, Brendan." I teased my fellow army trainee.

"Just as long as you don't have to carry a weapon, too, right?" He winked, and I laughed at his gentle teasing.

"It's good to see you again. How long have you been part of the Guard?"

"Only a couple of weeks. I'm just off scouting duty in the mountains close to the Golden Forest. But here's a secret; I think I like castle life much better."

"Everyone ready?" Aidric called at the head of our party. "Then let's go!"

We cheered as we headed out of the castle gate.

Excitement made its way through our group like a breeze as we headed down the hill from the castle into the city. For many of us—including me—it would be the first time exploring the city by ourselves. Winter was the season of social visits, negotiations between the nobles, and the time to find partners and enter marriage contracts. The whims of their families dictated most of my friends' schedules. Now that midwinter had passed, and spring drew near, even the most social nobles grew weary of the constant balls and parties. Which left the perfect opening for us to sneak out for the day.

Our four guards rode at the back, ignoring the rowdy group of nobles in front of them. I thought high school was full of cliques, but it was nothing like the court of Thavell. Even now that we were out here without parents and older family members, the group developed an order. Aidric and Jaclyn rode at the front, their closest friends behind them, and everyone else spread out after that. I hung to the back, enjoying the space and the piercing winter wind in my face.

A fine, dusty snow had been falling on and off for most of the week. Three or four inches lay on the ground. The main road into the city was clear of snow, but once the cobblestones ran out, it turned into mud. Our group slowed when we hit the slop. Most of the ladies pulled their long riding skirts up so they wouldn't drag on the ground. I pulled back a little farther, so the horses in front wouldn't kick mud into Willow's face. The slow place allowed me to get a good look at Windburn city.

The wealthiest part of the city sat closest to the castle. We passed large estates framing both sides of the road. Large fences and walls surrounded most of them. Each time we passed a gate, I'd get a glimpse of perfectly manicured gardens and huge, sprawling townhouses. I stood in my stirrups, attempting to see over one wall when a shadow overtook me.

Aidric and Midnight rode up beside Willow and me. The huge stallion huffed a greeting to my gelding.

"Trying to spy on our wealthy citizens, are you?" Aidric winked. My cheeks heated at his attention, but I knew it was impossible for him to see with my cheeks already rosy from the stiff wind. My conversation with Jaclyn this morning was too close to my mind relax with the prince next to me.

"They're fascinating," I told him. "Who all lives in them?"

"Most nobles have townhouses here, as well as homes in their lands. Where did you think they all stayed all winter?"

"I guess I thought they all stayed in the castle." I shrugged at his laugh. "Some of them do, but most stay here. We also have wealthy merchants, magistrates, and the like that live in this section. The next section is where the other merchants and some high-ranking workers in the castle live. The houses are still large, but closer together. After that is the market district where most of the bakeries, shops, and eating houses are. Past that is the hodgepodge of the rest of the city that leads to the business district by the docks. But we won't go that far today."

"When we passed through last summer, there was an open-air market on the main road. Is there still one in the winter?" I tugged on the bottom of my braid, tied with the purple ribbons the lady had given me on my first trip through the city. They were fraying because I used them so much, but I still loved them.

"There is," Aidric replied. "There aren't as many vendors

in the winter, but there are a few. Would you like to check it out after we eat?"

"That would be nice." I smiled.

Despite my discomfort, Aidric looked completely relaxed. I wondered if he knew about my conversation with Jaclyn this morning. It didn't seem like it. Aidric stayed next to me as we rode past the townhouses and into an area bustling with life. People on horseback and foot hustled in between buildings and through doors. In this portion of the city, people adored their buildings with roofs painted in the rainbow of colors I remembered from my first journey. Signs hung above each door, carved pictures letting everyone know what business it was.

Tristan and Annistyn led our group down a side road. They halted in front of a gray stone building. The sign depicted a goat on its hind legs, holding a tambourine. In a chain reaction, the rest of us halted.

"Guess we're here," Aidric said. He trotted Midnight to the front of the line and dismounted. Servants from the restaurant appeared to take control of our horses as the rest of us dismounted.

Maren grabbed my arm and led me inside. The roaring fire provided warmed my chapped hands and face.

"This is the place I told you about, the Dancing Goat," Maren whispered to me. "It's one of the best eating houses in Windburn." Annistyn appeared on my other side as we waited for the rest of our group to join us.

Inside, the first large room had three roaring fires with various pots and pans boiling over them. The wooden floors and wood paneling on the walls gave the place a rustic feel.

An ornate wood railing made the second story visible from the first.

The owner rushed forward to greet Prince Aidric. With the clap of his hands, people rushed to scoot tables together in a private room to the side to make enough room for all of us to sit.

"Well, ladies, let's divide and conquer." Annistyn disappeared into our group, reappearing at Tristan's side as he sat down. Making deliberation look like happenstance was a talent of hers. Annistyn wasn't the only one with that idea, though. There was shuffling and movement as everyone tried to grab for the best seats. I let myself get shuffled around, ending up sandwiched between Annistyn and Gemma, a girl I'd met a few times. A young man I hadn't met before slid in the space across from me. Maren winked at us from her seat towards the end of the table surrounded by eligible noblemen. Annistyn rolled her eyes and focused her attention on Tristan.

The owner served us personally. In seconds, crusty bread and mugs of hot tea appeared on our tables. I sipped the hot tea, letting the sweet liquid warm me up. My eyes slid to the head of the table where Aidric sat with Jaclyn on his right. The moment I looked, Aidric whispered something in Jaclyn's ear, and she covered a giggle with her napkin. I rolled my eyes and looked away.

"My knight master says the bandits have been hitting the southern mountain ranges hard this winter, we may head that way at the first sign of spring to see what we can do to help."

"That sounds so dangerous." Essie, seated on Tristan's other side, sounded terrified at the thought. "Aren't you scared?"

"It's so brave of you to protect others," Annistyn chimed in. "You'll be an amazing knight."

Tristan smirked at the two ladies taking up his attention. I rolled my eyes again.

"Hello? I'm Cyril." The quiet voice barely registered in the hubbub of our group. I turned my attention back to the person sitting across from me. He stared at me, waiting for a response. Realizing I was being rude, I sat my tea on the table.

"Oh! I'm sorry, I almost didn't hear you. I'm Lydia."

"Oh, I know who you are." He leaned forward on the table. "I've been wanting to introduce myself to you at the castle. My father and I arrived from Orsa recently."

"Well, it's nice to meet you. Was traveling to the castle difficult this late in winter?"

He shook his head, his sandy bangs falling in his eyes as he did so.

"No, Orsa's climate is milder than Windburn's. We didn't hit bad weather until we arrived at the mountain. But that's not important. We've heard a lot about you in Orsa. What's it like being the Gatebreaker?"

A server sat the first course of shrimp and mushroom soup in front of me, saving me from having to answer. Musicians arrived and played, drowning out the ability to have a conversation. I picked around the shrimp in my soup and smiled at Cyril, who still watched me as he ate. The musicians played through our meal of pastries stuffed with pork, potatoes, and creamed spinach. I attempted to get Annistyn's attention a few times, hoping her friendliness would get me out of this conversation, but she continued to ignore me in order to moon over Tristan.

The musicians didn't stop until the owner served us dessert and ushered them away. Jaclyn followed them and pressed some coins in their hands.

"So, Lydia, you haven't answered my question."

I took my time trying a bite of the custard in front of me.

"It's overwhelming," I finally told him. "Both in good ways and hard ones, but I'm honored that the king puts his faith in me. And I want to do the job well."

There, that sounded like a courtly answer. Cyril titled his head to one side as I talked. He was cute. And might even be charming if he toned down the intensity. I nursed my mug of tea between my hands and sipped it while he studied me. The servers had kept it full for me throughout lunch.

"Have you thought much about your future?"

I gulped my drink of tea, scalding my throat.

"Um, what do you mean?"

He smiled, and suddenly I knew exactly what he meant. I nudged Annistyn under the table, but she kicked me back and refused to turn around. Gemma was no help, either. She snored quietly, her head propped on her elbow.

"Your future, Lydia. You're a ward of the king now. Surely you must think about your future.". He reached out his hand. I sat back, knocking into the back of my chair. Without missing a beat, Cyril pulled his mug of tea closer, like that's what he meant to do all along.

"I'd like to get to know you, Lydia. I have a feeling we'll hit it off. In the meantime, my father can broach the topic with the king. They are good friends, I'm sure it won't be any problem."

"I... uh... I mean... that is..."

The scraping of chairs against the floor drowned out my

inane babbling. Cyril used the distraction of everyone standing to grab my hand and press his lips to it.

"I'm sure we will speak again, soon."

"Shall we head to the market before going back to the castle?" Aidric called over the noise. Everyone met his suggestion with a cheer.

As we exited the restaurant, Maren and Annistyn found me again.

"How did your meals go?" Maren asked slyly. She batted her eyelashes at a blonde-haired boy as he passed. He winked back.

"Not as good as yours, it seems," I teased.

"Oh, don't say that, Lydia," Annistyn snickered. "You got a marriage proposal."

"What?" Maren yelped.

"You were listening! I knew it." I punched Annistyn in the arm. "You could've helped me."

"You were doing fine."

"I sounded like an idiot."

"You didn't tell him yes or no, it was perfect." She linked her arm in mine and pretended to dry imaginary tears. "Maren, our little girl is growing up."

"Oh, hush," I growled.

"Is anyone going to tell me what you guys are talking about?" Maren grumbled.

"It was just Cyril from Orsa." Maren nodded her head in an understanding I didn't get. "Claims his father and the king are best friends. Mark my words. Lydia will be married before the week is out."

Maren outright laughed this time. I glanced over my shoulder, but Cyril was nowhere in sight.

"Who is that guy?"

"His dad is the Duke of Orsa," Annistyn whispered. "He thinks because it's one of the biggest cities in Thavell he can have whatever he wants. His son is just as pompous. I thought they weren't coming this year, but they showed up a couple of weeks ago."

"What about you and Tristan, Annistyn?" Maren asked. "I saw Essie trying to weasel her way in there."

"I don't know. I'm losing interest in Tristan." Annistyn shrugged. But, I knew my friend better than that. I tugged her faster down the street.

"Let's forget about boys and go shopping."

Our group spread out as we made our way to the market. Annistyn led us down a few less crowded side streets. I peeked into every building we passed. As we walked, the colors of the city came alive. The roofs in this section varied from pitched to flat, and they were all painted in a dazzling array of colors. Fuchsia, turquoise, violet, and cherry. The city fascinated me.

The market came into view as we arrived back at the main road. Annistyn, Maren, and I walked up and down the rows of wares. I pulled the hood of my jacket over my hair, both for warmth and the hope that no one would recognized me. I'd had enough of being the Gatebreaker for a day.

We passed tents filled with homemade creations. Baskets, fabrics, dresses, shoes, jewelry, and cosmetics. Anything someone might need or want. Annistyn and Maren pulled ahead of me as I paused at every tent. My head buzzed with the activity.

I stopped at a tent with jewelry on display. This jewelry didn't sparkle like the other tents I passed. As I studied it, I wasn't even sure I'd call it jewelry. Each piece had a rough stone hanging from a leather thong. The stones reminded me of the tourist places back home where you could mine your own gemstones in running water. The tent stood empty. I reached out and touched a deep black stone.

Fire raced up the inside of my arm. I jerked my hand back with a gasp. As soon as I let go, the pain vanished.

"Careful, dearie. That's ochrodite. This particular amulet holds wards against magic."

An old lady came through the back of the tent, her white hair hanging down her back. She leaned on a walking stick covered from top to bottom in various stones, many of them the same type she had for sale at her table. The shine on the unfinished rocks flickered in the late afternoon sunlight. I rubbed my forehead and looked away.

"It keeps the wearer safe from all magic directed at him. But it's no use if you've got magic yourself. It will just burn."

"So, a non-Wielder is supposed to use magic to stop magic?" Tristan's skeptical voice made me jump. I turned my head, my hood tumbling from my hair. Tristan stood behind me with his arms crossed, his eyebrow raised at the woman.

"People can go about their business however they please," the old lady said with a shrug. "I just provide them with what they request."

"Cheap jewelry?" Tristan asked.

"These amulets may not be pretty to the eye, but they do what they're meant to."

"What does this one do?" Tristan asked, picking up a rough stone that was deep blue, almost purple.

"Gives you pleasant dreams, darling," the lady replied. "Just whisper what you'd like to see before you go to sleep at night and hang it round your neck. Nothing is off limits." She winked. Tristan blushed crimson and set the stone back down.

"I think this is all a crock," he claimed.

I wanted to learn about the amulets, but from the look in the old lady's eyes, she was about to let Tristan have it. Their arguing voices carried as I walked away. The buzzing still filled my head. I rubbed my forehead again.

Something pinched at my side. I looked down just in time to see a young girl snatch the purse she'd cut from my belt and take off running.

"Come back here!" Without thinking, I took off after her.

"Lydia!" Tristan yelled my name, but I didn't look back. This child was fast, and I didn't want to lose sight of the little thief. She raced ahead of me down an alleyway. I followed, certain I would catch up with her in no time.

I underestimated her home field advantage, though. The child knew the streets of Windburn way better than me. She dashed left and right and up and down side streets almost quicker than I could see. Soon we were out of the merchant district and into another section of houses. These streets weren't like the ones we'd traveled down earlier. There didn't seem to be any rhyme or reason to how the small, square houses arranged themselves. In some places they were three stories high. The path twisted in and out of them, becoming wider and narrower haphazardly. The only thing that still looked like the rest of Windburn was the multi-colored roofs.

My months of being pampered in the castle showed. My fitness had declined since I stopped my training, and the longer I ran, the more winded I became. But no way the petty thief was going to get away with stealing from me! My temper spurred me on. Just ahead, I saw her turn a corner into a small courtyard between two levels of houses. I was right on her heels. I turned into the courtyard and stopped short. The girl was nowhere to be seen.

John sat on a bench in front of me. He stood when he saw me. Stunned, I took a couple of steps forward. The gate to the courtyard slammed shut behind me.

"Lydia, John and I need to talk to you."

I knew that voice. I whipped around.

The lady from the Golden Forest had returned.

CHAPTER TWELVE

"*W*hat's going on?" I demanded. "What are you doing with *her?*" I turned to the side so I could watch both John and the lady. John threw something. I reached up and caught my purse. But I couldn't keep my eyes off my friend.

"We thought you were dead," I told him.

"I know, I'm sorry—" He took another step toward me. After all these months, he didn't look any worse for wear. In fact, his leg and arm muscles bulged from under his clothing. "We needed to talk to you, away from your friends."

"No." I stuffed my purse in my jacket and reached out my hand. "John, you need to come with me. Come with me back to the castle. I'm trying to find a way back home. The king is helping me."

Chills skated up my bones when I realized John wasn't responding. He tucked his hands in his pocket. My hand dropped to the side.

"The king?" the lady asked, interrupting me. She looked much like I remembered. The first person we'd met after coming through the gateway. And the person who told me about my magic.

"I told you not to trust the king."

"He's the only one around here making any sense." My temper flared at her attitude. "Why should I listen to you?"

"Lydia, we can trust her," John said.

"And why should I trust you?" I demanded. "You almost got us killed."

John's face fell as my words hit their mark. Maybe later I'd regret them, but right now I wasn't backing down. If it hadn't been for him going behind our backs with Reynard, nothing bad would've happened last autumn.

"Lydia, I didn't know that was Reynard's plan. He told me we were just going to put everyone to sleep and sneak you, Erin, and Murphy out of there. If any of us had known what Reynard was really up to, there's no way we would have gone along with him."

"John's right," the lady said. She locked the gate behind her. "Reynard went off plan. That was not the intention."

"The intention for what?" I asked.

"The rebellion." She said it so matter-of-factly. The breath rushed out of my lungs in a large whoosh. The rebellion. A full-scale rebellion. This wasn't possible.

"I don't want to hear this. I won't be part of a rebellion."

"Well, you can't stay where you are," the woman continued. "The king is only using you to further his own ends. There is no search for your way home. He's lying. He will never let you go."

"And how do you know?" I asked. "You told us there was no way for us to get home."

"I may have spoken too soon," she admitted. "At the time,

I didn't realize what powers you actually possessed. I also wasn't sure the six realms truly existed. But, with a little more work, there may be a way to get you all home."

"Don't you see," John added, "this is why you need to come with us. The rebellion has been trying to open the realms for years. They're stronger now, and more organized. If they can open the realms, then maybe we can find our way back home."

"The king already promised me a way home. Why should I believe you, but not him?" I argued.

"Because the king only works for himself." Bitterness laced the woman's voice. "And he only cares about power. Doesn't he have you bringing magic Wielders out of the woodwork, now? Isn't he collecting all the strongest Wielders in the castle? Why do you think he started the Scholars in the first place?"

"He's trying to build trust in the crown again. He's giving Wielders a safe place to understand their powers. Magic that goes wild would be bad for everyone."

She snorted at my response.

"Don't you think, maybe, those people were trying to stay hidden for a reason?"

I would never admit that was exactly what I'd wondered myself. By her smirk, I knew she guessed anyway.

Ignoring her, I turned my attention back to John.

"John, please come back with me. Erin misses you. Murphy misses you. *I* miss you. I believe you didn't know about Reynard's place. Now make it right and come back. If you're not with us when we open the gate again, then what happens? What if you get stuck here?"

"Lydia, why don't you tell John what the king said would happen if he returns?" I shot her a glare.

"It's okay, I already know. Lydia, I'm not coming back with you just to get stuck in a dungeon."

"The king has to say that, but come with me and I'll talk to him. I'm sure I can reason with him, convince him to let you be free—" My voice faltered as John shook his head.

"Lydia, the king and prince are not everything they say they are. They aren't concerned about the kingdom. King Bleddyn is notorious among the commoners for his dislike of Wielders."

"You're wrong," I insisted. "He wants a better life for the Wielders, for everyone."

"Lydia, over a hundred Wielders came to the castle yesterday. You marked thirty of them for the Scholars. Last night, someone kidnapped and branded twelve of them."

His words hit me like a slap in the face.

"The king outlawed branding years ago."

"Well, I guess he started it again." John's voice softened when tears pricked in the corner of my eyes. "Why do you think he wants everyone identified? He wants to know who's a Wielder and who isn't. What do you think he's going to do when he knows everyone in the city or in the kingdom who has magic? Just leave them be?"

"The king wouldn't do that." I couldn't believe it. If the king was really doing this, it meant I was helping him hurt people. "Besides, Aidric wouldn't stand for it."

"I know this is hard to hear," John said. "But you have to believe me."

He took another step closer, but I backed up again. My

head still buzzed. This was too much to think about right now.

"If I come with you now, what happens to Erin and Murphy? Do we just leave them?"

Pain crossed John's face. The woman slapped a hand to her forehead like I was some irrational child.

"You're the person in the most danger right now. We will get them out as soon as you're safe."

"And you're okay with that?"

John refused to answer.

"The king has been nothing but nice to me." I knew I sounded hysterical, but I couldn't stop talking. "He's given me a place here. He has lavished titles and money on me. I'm one of the most powerful people in the kingdom because of him, and he continues to protect me and my friends. Why would I betray him?"

"So, you'd rather have titles and power than do what's right?"

I saw red. Before I could respond, John stepped in to defend me.

"That's not fair." He pointed at the woman. "Now lay off."

A rush of affection for my friend surged through me. I wanted to hug him; it'd been so many months since I'd seen him. And now here he was, safe and healthy. But something held me back. I studied the courtyard. The walls were at least eight feet tall and constructed from a brown plaster material. The gate was made from the same thing. Now that it was closed, it blended seamlessly into the wall. People passing by would have no idea I was here. That was a problem.

"I'm leaving."

"Lydia, come sit down," John insisted. "Let's talk about this."

Icy wind hit me in the face. I sucked in a breath, clearing my head a bit. John fiddled with the hilt of his sword, his eyes darting between me and the woman.

"If you don't want to come back with me, whatever. I won't tell anyone I saw you. But I'm leaving. Right now."

"No, Lydia"—the woman stepped between me and the gate,—"you're not."

Everything inside me froze. I glared at my friend.

"So, this wasn't to talk to me, it was to kidnap me?!"

"We're not kidnapping you, Lydia," John claimed. "We're keeping you safe."

"Come on, John," I scoffed. "Taking me from where I want to be to where I don't want to be against my will is the definition of kidnapping. Nothing you say changes that."

He looked away, his face red with shame. Good.

"Lydia, why won't you believe me?" John pleaded. The hurt in his voice thawed my heart the tiniest bit. "Please, trust me. I want to get home, too."

"Then why didn't you trust me?" I asked. "Why didn't you trust any of us? If you had told any of us what you were up to with Reynard, we wouldn't be in this position. You're with a rebellion, John!"

"You didn't trust us either, Lydia. You didn't tell us about your magic, and you didn't tell us you were the reason we were here."

"I didn't know." The words forced themselves out through my clenched teeth, trying to hold back my tears. "I messed up, I know that. And I've spent every waking minute of the past few months trying to fix it. The king is the only one who is trying to help me."

"The king's not going to help you. But we can."

"I don't believe you," I whispered.

While I pleaded with John, I called on my magic. I'd level this courtyard and the entire street to get out of here if I had to.

But something was wrong. Each time I reached for my magic, it slipped out of my grasp. It was like trying to grab fistfuls of water. My brow furrowed as I tried again.

"Having trouble finding your magic?"

"What did you do to me?" I wanted nothing more than to wipe that smug smile off the lady's face. I fought to keep my voice even. Panic would do me no good. But without my magic, I was helpless. I carried no weapons. None of my friends or even the guards knew where I was. I cursed myself for not sticking a dagger in my belt. How many times would I have to pass out or get trapped to realize I couldn't rely solely on my magic?

"Did you enjoy the tea at lunch?" she asked. "Someone on the inside slipped you a special tea that's made to dull powers."

"Did you know about this?" I demanded of John. He hung his head. I turned away.

"How did you find a tea like that?"

"I was the one who brought it into the country," the lady said.

They had me. There was no way I was getting out now.

"Lydia, please—come with us," John pleaded again.

I needed to stall, needed to bide time until my magic returned. But magic wasn't the only thing slipping from me.

My thoughts scattered, thwarting my ability to come up with a plan.

"I'm leaving," I repeated, hoping this time he'd listen. Magic or no, I'd fight with everything I had. "I'm going back to the castle."

"Lydia," John groaned, pulling the syllables through his teeth. "Don't make me do something I'll regret."

"Making you? You're the one trying to kidnap me. I'm not making you do anything."

"For once in your life, could you not be so stubborn?" John's groan rumbled in his chest. He hadn't expected my refusal.

"You have to get away from the king—"

"John, don't!"

He ignored her and plowed ahead.

"We think he's trying to use your magic to gain his own powers."

"That's… it's not even possible."

But was it possible? The woman smirked again, watching the seeds of doubt grow in my mind.

"Lydia!" Aidric screamed my name from the street.

"I'm her—" The woman grabbed me around the chest and slapped her hand over my mouth. I growled and fought against her. Roots snaked from the ground, wrapping around my arms and mouth. The root blocked my scream of rage.

"John, it's time to go."

John stood in the middle of the courtyard, his sword half out of its sheath.

"I don't want to force her," he argued.

"She'll understand later," she grunted, dragging me across the courtyard. I screamed again.

Magic rushed through my veins and exploded the roots. I stomped on the woman's foot, her grip loosened. I yanked away from her and darted across the courtyard. A huge fireball shot toward me and landed in my path. Flames shot up on every side, trapping me.

"Aidric! I'm here!" I reached for my magic, but the effects of the tea hadn't completely worn off yet. I growled in frustration, only able to see bits and pieces of what was happening through the flames.

The woman whistled, and three men ran from the house. She was like a commander of an army or something, always one step ahead of me. The fire receded when one man reached me. I threw a punch, but he caught it with ease and wrenched my arms behind my back. My shoulder twisted and my knees gave out with the pain. Before I could recover, the man had stuffed a piece of fabric in my mouth and tied my hands together. He grabbed my legs to bind them, too.

I yanked one leg loose and kicked out. The man jumped back, holding his bleeding face.

The gate exploded open. Another fireball rained flames, but it was too late. Tristan, Aidric, and Murphy charged through. I rolled out of the way, unable to free my arms or use my magic.

"John!" Murphy stopped, staring at his friend in the middle of the courtyard. "What are you doing?"

"Trying to save everyone!" Seeing Murphy broke John out of his trance. He unsheathed his sword and stopped Aidric from reaching me. "Trust me, Murphy."

"Last time you tried to save us, I almost died!" Murphy spotted the man with the bloody nose grabbing me again. He jumped over the bench and attacked, forcing the man to let go.

I tried to pull my legs under me, but then the woman had a hold of me again. No matter how I twisted, she didn't let go. While the second man distracted Tristan, the third tied my legs. Together, he and the woman carried me toward a smaller door on the far side of the courtyard.

"Aidric!"

The gag muffled my scream, but it was enough. Aidric looked up and saw what was happening. He locked swords with John and pushed him out of the way. When John stumbled, Aidric rushed for me. John regained his balance and launched himself off the back of the bench, landing squarely in front of Aidric again. My captors carried me closer and closer to the door.

"Tristan!" Aidric called, his attention on his opponent. John started a complicated pass with the sword. Aidric worked to keep up. Last year, John had revealed a natural talent for swordsmanship, and it looked like he'd kept up his practice while he was on the run.

Tristan fought one man from the house when Aidric called out. He buried his sword deep in the man's collarbone in a move so fast his opponent never saw it coming. The man dropped to his knees.

We'd reached the door. The woman tugged on the handle, but it didn't open. No amount of my thrashing made my captors lose their grip. My chest heaved; my magic still slipped from my grasp. No one was going to reach me in time.

Tristan pulled something from his belt and threw it. The man holding me fell, one hand clutching the dagger in his throat. Blood splashed across my face. The male tumbled into the woman, and I dropped to the ground. The woman rolled away from the body and was back on her feet, the bloody dagger in her hand.

Pain laced through my shoulder and up my spine. Stars popped into my vision. I rolled over to come face to face with the man's body still leaking blood onto the ground. I heaved myself upright and scooted back until I hit the wall.

Tristan rushed forward, pulling up short when the woman threw a fireball his way. His own air magic held it at bay, but he couldn't get past it. There was a yell across the courtyard as Murphy's opponent landed a blow to Murphy's chest. I screamed again as the sword cleaved through Murphy's shirt. But there was no blood. And no cut on his chest. Murphy took advantage of his opponent's confusion and swiped his legs out from under him. His sword went flying. Before he could stand, he found Murphy's axe at his throat.

"Spirits curse it!" the woman yelled. She started for me again, but a gust of air pushed her back. She cursed again. "Retreat!"

Aidric swung his sword at John, who dropped and rolled out of the way. Before Aidric could stop him, John gripped a stone hanging from a leather cord around his neck. He looked over at Murphy.

"Tell Erin I'm sorry and I love her." A clap reverberated through the courtyard, making my ears ring. John, the woman, and the man on the ground in front of Murphy burst into flames.

"No!" The gag muffled my scream. Murphy reached for John, but the flames disappeared and all of them had vanished.

CHAPTER THIRTEEN

J couldn't look away from the scorched spot on the earth where John had been seconds ago. Someone moaned. The man Tristan cut down was waking. Tristan yanked the leather cord from around his neck. After making sure he wouldn't escape, Tristan rushed to my side and cut the bindings from my legs and arms. I ripped the gag from my mouth.

"Thank you," I whispered, my throat sore from screaming. My whole body shook, but I wasn't sure why. Tristan helped me stand and held onto me when I swayed. Stars filled my vision again.

"Murphy." Aidric knelt and inspected the ash where the woman disappeared. "Find Brendan, Preston, and Wendell. They should be in the market with everyone else. Send Brendan to find Nadine and bring backup. Tell Jaclyn to convince everyone else to head back to the castle without alerting them to the problem. She can do it. Tell Brendan to bring some irons back. I know a peaceful place our guest can recover."

Murphy nodded grimly. His eyes widened when he spotted me. Abandoning his earlier plan of action, he rushed over.

"Lydia, are you okay?" He knelt in front of me. But that wasn't right. Somehow, I'd slid back down to the ground without noticing. "Where are you bleeding?"

"Bleeding?" The fuzziness from the tea had worn off, but now a different fog trapped me. I pulled a cloth out of my pocket and wiped my face. My stomach churned when I saw the blood.

"It's not mine." Tristan and Aidric now stood behind Murphy.

"It's from..." My voice broke and I waved in the general direction of the man, unable to look. "It splattered when Tristan saved me. Thanks again, by the way." Tristan nodded.

"Thank you all for coming." Tears suddenly flooded my eyes. "I didn't know what was going to happen."

I pointed at Murphy.

"What aren't you bleeding? The guy tried to run you through with his sword."

Murphy looked down at his cut shirt.

"Well... uh... I think when you healed me last fall you somehow made me impervious to injury."

A cackling laugh busted out of me, much to the surprise of the three guys.

Aidric patted Murphy on the shoulder.

"She's in shock. I'll take care of her. Bring Willow on your way back."

"It's going to be okay, Lydia," Murphy told me. He handed me a clean handkerchief from his own pocket and left to fulfill his orders. The man on the other side of the courtyard moaned. Tristan left to take care of him, leaving me alone with Aidric.

I used the handkerchief Murphy gave me to wipe most of the blood off my face and arms. There was nothing I could do about my clothes, though. Aidric surveyed me, his face still grim.

"What?" I asked.

In response, Aidric reached forward and pulled me into a fierce hug. My head swam and I couldn't help the squeak of pain that escaped me. Aidric let go just as fast.

"I'm sorry, I didn't mean to hurt you."

"You didn't." My head cleared some. My body tingled from Aidric's sudden affection. "What was that for?"

He sat back on his heels in front of me.

"I looked up, and you were gone. Tristan was screaming after you. If it wasn't for the old lady, I wouldn't have known where to look."

"What old lady?" He wasn't making any sense.

"It doesn't matter. What possessed you to run after that girl, anyway?"

"She stole my purse," I argued. I pulled the purse from my pocket. Coins still dropped from the slit in the fabric.

"And you couldn't have just gotten a new one? My father won't let you run out of money."

He took the purse from me, and a necklace fell from the opening into his hand. Aidric let the delicate silver chain run through his fingers. He held the red stone up between us. I looked down at the ground.

"I can't wear it anymore. So, I've been carrying it in my purse. But you're right, it was stupid. Over a necklace."

Aidric put the necklace in my palm, and I clasped my hand around it.

"What did they want with you?" He asked.

"They wanted me to join the rebellion."

Aidric slid off his heels onto the ground. He muttered something I couldn't make out.

"I told my father these attacks were a sign of an organized rebellion. The uptick in raids of the villages most loyal to the crown, the attacks on army posts, defections from different fiefdoms. There's no pattern, but there was something intentional about it. I wonder if Reynard's attack went into this?"

"They said he went off script." Bits and pieces of the conversation came to mind. "What happened in the forest last fall wasn't planned."

Aidric blew out a breath, causing a strand of hair to fly in the air.

"Sarge tried to convince me to go with them. She said the king has some dastardly plan to steal magic or something."

"Who's Sarge?"

"The lady who was here." I chuckled at myself. Aidric watched me like I'd gone crazy. Who knew? Maybe I had. "I made the name up. She never told me her real one. But this isn't the first time I've met her."

Aidric hit his fist against the ground.

"Stealing magic isn't even possible, is it? Children inherit magic from a parent."

"What about me?" I asked. "My world doesn't even have magic."

Hoofbeats sounded in the street by the courtyard. Tristan drew his sword and opened the gate.

"It's Murphy and Preston," he called.

Aidric breathed a sigh of relief. I made to stand up, but my head swam again. Murphy and Preston appeared, with Willow and Midnight in tow. Aidric turned back to me and swept me up into his arms.

"Aidric, no. You shouldn't."

"I don't care," he told me. "I'm not letting you out of my sight until I know you're safe."

"Brendan left to bring reinforcements. Lady Jaclyn convinced your peers to return to the castle for some skating by the bay. Wendell escorted them," Murphy reported.

Seeing us coming, Willow bowed his front end so Aidric could settle me easily. I wanted to insist I knew how to ride, but found keeping my body from shaking was the most I could manage. Murphy saw me shivering and tucked his cloak around me.

Aidric nodded and settled himself behind me on Willow. I leaned into his warmth at my back. Murphy handed him Midnight's reins.

"Can you all take care of everything here?"

"Yes, Your Highness." Murphy saluted him.

"Make sure our guest makes it back in one piece," Aidric told Tristan. "I'd like to have a conversation with him later."

"Of course, my prince."

I pulled Murphy's cloak tighter as Aidric pulled me close and we headed back to the castle.

"Just start from when you woke up today," Nadine instructed.

Gabrielle drew the curtains in my sitting room as the

sun sank below the horizon. Any other time, the mismatched group arranged around my fire would have given me a chuckle. As it was, my bones ached from the healer who'd arrived in my room a few hours ago. Much of what happened once we made it back to the castle was a blur. I remember Aidric carrying me and calling for Gabrielle. The healer had arrived and sent Aidric away, then practically force fed me broth and watched over me until I fell asleep.

I'd woken hours later and found Aidric hovering outside my door like a mother hen. As soon as I'd eaten again, he'd notified the king I was awake. I'd no sooner slipped a clean dress over my linen nightshirt when the king arrived with a group in tow.

Now, the king sat in front of me. Nadine and Olma stood behind his chair, flanking him on either side. Murphy and Tristan huddled together on an ottoman. Aidric stood next to the chair he'd pulled directly in front of the fire for me. He acted like my personal sentry, jumping at every noise, and standing with his hand on the hilt of his sword. He hadn't even changed his clothes since we'd returned.

Nadine coached me through repeating everything that had happened that day. I walked her through my morning in the library, with only the barest details of why I'd been there. I mentioned speaking with Jaclyn, not daring to look at Aidric as I glossed over the fact that she'd been looking for me.

"Who did you sit with at lunch at the Dancing Goat?"

"I sat between Annistyn and Gemma and across from Cyril of Orsa."

"Did you talk to anyone?"

"Not much, musicians came to play. I spoke to Cyril a little."

"What did you talk about?"

I twisted my hands in the blanket over my lap.

"I don't think it's that import—"

"Lydia," the king said kindly, "we don't know what's important, that's why we need to know everything."

"Well, it was the first time I'd met him, so he asked me a few questions about myself, told me where he was from..."

"Anything else?" Nadine asked.

"Um." I blushed. I kept my eyes on the floor, unable to meet anyone's eye. "He asked me about my future and told me his father is friends with the king and would discuss our future—together."

Tristan snorted and quickly transformed it into a hacking cough. I glared at the smirk Murphy wore. He thumped Tristan's back to hide his amusement. Aidric's hand clenched on the back of my chair.

King Bleddyn glanced at Murphy and Tristan, amusement crossing his face. He cleared his throat.

"Well, I'll speak to Bertram on that matter another time. Please continue."

Details became hazier as I described seeing John and talking to Sarge, as I called the lady in my head.

"I couldn't believe it was Sa—the lady, again."

"What do you mean, again?" Nadine asked.

"Oh, right. I never told you. It didn't seem important. She found us when we came through the gateway."

I told them what I remembered of that first meeting. And for the first time, I told everyone about the second meeting. When she'd told me about my magic.

"I didn't believe her. It didn't make any sense. And then she transformed into a wolf and vanished."

"She what?!" King Bleddyn's voice boomed in my small room. He held up a hand. "I apologize. I didn't mean to yell. What did she turn into?"

"A wolf. Larger than any wolf I've seen, though. Brownish color, I think?" It had been nearly six months since we'd arrived in Adylra. Details were fading.

Abruptly, the king paced in front of the bookshelf. I paused talking and turned my words over in my head, afraid I'd upset him.

"Keep going, Lydia. Tell me what happened after."

I made it until the man grabbed me and tied my arms behind my back. My voice failed me. When I looked down, I realized my hands were shaking. Thankfully, Aidric, Tristan, and Murphy took up the story from there. I clenched my fists, willing myself to be calm as they rehashed what happened. The surge of emotion had one benefit, though. My magic responded to my fear and curled under my skin. The tea had finally worn off.

Nadine pulled a small leather book out of her back pocket and made notes after we finished telling the story.

"If this woman is right and there's a bigger revolution in play, we need to go back and look again at the raids that have been happening this past year. Maybe they're connected."

"Aidric has a point." Nadine tapped her quill against her chin. "If we can find something that connects them, that may help us pinpoint a home base."

"There is no revolution." King Bleddyn quit pacing and returned to the group. "There is no rebellion. Just because a group of malcontents call themselves rebels doesn't mean there's a larger threat."

"It seemed serious today, Father." King Bleddyn shot a look at Aidric, and he softened his tone. "If we had been a few seconds later, who knows what they would have done to Lydia."

"This is not the time for this conversation."

Aidric glanced at me and stopped talking. I looked between Nadine, Olma, and Aidric. None of them seemed interested in continuing to talk.

"Wait—" King Bleddyn cocked his head in my direction. I plowed ahead anyway. "We made a deal that I would be part of the conversations that had to do with the Gatebreaker and what that meant. Whether or not there's a bigger rebellion, these people want me for something. And I want to know why that is."

Everyone froze as I stared down King Bleddyn. After a tense minute, he threw up his hands in resignation.

"You're right, Lydia. I told you that." For a moment, the only sound was King Bleddyn scratching his beard. "If these people are connected to Reynard, then they may have people inside the castle. They knew about Lydia's whereabouts, and they knew enough about the trip today to plant someone in the restaurant. Nadine, first thing tomorrow I want someone there questioning the owner and the staff."

Nadine nodded.

"What do they want with me?" I asked.

"I don't think you understand how unique your powers are, young lady." It was the first time Olma had spoken since he arrived. "Not only do you have control of all eight affinities, but you learn faster than anyone I've met, you have an instinctual feel for magic that's unparalleled, and you've demonstrated being able to draw magic from other sources and control it. Even before magic left these lands, magic like yours was legendary. And the more rumors grow of your abilities, the more you're going to be sought after."

My hands unfurled in my lap. Me, legendary? None of it made any sense.

"I still think we should make sure the recent raids aren't connected," Aidric put in.

"So, we shall," the king agreed. "We will check on the raids, we will talk to the restaurant owners, we will inspect the houses near the courtyard where they ambushed Lydia, and tomorrow I will speak to our friend and find out what we know. But right now, we all need to retire and get some rest, especially you, my dear." He gave my still shaking hands a pointed look.

Everyone stood and moved toward the doorway. I stood and gave Murphy a hug.

"I'll fill Erin in on everything," he whispered. "Come visit us tomorrow if you can."

Aidric acted determined to keep his post at my side until King Bleddyn pointed him toward the door. "Nadine has already set guards on her door, and her maid plans to sleep on a pallet in her room for now."

Even though I didn't want Gabrielle assigned to a pallet on the floor, part of me felt relieved someone would be with me. Aidric's shoulders drooped. He opened his mouth to say something, but changed his mind and squeezed my hand before leaving. When he opened the door, I spied Millicent, Jaclyn's lady's maid, standing in the hall.

"Prince Aidric, my lady has been fretting with worry. She heard there was a battle, but you didn't send a no—"

Aidric held up a hand and Millicent stopped mid-word.

"Tell Jaclyn—"

The door shut behind him, cutting off his words. Olma, Nadine, and King Bleddyn finished up a conversation about logistics and made for the door.

"Uh, Your Highness. May I speak with you, privately?"

King Bleddyn waved Olma and Nadine on. He sat down in the same chair and invited me to do the same. When I didn't say anything, he sat forward.

"This is your meeting, Lydia. What can I do for you?"

"Sire, I told you John, and the lady claimed twelve of the people who joined the Scholars were branded last night. I thought branding was outlawed years ago?"

"It was one of the first things I did when I became king."

"Then why is it still happening?"

"Lydia, I can't be everywhere at once. You know there are still people who don't accept magic and Wielders. For years they've been branding Wielders under the cover of night. I assure you, I'm doing my best to stop it."

"But why was it just those who I marked strong enough for the Scholars?" Restless energy surged through me. I paced in front of the fire. "It's my fault these people are hurt. How can I keep identifying people when they end up hurt the next day?"

"Lydia, you have a gracious heart. But the people you see in the throne room come forward voluntarily. They undergo rigorous tests to make sure they have magic. These tests have been happening for months. You marking them for the

Scholars is just one step. They declared themselves as Wielders months ago."

The restlessness leaked out of me. I sat back down. The king's words didn't bring relief, but they did calm me some.

"Twelve brandings in one night are more than I've heard of before." The king tapped his knuckles. "I'll look into it. This can't keep happening if we want people to trust us."

"How can we be sure it's not my fault?"

"One thing I've learned, Lydia, is that Magic Wielders cannot hide their powers forever. There always comes a time when their magic slips out, or they're forced to use it. You are a prime example. If you hadn't used magic, your friends, my son, and myself would have died. Wielders shouldn't live in fear of revealing their magic. And that's what we are trying to do. I want Wielders to be free from the fear of being found out."

He leaned forward and gripped my hands in his.

"You, dear one, are helping people come forward. You are the example they look to. Since the announcement of your arrival, more people have petitioned to join the Scholars than ever before."

"But does it matter if people are getting hurt?"

"Of course it matters. If it helps, I'll recruit some volunteers from the new group of army trainees to mix in with the groups brought to the audience from now on. We will take different routes to and from the castle. We will have the Wielders come prepared to stay, so if we accept them into the Scholars, they can move into the safety of the castle that day. Does that help?"

I sat back and nodded.

"Good." The king chuckled. "You know, when you asked

me to stay, I thought for sure it was to ask me about your marriage proposal."

My back snapped straight like a rod.

"I forgot about that."

"So, would you like to accept?"

My mouth dropped open, flabbergasted by the king's question.

"Do I... huh?"

King Bleddyn's serious face slipped as he erupted into peals of laughter. Despite myself, I smiled.

"I'd heard Bertram's son was as bold as his old man, but this takes the cake." King Bleddyn wiped his watering eyes.

"Sire?"

"From your reaction, I can assume marriage doesn't work the same way in your homeland?"

"No, sir."

"Lydia, I've been fielding marriage requests since the moment you arrived at court."

"I didn't know." From who? I wanted to ask. I'd be interacting with my fellow nobles differently from now on.

"Nor should you. As a ward of the king, your future is my responsibility. I won't bother you with anything that's of no concern. I'll let Bertram know what I let everyone know. An offer for betrothal will come at my discretion, and no amount of negotiation will make me change my mind."

"But, Sire—"

"I know, I know." He stood and stretched his arms. "You're not staying, so it's a moot point. I find its best not to tell my nobility that the Gatebreaker will leave us soon. So, I tell them the same thing I would if you were staying."

"Thank you, Your Highness." I walked with the king towards the door.

"You could, you know?"

"I'm sorry, what?"

"Stay. Just say the word and Thavell will welcome you home."

I remained silent as he opened the door and walked into the hall where the spiral staircase began. Before he started down them, he looked over his shoulder.

"Oh, Lydia,"—he paused with one hand on the stair rail—"while you're here, it is my responsibility to keep you safe. I'm asking you to stay within the inner wall of the castle grounds. I don't want to order you around or have you guarded constantly. You'll stay safe as long as you don't leave."

A chill ran up my spine. I curtsied.

"Of course, Your Majesty."

He nodded, satisfied.

"Thank you. Now get some rest."

CHAPTER FOURTEEN

Gabrielle slept on the pallet next to my bed despite my protest. She readied me for my usual lessons with Lord Barwick, but when it was time, I couldn't leave my room. One look down the spiral staircase and I started shaking again.

Without having to ask, Gabrielle rang for a messenger and sent a note to the lord that I was under the weather and wouldn't be able to attend today. She started a fire and told me the legends of magic she grew up with while she mended clothes.

Erin and Murphy showed up after lunch. Gabrielle disappeared when Erin threw herself on my shoulder. Her red-rimmed eyes and tear-streaked face broke my heart.

"I'm so sorry, Erin."

"What is he thinking?" she cried.

"I don't know." Worry for my friend knotted in my chest.

"Do you believe anything he said?" She pulled away and faced me. I wrapped my arms around myself.

"I don't know." Murphy had filled her in on most of the

details last night and I told her everything again. "Old Sarge didn't want him to tell me about the king trying to steal my powers, but he did anyway. I believe he really thought he was trying to help me. But that doesn't mean he can just take me without explaining what's going on. Spirits, I just want to beat him in the head."

"Spirits?" Murphy asked.

"It's easy to pick up on." I shrugged.

"Why does he have to be such an idiot? I can't believe he fought Aidric and tried to kidnap you!" Erin beat a throw pillow into submission.

"He wasn't happy with how things were going," I assured her. "It doesn't excuse him completely, but he got mad when Sarge tried to take me."

"I know it's terrible of me, but I'm sad I'm not the one who got to see him yesterday." She leaned her head on my shoulder again. "I can't quit worrying about him. This is the longest I've ever been without him. It's like part of me is missing."

"Erin, he told me to tell you he loves you. That I believe."

"I miss him, too," Murphy added.

"Me, three." No matter what, John was my friend. We had to get him back. If only there was a way for us to speak to John alone. Maybe together we could figure this mess out.

"Do you think he's still in the city?" Erin asked.

"I have no idea. Next time I see Lord Barwick, I'll ask if he's ever heard of something like that. But traveling with magic had to take some serious power. I can't imagine they went far."

"You know, we have one night off every week. Nadine lets us go into the city—" Erin started.

"I want in," I announced with no hesitation.

"Want it on what?" Murphy asked innocently.

"I know you two." They avoided my gaze. "I know you're already concocting some big plan. But the king restricted me to the palace grounds last night."

Murphy groaned, but Erin grinned.

"That just means we need to be creative."

She wiped her eyes one more time and unrolled parchment she had in her bag.

"Well, while you two were out getting into trouble yesterday, I kept digging about the realms."

Murphy moved to my other side on the couch and all three of us peered down at the notes Erin showed us. She'd drawn at least a dozen pictures of caves, sparkly lakes, and circles of mushrooms. She pointed to some words on one page.

"Lydia, that old tome you pulled off the shelf was a book of fairytales."

I scowled.

"No, it was really helpful!" she insisted. "It took me a while to translate, but most of the stories talked about people finding themselves in other realms. They slip in through a lake, or cave, or even fairy circles. But—"

She scooted her drawings to the side and flipped over another piece of parchment. This one had drawings of various wrought-iron gates. I ran my finger across one that looked familiar.

"I found another book of stories written in common language. So, they wrote it after magic went away. Again, there are the stories of different realms. But in all of them, a person dreams of a gate, and then one appears. That's how they travel between the realms."

"That sounds like—"

"Exactly." Erin nodded. "It sounds like something has always separated the realms. When magic was wild, people fell through these entrances to the realms. But when magic was locked away, these gates appeared and locked off the realms."

"But who created them?" Murphy asked. Erin shrugged.

"If we can figure it out, maybe we can figure out how to find them. And maybe one of them will lead us home. Erin, have you compared anything else between the books of stories? Descriptions of the places or people?"

She pointed to her third piece of parchment.

"Already on it. The books... uh... ended up in my room. I'm making lists of the landscapes, characters, magical creatures, types of magic, anything I can think of. I thought we could compare them and maybe that will help us learn about the different realms."

"Great work!"

"Tell me where you keep the books and I'll work on the lists the nights you have watch," Murphy added. I scanned the information Erin laid before us.

"If we keep this up, we're bound to find something. We have to keep following the breadcrumbs."

Someone knocked at the door. Erin and Murphy looked at me, but I shrugged. She made the notes disappear as I opened the door to reveal Aidric. He held flowers in one hand and a basket in the other.

"Oh, I'm sorry." He spotted Erin and Murphy behind me. "I didn't mean to interrupt. I'll leave."

"No, it's okay," Erin told him. "We have to get back."

"Keep me updated," I told her as they squeezed by, leaving me alone with Aidric. Where was Gabrielle when I needed her?

"May I come in?" Aidric asked.

"Yeah, of course." I moved out of his way. He set the vase of flowers on a side table and carried the basket to the larger table by the window. He spun in a circle and rubbed the back of his neck.

"I heard you haven't left your rooms all day. I thought I'd bring you some dinner."

"Isn't there a ball tonight?"

He stepped forward and the late afternoon sunlight made his skin glow. The urge to reach out and run my hand up his arm overtook me, but I resisted.

"If you've been to one ball, you've been to them all."

"Won't you be missed?" I raised an eyebrow.

"I'm the prince, I can do what I want." His grin was infectious and I was powerless to resist it. He pulled out a chair for me. I didn't move from where I stood in the middle of the room. Jaclyn's words stuck in my mind.

"Does Jaclyn know you're here?"

Aidric's grin faltered. "It doesn't matter."

"It does, Aidric. You're going to be king one day. And she's going to be queen. Everything you do matters. But me," —I touched my chest—"I'm nothing. Not really. Maybe I have a role to play while I'm here, but then I'll be gone."

"Is that what she told you? That you're nothing?"

"No, but she reminded me I'm leaving. And the people left behind are the ones that have to deal with the consequences of my choices."

"That's not true—"

"She's right, Aidric. We're fools to think otherwise." Somehow, as we talked, we'd gotten closer together. Now I had to look up to stare into his eyes. I was like a moth, always drawn to his flame. His hands grasped both my arms. This close, the sunlight illuminated the gold flecks in his eyes.

"What do you want, Lydia?"

I leaned my head against his chest and breathed in his snow and salt-water scent. This time, there was no magic connecting us, bleeding our emotions together. But I knew what he was thinking the same thing I was. And just like before, it didn't change anything.

"It doesn't matter what we want. And tomorrow, you'll remember that."

He let go and turned away. Goosebumps raced up my arms. Once again, he pulled the chair out.

"And tomorrow, we'll deal with it. But please, for tonight —will you have dinner with me, my friend?"

I smiled.

"That, I can do."

So, we ate dinner together and talked long into the night. We swapped stories from our childhoods. He discussed his theories about the rebellion. I told him what Erin, Murphy, and I suspected about the realms and the gates. I confessed identifying Wielders for the Scholars worried me after learning about the people who were attacked and branded. Neither of us had any answers, but giving voice to my worries and concerns helped ease the knot in my chest that was my constant companion these days.

At some point, we moved to the couch. I crossed my legs, and Aidric propped his feet up, letting one drop against mine.

It was the only physical contact we allowed ourselves. Having Aidric all to myself was bittersweet. I never let myself think about how much I missed him. And even now I knew we couldn't let this happen again.

The candle burned low. When it was little more than a puddle of wax on the holder, we knew our time was up. I walked Aidric to the door. His arms circled my body, and I let myself lean into his touch. The desire to look up and kiss him was strong. But even though we were alone, he was still engaged to Jaclyn. And that was a line I knew neither of us wanted to cross.

Before he left, he lifted my chin and brushed my hair out of my face.

"You're not nothing," he whispered. "You've never been nothing. And even when you go home, part of you will always live in my heart."

CHAPTER FIFTEEN

"Lydia." Lord Barwick's baritone voice woke me up. "You need to learn this."

I sat across from him in his study, memorizing a book of spells. I'd drifted off halfway through a spell to clean a puddle.

"Spells are not my strong suit. Usually I,"—I twiddled my hands in the air—"and the magic does what I want."

Barwick pushed his glasses up on his nose.

"While that's nice and all, sometimes you need to be more precise."

I snorted. Barwick might be a high-ranking lord, but months of lessons with him had taught me he had a good sense of humor.

"Are you saying your magic has never done something —unexpected?"

My thoughts turned to the display at midnight, finding myself all the way across the castle at night, and—most recently—making Murphy invincible.

"I get your point," I sighed, returning to the book.

For the past two weeks, my days had returned to a routine. The first three days I spent in the throne room in a rotation of more and more extravagant outfits. The next three I spent in lessons with Lord Barwick. But the incoming Scholars class kept him distracted, so most of my lessons were me memorizing spells and studying magical theory.

At night, when I wasn't avoiding Cyril at the banquets and balls, I huddled in Erin's room with her and Murphy researching everything we could to understand the realms.

"Lord Barwick, my father said you wanted to study this?"

My eyes stayed frozen to the page in front of me as Aidric entered the room. We'd barely spoken since the night after the ambush in the city. It was for the best. Really. It didn't matter that butterflies fluttered in my stomach every time he looked at me, or that he visited me in my dreams.

The rust stone dangling in Aidric's hand caught my interest, though. It was the one they'd cut off the prisoner in the courtyard. I slammed the book shut and grabbed it from Aidric before Lord Barwick even got his glasses on.

"Now, Lydia. Be careful with that."

I held the stone up in the sunlight. The pockmarked surface reminded me of the landscaping stones in front of my school. The surface scratched my skin when I rubbed it with my finger.

"Have you figured out how it works yet?"

"No, we haven't." Lord Barwick shook his head. "None of the fire incantations make it do anything. Our best guess is it's spelled to the creator, or there's only a certain word that can set it off."

I tossed the stone in the air and Aidric snatched it before

it came back down in my hand. He smirked and handed it off to Lord Barwick. I rolled my eyes.

"Well, we know Sarge is a fire Wielder," Aidric started. My nickname for the strange woman had caught on. "So that would make sense. They must only work synchronously as well. Since our friend downstairs didn't have it in his hand when she set them off, they left behind him."

"Fire as a conduit for travel; I've never seen it's like," Barwick mused. Without taking his eyes off the stone, he waved Aidric and me away.

"Lydia, you're done for the day. Take care and I'll see you next week."

I made a dash for the hall behind Aidric.

"Didn't you just get in there?" he asked.

"Mom always said never look a gift horse in the mouth."

"What does that mean?"

"I don't really know." I giggled.

Aidric and I walked down the hallway together.

"What are you going to do with your free afternoon?" Aidric asked.

"I'm working on a theory I need to research. I was thinking about heading down to the Scholar library on the lower levels."

"That place gives me the creeps." He shivered. "You're not going to visit your friend Cyril? You guys looked cozy at the banquet last night."

It was my turn to shudder. Somehow, he'd grabbed the seat beside me. Then he talked my ear off all night long. I glared at Aidric's smirk.

"He's very charming, you know."

"Is that right?"

"Oh, yes." I twirled my hair around the end of my finger. "In a know-it-all, pompous, thinks he's the smartest guy in the room kind of way."

We went our separate ways and his laughter followed me down the stairs.

My feet carried me to the library set up for the Scholars on the same level as the classrooms and dormitories. People were moving into the dormitories every day now, but lessons wouldn't start for another week. So that left the library deserted. I waved my hand, and the torches on the wall sprang to life. I smiled. Take that Barwick and his annoying spells.

The torches burned down an hour mark as I browsed the shelves. Most of these were basic spell books or explanations about each of the affinities. My hand lingered on a book about healing, but I moved on. I wasn't here to learn about my magic right now. And as much as I wanted to figure out how I'd made Murphy impervious to blades, he was fine with it right now. I had other things to concentrate on.

Of Elves and Fae. The gold lettering glinted in the torchlight.

"This looks promising," I muttered, pulling the dusty book from its place on the shelf. I found a table and displaced another puff of dust when I slammed the book down.

"Maybe I should have memorized that cleaning smell," I grumbled.

I conjured a ball of light above my head and pulled out my parchment to read. Another hour mark burned down while I skimmed the information about elves and faeries. The author questioned if they were different beings or not. He had compiled all the stories of the two races and made charts listing which traits belonged to elves, which to faeries, and which traits belonged to both. Diligently, I copied the traits he described. Looking at the information I'd written, something clicked. I sketched out the eight-point affinity star.

Over and over, the author described elves in terms of how they valued purity and their ability for healing and creating illusions. All these things were characteristics of a light affinity. I wrote *elves* under the bottom, right point of the star.

In contrast, he described the faeries as tricky, flighty, and quick. They used their magic for manipulation, sleight of hand, and binding. I wrote faeries on the point of the star with the air affinity.

I wrote the name of the realms on the side of the parchment and matched them up to each of the points. Mermaids with water seemed obvious. So did dragons with fire. From the way Jaclyn described phantoms, they lined up with aether. That was five affinities that related to a realm and magical being. I circled the points for light, spirit, and earth. If Thavell was the human realm, what affinity would it align with? Humans could have all the affinities. Hadn't Jaclyn mentioned something about eight spirits that created the realms? That had to mean something, right? But then why were there only six realms?

Throwing my quill down, I nestled my head in my hands. Every time I thought I was onto something, it unraveled. Was there really a connection here, or did I just want everything to fit into a neat box? I groaned and slid my head down until my forehead rested on the table. I'd been down here so long I was hearing things. The sound of a fire crackled in my ear.

"Ash!"

I jolted up to see the little ash sprite sitting on the table.

She'd heeded my warning and left after I found her the first time.

"I hope you don't mind," when she quirked her head at the sound of the name. "I didn't know what to call you. Sorry, it's not very original."

She fluttered her wings and smiled at me. I took that as a good sign.

"It's good to see you. Have you been well?"

She nodded.

"I really wish I could understand you," I told her. "But I don't even know how I'd go about it. It's not like talking with a horse, is it?"

Ash crossed her arms and huffed. I laughed.

"Yeah, I didn't think so."

Ash fluttered to the top of my shoulder and peeked into the library. Satisfied we were alone, she jumped back down on the table in front of me. She snapped her fingers. Flames erupted on the table. I scooted away before they caught my sleeves on fire. Ash laughed when I panicked. The flames burned bright for a minute and then vanished, Ash with them. A small piece of parchment laid on the table where the sprite and flames had been.

The familiarity of the fire trick made me nervous. I looked over my shoulder, but I was still alone. I poked the note. Nothing happened. Feeling silly, I unfolded it. Three words stared back at me:

Howling Moon, midnight

STUFFING the note in my pocket, I frantically rolled the notes I'd written and slammed my book shut. Grabbing everything in my arms, I raced for the library door. I crashed into the person on the other side in a pile of parchment and books.

"I'm so sorry," I said. "I'm so clumsy, let me get these."

My victim picked up the books while I separated the mixed-up parchment. When I looked up, she took a step back. I remembered those steely eyes.

"You're Dana, right?"

She nodded. I held out her parchment. She snatched it and shoved my book in my arms.

"I'm Lydia. It's nice to meet you."

I extended my hand. She flinched like I'd smacked her.

"I know who you are."

I let my hand drop.

"I'm sorry, have I done something wrong?"

"You're the reason I'm here."

"I'm sorry, I don't understand."

Dana scoffed. I bit my lip to stop myself from snapping at her.

"Don't act like you're not part of this. I saw you standing up there with the crown on your head. If it wasn't for you, I'd be home."

"Then go home." I lost the hold on my tongue. "You don't have to be here."

"I hid my powers for two years until the steward heard I'd saved Kylie when she gave birth. The next thing I knew, I was being tested and ended up in the throne room. If you're so powerful, why didn't you hear what I sent you? Why didn't you help me hide my powers?"

"I don't know what you're talking about. You wanted to join the Scholars. If you don't like it, go home."

"That's just like a noble," she sneered. "Nothing is voluntary with the king. He knows where I live. He knows who my family is. I tried to not do the tests and the next thing I know, the steward had my father in the stocks, accusing him of stealing from the blacksmith. Do you think that's a coincidence?"

"The king only wants people here who know want to be here," I threw up my hands. "Why would he care if some girl from Windburn shows up or not?"

Dana yanked up her sleeve and thrust her arm into my path. There on the inside of her wrist was an eight-pointed star with solid triangles above water, aether, and light. The brand was still red and swollen.

"If the king doesn't care, then how do you explain this? They broke into my house the night after they dragged me before you."

"I don't have time for this." My voice shaking, I backed away. At the end of the hallway, I turned and ran.

CHAPTER SIXTEEN

Isprinted all the way to Erin's room. Thankfully, she was there. Completely breathless from the run and my conversation with Dana, I thrust the note into her hand.

She dropped onto her bed when she read it. I dumped the rest of my stuff from the library on her desk and slid down onto the floor.

"Do you think?"

"It's his handwriting," I said. Pained hope flickered across Erin's face. "But what does Howling Moon mean?"

"It's a tavern," Erin answered. She flipped through a book, opening it to a map of Windburn. She traced the route from the castle to the tavern with her finger. "On the south side of the city, near the shipping docks."

"Where's Murphy?"

"His unit is out in the city on patrol. He won't be back until the morning."

"Well, I guess you and I are going to meet John, then."

My heart squeezed as she tried to temper her excitement.

"Lydia, you can't. Do I need to remind you the last time you met John in the city things didn't go well?"

She had a good point. And I couldn't deny even the thought of leaving the castle made my heart catch in my throat. But I knew Erin would go no matter what.

"Erin, I'm not letting you go alone. They got the slip on me last time. But I have my magic, and you're more than capable of holding your own. This is the first time John's reached out to us. We're not giving up on him."

"Let's do it."

Begging away from the ball that night was easy enough. I had Gabrielle send a note that I had a headache. To my surprise, no one bothered me.

The winter night was cloudy, perfect for sneaking around. My purple cloak blended into the darkness perfectly. I met Erin near the wall by the bay. Together we climbed up into an abandoned watch tower Aidric had shown me. I called some water from the bay towards us. Directed by my hands, the water formed steps leading down to the docks on the other side.

Erin let out a low whistle. She tested a watery step with her foot and then rushed toward the ground.

"Impressive," she whispered when I joined her. The water collapsed with a splash. This area of the docks held the pleasure boats and ships of the king and nobility. No one sailed for fun in the winter. The shipping docks were more active this time of year, but they were on the other side of the city.

I reflected the light away from us and drew shadows closer until we were invisible to anyone passing by.

"This is my favorite trick of yours," Erin told me.

"It comes in handy. But the illusion fails if we run into anyone," I warned. With an hour until we needed to meet John, we made our way around the docks. It was the long way around, but less chance of us running into someone or being spotted by another Wielder. I kept the hood of my cloak pulled up, just in case.

Windburn was eerily silent. We spotted a few people here and there, but they all darted from street to street, eyes open for anyone watching. We discovered why when we passed a bulletin board.

Curfew in effect
By order of Olma, Steward of Windburn

"THAT'LL DO IT," I muttered.

"I'm assuming we're going to pretend this is a coincidence, right?" Erin asked.

"Of course," I told her.

We made it to the tavern right at midnight. As quiet as the street was, the tavern was packed. Erin and I squeezed in unnoticed, but there were too many people to stay concealed. Everyone ignored us as we scanned the room.

"I don't see him," Erin whispered. I nudged her with my elbow and pointed to a door ajar on the other side of the room. A tiny silver horse sat on the handle. Erin picked up the delicate figurine. The door led to a long hallway. We followed it and turned left, where another silver horse awaited us. Another hall led to a door where a horse waited on the handle. We heard muffled voices behind the door.

"We've come this far," Erin said. She gripped the hilt of the dagger. I let my magic simmer underneath my skin. Flames danced in the palms of my hands. Sarge didn't know it, but she'd given me a new trick. I'd been practicing throwing fireballs since the ambush.

The door opened on a puff of my conjured wind, revealing a circular room surrounded by a dozen alcoves, all blocked from view by shimmery curtains. Erin pointed. Across the room, a final silver horse perched on the wainscoting outside an alcove. I used a bit of shadow to shield, hopefully making us unnoticeable as we crossed the room.

Despite the soft voices, I couldn't make out anything going on behind the curtains. I blinked and the magic shining off them scalded my vision. Another blink and it vanished. Someone had spelled the curtains to keep anyone on the outside from knowing what went on behind.

Erin pocketed the last horse. She glanced in my direction, but I shook my head. Whoever spelled these curtains made it impossible for me to manipulate them with magic. She drew her dagger from its sheath and threw back the curtain.

"Erin!" Dark circles painted John's eyes. Patches and loose threads decorated his clothing.

Erin dropped the dagger. John's cry undid her. She threw herself into her boyfriend's arms as he caught her up in an embrace.

I let the curtain fall back between us, giving them time together. As soon as the curtain fell, the faint voices started again, obscuring anything that happened on the other side. Pulling my cloak tighter around me, I hid in the shadows next to the alcove. No one came or went while I waited. Using my vision, I studied the magic on the curtains. Symbols were written in air magic; I didn't recognize most of them. Even the walls were warded. I probed one symbol with my magic, trying to understand how it worked. Like a snake, the magic on the curtains shocked mine. I recoiled, the shock reverberating through me. I rubbed my chest.

Erin's arm appeared from behind the curtain and pulled me in. John wrapped me up in a hug.

"Lydia, I'm so glad you came. I'm so, so sorry. For every-thing. I've been so blind."

My muscles relaxed, and I hugged John back. When he pulled away, I noticed both he and Erin were teary-eyed. We sat around a small table. Erin perched on John's lap. He wrapped an arm around her waist. Erin offered me a cup of tea, but I declined. Any kind of tea was off my menu for the moment.

"Lydia, can you ever forgive me?"

Words lodged in my throat. I studied my friend as I thought about what to say. John's blonde hair, broad shoul-ders, and square jaw looked just like I remembered. A scruffy, dark beard now covered his chin and cheeks. While we'd been separated, John's birthday had come and gone. But the hardness in his normally bright blue eyes made him look older than eighteen. And despite knowing this was my friend, the memories of him standing next to Reynard, cutting down other soldiers, and dueling with Aidric still haunted me.

Erin squeezed John's shoulder as she watched my face. Even without magic, Erin read my thoughts. John understood too. He dropped his gaze to the table. I reached out and took his hand, quelling the part of me that remembered the panic in the courtyard.

"John, you're my friend and I love you. I forgive you, but —I need time."

He nodded, squeezing my hand.

"I deserve that, Lydia. And I'll do whatever it takes to make it up to you."

"You can start by telling us what you were thinking," Erin said. She slid off his lap so she could face him. He kept his hand on her knee. "Tell us everything, John."

So he did. He told how Reynard had invited him to take private sword lessons. After a few weeks, he'd invited John into the city for dinner. That was when he revealed my magic. My brow furrowed; I had no idea how Reynard would have known about my magic at that point.

John didn't know about the larger rebellion until after the failed coup. They took shelter in a remote village outside the forest, close to the stronghold of Fenwood. There, they scolded Reynard for doing his own thing. That was where John met Sarge as well.

"What's her name?" I asked.

"I don't know. She told me to call her Morghan."

I snorted.

"What?" John asked.

"It's in a book of legends Erin pulled from the library. Morghan's supposed to be one of the eight spirits. She often takes on the form of a wolf. And she's the creator of war."

"Yeah, that sounds like her, all right. She convinced me you were in danger, and I agreed to come back to Windburn with her—and you see how that went. Her magic rocks transported us two streets over. We split up, and I've been on the run ever since. There're drawings of me at every signpost. Apparently the king is offering a reward for my capture."

"I didn't know," I told him.

"King Bleddyn keeps a lot of cards close to his chest."

I didn't want to admit how right John was.

"Are you safe here?" Erin asked. John nodded.

"I've been doing the owner favors to earn my keep. He's in with the rebels, so he's not interested in turning me in as long as I keep him happy. I knew this place would be perfect because no one can hear what we're talking about."

John propped his elbows on the table, leaning forward to stare at me.

"Lydia, I needed you to come tonight because you're in danger."

"John, if you think the kin—"

John held his hands up in protest.

"This isn't about the king. I don't believe anything he says, but that's not what I'm talking about. It's the rebellion. Like Reynard, most of the leaders are Wielders who fought in the civil war years ago. They know more about magic than anyone. And they've discovered something—"

John's pause made me tense. Erin laid a hand on his arm to encourage him to continue.

"We know the Golden Forest is the center of magic, and that's why magic was trapped there for so many years. A couple of decades ago, before the civil war, the Wielders released the magic in the forest. That's it, right? But there are the other realms. They're real, you guys."

Erin sucked in a breath. We knew it.

"The rebels have tons of old information about them. They have access to letters written by inhabitants of these other realms. Elves, Faeries, Merpeople. They can communicate with them."

"But how?" Despite the eavesdropping spell, I whispered.

"I don't know," John admitted. "This group has had decades of experience keeping information secret. When you're with them, you only know what you need for your missions. The information I have I've been able to piece together bit by bit."

"What I do know is these beings aren't like humans who can have magic or not. Their very essence is magic, without it —they die. So, when each realm locked themselves behind barriers, it stopped the magic from leaking out. But over the years, the magic has faded. And now they're desperate. But it's not just the realms. Without each realm being connected like before, the magic here in Thavell is unstable. It comes from the forest, but it has nowhere to go. Humans don't account for enough of it."

"Morghan wanted me to convince you to come with us so you can break the barriers and open the realms again. If it was just her, that would be fine. That's how the rebellion started. They wanted to balance magic and let Wielders be free to practice their magic without persecution."

"Your alliance with King Bleddyn is doing what he wanted. Wielders see you and hear about you; they're trusting the king more. He's always spoken against what his father did, and people are believing him."

John paused; his mouth set in a grim line.

"Isn't that what the rebellion wanted? Freedom to use their magic?"

"Not all of them. There's been so little progress for so

many years, people are getting nasty. Since the Battle of the Forest, Reynard has gathered more supporters. These people aren't happy with peace. They want an uprising. And they won't be happy until the king, the prince, and anyone loyal to them are dead."

"Like me," I said.

"Yeah." John rubbed his hand across his face. "They know they need your magic. But they're trying to capture you and force you to use your magic for them. As an example of what happens when you're loyal to the king."

With each of John's words, my world shrunk until the only thing that existed were my memories. The first man I killed, fighting in the forest, the lifeless eyes of the man in the courtyard. It would keep happening. The fighting, the horror. Because of me. And I couldn't stop it.

I didn't notice my hands were shaking until Erin knelt beside me. She covered my quivering hands with her own.

"Lydia, we won't let anything happen to you. I promise."

"Erin's right, Lydia. Take me back to the castle. I'll tell the king everything I know. Who cares if he throws me into the dungeon. I won't let them hurt you."

The love of my friends bolstered me. I drew a deep breath and let it out slowly. It took a minute to remind my body danger wasn't imminent. With my head cleared of flashbacks, another idea occurred to me.

"John, are you still connected with the rebels? Doing work for them?"

Erin hummed in question. But John's eyes lit up.

"Yes."

I pulled blank parchment out of my purse.

"Give me everything you know. Names, numbers, anything. If you know the next target, even better."

"Lydia, what are you thinking?"

Erin watched nervously as John started writing out everything he remembered.

"I'm going to take this information to the king. And if I can leverage it, well, maybe John won't ever have to see the inside of a dungeon. But, John, we'll need more information. It means you'll have to stay here and keep doing work for them."

"John, no!" Erin protested. "I just got you back. If the rebels find out you're passing information to the king, they'll kill you."

"I hope they try." His dark words made Erin even more frantic.

"There has to be another way. Isn't there somewhere you can just hide until we find a way home? Or come back to the castle. Surely Lydia can talk King Bleddyn around."

"Erin, if John comes back now, King Bleddyn will throw him in the dungeon." I shook my head. "I know it's dangerous. John, if you'd rather find a place to hide, that's fine. I'll take what you can give me now and see what the king says."

John took both sides of Erin's face in his hands and kissed her deeply.

"Erin, I need to do this. Let me make up for some of the harm I've done. And if we know the rebels' plans, we have a better chance of keeping Lydia safe."

Erin didn't look happy, but she nodded in agreement.

"Should we meet you back here in a week?" I asked.

"Someone can meet me here, but not you." John held up a hand before I protested. "It was dangerous enough asking you to come tonight. I only risked it because I had to talk to you in person."

He stood and tapped on the wall behind us. A knee-high door appeared.

"These alcoves have escape hatches. They started reappearing with magic a few years ago. They lead to different parts of the city every time you go through one. So, once you get in, don't lose sight of one another."

John pulled me into another hug.

"Thank you, Lydia. Stay safe."

He tugged Erin into the opposite corner. I turned my back and collected the notes he'd written to give them privacy. Erin wiped a tear and opened the small door. We'd have to crawl.

"I'll see you in a week, babe," John said.

Erin nodded and made her way into the tunnel. I followed right behind her.

CHAPTER SEVENTEEN

The only thing good about the tunnel was that it was warm. Erin and I heard the wind whistling outside, but we didn't where the dark tunnel lead. Afraid to lose her, I crawled so close I kept landing on Erin's foot. She didn't complain. In fact, we both stayed silent as the dark tunnel twisted on and on.

Finally, Erin ran headfirst into a door. I gathered shadows again as she pushed on it, and out she tumbled into the street. I landed right behind her. When we turned around, the door had vanished. I shivered and pulled the hood of my cloak back over my hair.

We stood under a thin awning. Across the street, the sign for the Dancing Goat swung in the howling wind and sleet. I breathed a sigh of relief; we weren't too far from the castle. Erin assessed the empty street, silent as a tomb.

"I'm sorry," I whispered.

"It's okay," she told me without turning in my direction. I swallowed the lump in my throat.

"Really," she insisted. "It's a brilliant plan. I just wish it didn't have to be so hard, you know?"

Not trusting my voice, I nodded. I knew exactly what she meant. These days nothing was easy.

We didn't need the cover of shadows on the way to the castle. The pouring sleet made it almost impossible to identify anyone who wasn't right next to you. It also made the brief journey difficult. We avoided the worst puddles, but the sleet made everything slick, and we frequently had to jump out of the way of horses sloshing down the street. Eventually, we made it back to the edge of the wall. The sea raged too hard for me to grab it for stairs again, so I lifted us over the wall on a puff of wind.

The effort made spots flare in my vision, and we had to rest in the outpost for a few minutes before starting the trudge again. Early dawn light peeked over the horizon by the time I left Erin in her room. Thankfully, the terrible weather meant a late start for the people in the castle. I only had to dodge a few servants before hauling myself up the stairs to my room.

"Where have you been?!"

My soul left my body when Aidric's voice rang across my sitting room. Water fell from the sky, dousing him from head to toe. His feet slid out from under him as he rolled and spluttered under the waterfall.

"Aidric?! What do you think you're doing scaring me like that?"

I waved my hand and stopped the water, leaving the sopping wet prince to struggle to his hands and knees on his own.

"That's how you defend yourself against intruders?"

His curls laid flat against his head, and water still dripped from the end of his nose. He was so angry his eyes could have burned right through me. I burst out laughing.

"It... wasn't... intentional," I gasped out between laughs. I doubled over, supporting myself on a nearby table. "Just happened. You should see yourself!"

A fresh wave of laughter hit me. I had to sit down to keep from falling over. Aidric glared at me the whole time. He made his way in front of the fire and wrung out his clothing. Once I had control of myself, I twirled my finger in his direction. A cyclone of air surrounded him, twisting from his head to his toes. When it disappeared, he was dry.

"What are you doing sneaking out at night?" he spat at me.

"What do you mean, sneaking out?" I asked, the picture of innocence. Aidric grunted and grabbed a piece of bread off my table, stuffing it in his mouth. I crossed my legs, tapping my toe in the air. He wouldn't get anything out of me with that attitude.

"I came to make sure you were okay, and you weren't here. So, I waited. You never came back."

"Hm," I hedged. "I went for a walk. The cool air clears my head."

Aidric gave a skeptical look out the windows at the buckets of sleet still falling from the sky.

"My father had a good reason for asking you to stay on castle grounds."

"Your father ordered me to stay on castle grounds, actually. And wasn't it you who told me I didn't have to do whatever your father told me?"

I'd cherish the incredulous look that crossed Aidric's face

forever. It annoyed me to no end that he was always one step ahead of me. For once, I had the upper hand.

"Not when it's your safety at risk," he sputtered. "Everyone here is trying to protect you. And this is how you repay us?"

"I won't apologize," I growled. "I'm sick and tired of everyone trying to protect me. Like I'm some porcelain doll ready to shatter. When is your father going to realize I have more than magic tricks to contribute?"

"Like what?"

"I have proof of the rebellion."

Aidric fell silent, regarding me like an opponent he didn't expect. Maybe it was my imagination, but I swore there was pride in his expression.

"Well, perfect timing. I'm here to escort you to your first official council meeting."

Aidric waited while I rushed into my closet. Gabrielle wasn't around to help me pick out an outfit. I bit my lip, hoping she wasn't out looking for me. I needed to do a better job of telling her if I was going to be out. Gabrielle never asked where I'd been, even when I knew she suspected I was up to no good. There was nothing for it now, though.

I yanked my soaked clothes off and pulled on the first thing that looked presentable. A white shirt with full sleeves that tied back at my elbows went over my undergarments. Then a simple emerald overdress that laced up the front. This early in the morning, full court regalia wasn't necessary. But if this was an official council meeting, I knew I had to impress. My knee-high boots I exchanged for brown hose and tan leather flats with jewels sewed on the toe.

I pinned a broach on my chest and put a headdress over

my braided hair. Nobles showered me with gifts every day. I couldn't keep everything straight, so I tried to wear at least one or two gifts with each outfit, hoping this way I could keep people happy. I wasn't made for a place where any detail of an outfit could offend someone. A knee-length navy coat went over everything. I made sure the notes from John were still safe in the purse attached to my belt and followed Aidric to the meeting.

He didn't lead me to the throne room, but to the king's chambers. As we passed the dining room, a wave of nostalgia struck me. Not even a month had gone by since King Bleddyn had invited me to dinner. Yet somehow it felt like years.

The king's private study was situated over the dining room. Falir opened the door when Aidric knocked. He smiled when he saw me and led me to a seat at the side of the room. I surveyed everyone gathered. Nadine and Olma, I'd expected. Lord Barwick sat next to the fire, using the light to read some manuscript. There was no sign of Harman, his new assistant. To my surprise, a low-ranking noblewoman stood at the side of the room. An elaborate scarf covered her close-cropped gray hair. I wracked my brain for her name. It finally came to me: Baroness Mirela of Serova, a small fiefdom known for its lakes. I couldn't remember where it was located, though.

Aidric perched on the side of his father's desk. King Bleddyn reclined in his chair. Once Aidric and I settled, he clapped his hands.

"Now that everyone is here,"—he threw a look in his son's direction, Aidric ignored it—"I'd like to welcome Lydia to her first council meeting. As the Gatebreaker, I thought it best she knows what is going on in the kingdom to better understand her role."

He didn't mention that I'd made him promise to include me. I smiled when everyone nodded in my direction. King Bleddyn stood and flipped a large tapestry around, revealing a large map of Thavell.

"Let's get started."

The council meeting lasted hours. I tried to pay attention to everything, but many of the topics went over my head. They discussed grain prices in Orsa. A sickness that had overtaken the outpost, Terin, on the northern shores. A noble who was upset because his neighbor planted crops over the boundary between their lands. Needles with different colored threads tied to the end decorated the map. Aidric moved them around as everyone gave reports.

"Lord Barwick, do we have an update on the concentrated levels of magic?"

Lord Barwick started, pulling his eyes from the manuscript.

"Yes, my king." He took over the map, placing golden threaded needles around the map. When he stepped back, the threads connected four spots: the Golden Forest, Windburn, an area off the coast of Orsa, and somewhere left of Alvale.

"Since we noticed the concentration of magic in the land in the Golden Forest last year, my scouts have been measuring across the country. They've identified these four places as the areas with the highest concentration of magic."

My eyes widened at the sight of the map. I pulled out the notes from John and flipped through them.

"Do we know what's causing these concentrations?"

"No, sir. But these areas also have the largest population of Wielders. They also seem to be the places more magical creatures appear. We just got a report of a new flock of birds that burst into flames with no injuries near Orsa."

King Bleddyn scratched his beard.

"Could these spots be related to the realms?" Baroness Mirela asked.

"I'm not sure if we're ready to admit to the existence of the realms yet," Olma stated. I shot him a look, but remained quiet. The conversation I overheard between Olma and the king was still fresh in my mind. They knew the realms existed, so why wouldn't they tell the council?

"Well, the realms are common knowledge at this point. You don't have to be ready to admit to what's right in front of your face."

I resisted the urge to chuckle. Mirela seemed alright to me.

"Uh, Your Majesty?" All eyes turned toward me. "I don't know why there's a concentration of power in these places, but I know we aren't the only ones aware of them."

"Well, let's hear it," Mirela said. I hesitated.

"Lydia, these people are my friends and closest confidants. You can say anything in front of them."

"Alright." I straightened in my chair. It was time to play ball. "But the person who got me this information is risking his life to bring it to us. Before I reveal it, I want your word that should he need to seek shelter, he will receive clemency and you will clear him of all crimes he's accused of."

"Girl, if you have information that would benefit your king, you will give it to him. Anything less is treason."

"The information I have now, I'll gladly give. But if my

source doesn't have assurance from me, he will go into hiding and this is the only information we will get."

Mirela *humphed* and sat down. I held my chin up, daring anyone else to challenge me. Olma tapped his fingers on the arm of his chair but said nothing. Aidric gave me the tiniest of nods. King Bleddyn studied the map for another moment before turning to me.

"I take it this has something to do with your rebel friend— John, is it?"

"Possibly."

"Can I ask how you came into this information?"

"My magic works in strange ways, Sire." It wasn't a lie, but I wouldn't admit I'd left the castle grounds. For the tilt of his head, I could tell King Bleddyn saw through my non answer, but he didn't argue.

"I won't pass up the opportunity to have an inside man. You have my word, Lydia. If we receive timely reports that benefit us, then John may return to the castle if he is in danger. I will clear him of all crimes. I'll even allow him to work here to stay close as we unravel the mystery of your arrival. But I expect him to stay as long as possible. And just so you know, all our spies have ended up dead. This isn't a game."

"I know, Your Highness. Thank you."

I took the initiative to work on the map. Using notes John made, I planted needles in each spot he'd mentioned a stronghold. Once I finished, I knew my hunch was correct. Each rebel base lined up with the areas Barwick marked.

"These are the bases of rebels. They weren't lying when they tried to ambush me. They're organizing a revolt."

Mirela cursed and Lord Barwick put down his

manuscript to pay attention. He took the papers from my hands and, with a wave of his, they multiplied until everyone had copies. He smiled at my impressed look.

"This is why you need to memorize spells." He winked.

"Do we have any way to verify this?" Olma asked. "What about our prisoner?"

"We found him dead before we could question him," Nadine replied.

I tried to push that information out of my mind. Instead, I pointed out the numbers and information John had given me.

"There's a group who only wants to live in peace and let their magic be free. But the bigger group is trying to stage an uprising. And unfortunately, John said that group is gaining ground. Their first plan of action is to capture me and force me to open the realms."

"But if you're in the castle, they would have to stage a full on attack to get to you."

I grimaced.

"John thinks that's exactly what they're trying to do."

We spent the next few hours going over the numbers and theories. Nadine discussed protection plans and extra watch shifts. King Bleddyn sat at his desk, rolling his staff underneath his hand while everyone brainstormed. I explained what I could from what I'd heard from John and even threw in my theory about the realms being locked by magical gates.

We didn't stop until Falir arrived to announce it was noon.

"This is a good start, my friends. This is information we can work with. We will take this up again next week. Nadine and Aidric, I'd like to get with you tomorrow morning to assess the troops we have in these areas."

With the dismissal, everyone made to leave. I gathered my copies of the notes so I could review them with Erin and Murphy later.

"Lydia, stay a moment."

I cringed to myself. Maybe I had been too bold. But it didn't matter if it meant John could return to the castle. I approached the king's desk. He passed me a letter. The official notice stated John had been pardoned for service to the crown. After I read it, King Bleddyn took his wax ring and sealed it.

"Now you have proof. I won't go back on my word."

"I know, Your Majesty. I trust you."

The king leaned back and twined his hands together.

"Do you, Lydia?"

"Of course." I wanted to tell him if I didn't trust him, I never would have told him about John.

"Lydia, I'm not sure how I feel about you dabbling in things like rebellion and spying. I don't have to get this information from you, you know. Your resources are limited. I have a feeling if I assigned your friends Erin and Murphy elsewhere, then the information from John would dry up as well."

"You could do that," I admitted. His implication about separating me from Erin and Murphy grated me. If King Bleddyn wanted to play like that, so be it. "But you won't."

The king's eyebrows disappeared into his hairline.

"And why is that?"

"You just told us all of your plants in the rebellion ended up dead. Maybe this is a terrible idea, and maybe my friends and I are stupid and naïve for attempting it. But you know I think differently than other people here. I didn't grow up learning your rules or knowing about magic. You're a great king. You won't turn down something useful. And I think you want to see how this plays out."

King Bleddyn smiled.

"You're smart, Lydia." He pointed at the door in dismissal. "Don't let it go to your head."

To my surprise, Mirela waited for me outside the king's chambers.

"Walk with me, girl," she barked. I complied.

"You probably don't know this, but I've known King Bleddyn since he was a babe. His mother was one of my best friends. She died giving birth to him. King Lewis wasn't the doting type, so I took Bleddyn in and raised him with my own children for the first few years of his life. I know the boy better than anyone."

"I didn't know that," I admitted, cringing inwardly at her calling the king a *boy*. My knees still shook from the mild confrontation I just had with him. We stopped at a window overlooking the city. Mirela leaned on her cane as she peered out the window.

"Why do you care?" she asked.

"Care about what?"

"About this." She waved her hand at the bustle of people below us.

"I don't know what you mean."

"Bleddyn's council knows everything. We know who you are, where you come from. And we know your only goal is to get back home. Helping us is just something to bide the time until that happens. But instead of just enjoying the luxury and doing what you're told, you stick that pretty little nose of yours everywhere."

Feeling self-conscious, I rubbed my nose. Impatient when I didn't answer, Mirela pressed again.

"Why do you care?"

My thoughts turned to Aidric and Nadine, the first people I met here. To Brendan, Rose, and Val, my training mates in the army. All the people who were joining the Scholars, it was because of me. And the magic that grew stronger every day within me, I still didn't understand it. I clenched my hands on the railing of the window.

"Somehow I've been dropped into the middle of the story that is still unfolding. But over and over I hear from Wielders, people who want to live their lives and use their magic. Maybe it doesn't matter what I do here. But I have this power in me, this power I still don't understand. And if I work to understand it, if I can make a difference while I'm here, I owe it to everyone who's helped me or died trying to protect me to try."

Mirela nodded, seeming to accept my answer.

"Then let me give you some advice. Don't embarrass Bleddyn."

"I didn't—"

She held up a hand to stop me.

"He won't forget it. And he will make sure you don't forget it, either. Mind your step and you'll be fine."

She walked away, leaving me to look over the city alone.

CHAPTER EIGHTEEN

The next week passed uneventfully. I paced in my bedroom the entire night Murphy was set to meet with John. Thankfully, he returned just before dawn, new reports in hand. I presented the findings at the next council meeting. John said Reynard was in Windburn, but nothing was happening yet. King Bleddyn ended the curfew since we'd discovered most people were circumventing it with underground tunnels, anyway.

"This blasted city always has more secrets," King Bleddyn muttered.

Pacing around the castle did me no good. My throne room appearances were over, and my lessons with Lord Barwick had lessened as he took on more responsibilities with the Scholars. Sitting around with Annistyn and Maren and playing political intrigue over embroidery didn't appeal to me. I needed to be useful.

With nothing else to do, I made my way to the Scholar's library. After my first encounter with Dana, I hadn't been back down to that level. But the first book I found had been helpful, maybe there were more.

"Welcome, students!" A voice echoed through the hall, catching my attention. I stopped outside the open door. "For those of you I haven't met, I am Lord Barwick, Grand Wizard of the Palace Scholars."

I'd forgotten today was the first day of classes. I peeked around the corner. Almost a hundred students sat with their back to me, dressed alike in the white robes of the Scholars. The room was an auditorium of sorts, with a half-moon of seats descending to a flat area where Barwick stood.

"This is Wizard Jamine. She will teach you the basics of magic use and history of magic."

Jamine appeared from the shadows, stepping up and waving at the class.

"And this is Wizard Simon, my second in command. You will start with him today as we introduce the basics of using gemstones. We hope that learning the basics of magic and the properties of gemstones together will help you incorporate the two. For now, I leave you in Simon and Jamine's capable hands."

The class applauded politely. Barwick climbed the stairs and exited out a door on the other side of the hall. I looked through the students, recognizing a few of them, including Arete and the older man I met after my first throne room appearance. Dana sat off to the side by herself.

Simon stepped up to the front.

"I'm honored to have you all here together. This is the largest and strongest class of Scholars we have ever assembled. I'm excited to see where your paths take you after you graduate from here. Many of you have known about your magic for years, some of you just learned of it recently. I'm afraid these first few weeks will be boring, but important. Many speak about magic as if it's guesswork. They talk about instinct."

Even though Simon couldn't see me, I blushed remembering my first conversation with him.

"That's not what we are doing here. Magic is not about trust or instinct. It is a finite resource. We will learn to control it, so it doesn't end up controlling you."

A murmur went through the class as the echo of Simon's pronouncement rang through the air. My magic jumped in my chest, like his words offended it. I looked at my hands, the golden threads weaved through my bones and veins, shining in my vision. My magic was part of me. Surely, I could trust it just as much as I trusted my heart or my lungs.

Simon waved a hand to quiet everyone down.

"Now, now. I know it's not what many of you have learned. But bear with me and Jamine and we will teach you to unlock all the secrets your magic holds."

Well, that sounded better.

Simon reached a hand into his pocket and drew out a green stone. Unlike the rough unfinished stone I'd inspected in the winter market, this stone was perfectly round and polished until the shone. The pearlescent green color reminded me of new leaves in the spring.

"Gemstones are the first step to gaining control of our powers. I'm here to help you understand the gemstone lore that is out there and wield your stones as well as you wield your magic." He waved a hand, and an orb of light illuminated a large piece of slate hung on the wall. Simon waved his hand again, and a list appeared in neat script:

Manalase- earth
Indoro- water
Adenite- spirit
Viridite- light
Ochrodite- metal
Cryoase- air
Daltelian- fire
Galcian- aether

He lined stones on the front table. I leaned into the room a little further to get a good look. The green one was first, then one of pale blue. The next one had mixed shades of deep purple and green. A stone that looked like liquid gold was followed by black, then a translucent silver. At the end of the row was a rust-colored stone. But something was off. I counted only seven stones.

"These are the gemstones and their corresponding affinities. Unfortunately, I do not have any galcian to show you. The mines of old Galan were emptied of it centuries ago. It's so rare I don't think even King Bleddyn has ever seen an example. From texts we know it is a delicate red stone, able to conceal and stop magic."

I gripped the purse hanging from my belt with Aidric's necklace still tucked inside. Could it be?

"Everyone, look under your seat."

As the students moved to do so, I crept into the room and checked under a seat in the back. Arete caught my eye and waved. I smiled at her before she turned around, her bag of gemstones in her hand. Luck was with me. A few extra bags were under the back row. I grabbed them all, ideas winding in my head.

"Now, retrieve the manalase."

No one paid any attention to me, so I sat and retrieved the light green stone from one of my bags.

"Just like earth holds plants, animals, invertebrates, dead matter, and all manner of things, its corresponding stone can store all types of magic within it. You can fill this stone with your magic, so you have a reserve of your own power when you need it."

"But be warned, once you give manalase part of your power, keep this stone with you at all times. If another mage touches it, they can access the power from the stone as well. Now, close your eyes and find your magic. Listen to my instructions and I will tell you how to fill your stone."

With everyone's eyes closed, I took the opportunity to sneak away. Following my original plan, I stopped by the library. But instead of searching for books about the realms, I grabbed one on gemstones and a book of spells.

Retreating to my rooms, I spent the rest of the day experimenting on my new collection of stones. It took me until nightfall to accomplish my goal. As soon as I did, I rushed to tell Murphy and Erin. On my way across the dark grounds, the sound of sobbing stopped me in my tracks.

Looking around, I spotted a dark shape by the rounded tower of the castle. I let a ball of flame erupt in my hand.

"Hello?" I called.

"Not you again!"

My flame illuminated Dana, tears streaming down her face.

"Dana, what's wrong?"

"Please, just go away."

Dana clearly still had a problem with me. My desire to

get to Erin and Murphy almost won out, but I hesitated. Today in class, she'd been sitting by herself. And now here she was again, all alone. I let the flame dim and leaned back against the castle.

"I'm just going to stand here. Ignore me if you'd like."

Stars sparked in the cloudless sky. Leaning my head back, I stared at them while Dana made good on my offer. Counting them passed the time. Occasionally Dana would sniff, but that was the only noise she made. When I was closing in on a thousand, she sighed.

"I miss my family."

Her words hit me in the chest, ripping my already raw heart. Seeing Dana so homesick was like looking in a mirror. Maybe I couldn't make everything right, but there was something I could do with her. I grabbed her hand.

"Come with me."

Dana followed me without complaint, from shock, most likely. I led her all the way to Erin's room. Thankfully, both Erin and Murphy were together.

"Hey, Lydia."

"Guys, this is Dana. She's one of the Scholars."

"It's nice to meet you, Dana." Erin joined Murphy on the bed to let Dana have the chair. I handed both Erin and Murphy viridite stones.

"Um, thanks?" Erin said.

"Just wait." I pulled a note out of my pocket. "Grip them in your hands and say *sceadwian*."

"Say what?" Murphy asked. Dana watched silently from the side of the room.

"Sceadwian, it's an Old English word. I needed something that no one would accidentally say."

"Well, you won't have to worry about that."

I glared at Murphy.

"Say it one more time," Erin said.

"Sceadwian, like 'said-we-an.'"

Murphy and Erin exchanged a glance.

"Sceadwian!" they chorused.

They vanished. A feral grin appeared on Dana's face. I clapped my hands in delight.

"It worked!"

"What worked?" Murphy's disembodied voice asked.

"You're invisible," Dana said.

"What? Oh wait, Murphy, I can't see you!"

"Now say, *onlucan*."

"Onlucan," the chorused again. And there they were.

"How did you do that?" Dana asked.

"Don't worry, I'll teach you." She set her shoulders, and I knew she'd learn easily.

"Erin, do you have a way to contact John before you meet him next week?"

"Yeah, why?"

"Tell him we have a new meeting location. You and Murphy won't be going alone. Dana and I are coming. We're going to see her family."

CHAPTER NINETEEN

*E*arly the next morning, Lord Barwick found me in his office, diligently copying spells over and over to memorize them.

"Well, Lydia, this is a pleasant surprise."

"You are right, spells can come in handy." And rewriting them came in handy, too.I didn't mention that part. There was something that bugged me, though.

"Sir, I was using the Scholar library yesterday and heard a bit of the first lesson. About using gemstones in magic. Why haven't we ever gone over that?"

Barwick stacked the papers on his desk before turning his attention to me.

"I didn't think you needed it."

"But Scholar Simon made it very clear that magic needed to be controlled."

My teacher leaned back in his chair, his face towards the sky as he pondered.

"Yes, Simon focuses on control. It's good for a group of young mages. In the past, there was a Wielder in Alvale who died when they overexerted themselves during a routine training exercise. Then, we found some old texts that discussed the practice of calling on gemstones for more power. And especially after your events in the fall, we realized we would be in trouble if any of the Scholars working for the crown found themselves where they had no reserves to call on."

"But tell me, Lydia. Is your body completely under your control, your emotions? Do you ever get sad or angry, act impulsively?"

"Yes, I do. Everyone does." I jumped in before Barwick got lost in a list of unanswerable questions.

"Well, it's the same with magic. It's innate in those of us who are Wielders. We need to learn control of our magic just like we need to learn to control our tongue or our energy. Stones help with that. They give us a solid focal point to work off, or we can use their properties to enhance what we know. I've been working with you for months now. Your control is as good as you can make it. And you know better than any of the Scholars downstairs that losing control of your magic—especially with the power you possess—is dangerous."

He stopped to write something on one of the books spread out before him.

"Your journey is unique. You learned your magic in a trial by fire, as it were. Learn about gemstones and use them if you want. It's never a bad thing to have more than one tool at your disposal."

"In the future, let Harman know if there are any books you need down in the Scholar wing. He can fetch them for you. We don't want any distractions now that studies have begun."

Barwick buried himself in his book and I went back to copying spells.

After my lessons, I found Tristan by the training courts. I joined the other nobles, watching the squires and knights spar. Once Tristan finished, I followed him outside.

"Tristan!"

"What can I do for you, my lady?" Snow caught in his mousy hair.

"I want you to teach me to throw daggers." Before he could say no, I laid out my reasons. "I'm helpless without my magic. You witnessed that. Some people can use magic and weapons, but I don't have that skill. I have basic fighting training, but I can't focus on a sword or a bow and arrow if I'm dealing with magic. In the courtyard, you took down that guy in a single throw. If I could do that, I'd have something as backup."

"Why the sudden desire?" he asked. I admired Tristan's ability to go with the flow. Nothing ever surprised him.

"It's never a bad thing to have more than one tool at my disposal."

"Then let's get to it," he said.

A WEEK LATER, when Dana and I met Erin and Murphy at the abandoned watchtower, I had two blades concealed under my skirt. Tristan had coached me every day in his knight master's private training area. My aim and strength weren't perfect yet. But with a target on my back, everything helped.

While Erin helped Dana up the ladder, Murphy grabbed me by the elbow and tugged me into the shadows.

"I don't like this. John is going to meet us on Berry Street, but none of us are familiar with this part of the city. Let us take Dana to her family. We will have her back before dawn. You need to stay here."

"I'm going Murphy, I have to do this."

"Why?"

"It's my fault Dana's here. I don't care if I didn't know, but the fact is, if I hadn't recommended her for the Scholars, she'd still be home. I'm doing this."

"Lydia, this isn't a good idea."

"I agree with Murphy."

Both of us spun around. Aidric leaned against the castle wall. Erin and Dana were in the tower now, out of earshot.

"Are you following me now?" I accused.

"Only when I think you're doing something stupid."

I bristled. Murphy stayed silent, clearly torn between defending me and agreeing with the prince.

"I'm doing this, Aidric."

"It would just take a minute for me to call for the watch and put a stop to this right now."

I gasped, shocked that Aidric would make a threat like that.

"You wouldn't!"

"Did you forget what happened the last time you were in the city? We almost didn't get to you, Lydia. Don't you get it?"

"I get it, Aidric, but I'm not going to hide. I have a duty to help."

"You can't fix everything, Lydia. This world is big and

there are people hurting all over. What does helping one person fix? How does it solve anything?"

"It helps her."

We faced off. Murphy decided it was time to bow out. He took two steps backward, then hurried up the ladder to the watchtower. Aidric slouched, and he blew out a long breath, forming a misty cloud in the air.

"You win Lydia." He threw up his hands while I smiled. "But I'm coming with you."

I didn't have time to argue. We needed to meet John. Without replying, I raced up the ladder. Aidric came right behind me.

When we reached the top, Dana squeaked and bowed low to the prince.

"Don't worry about all that," Murphy told her. "He's a pushover."

"Thanks for that, Murphy."

Dana's eyes widened as she stared between the three of us and Aidric. Seeing that we weren't concerned with his presence, she stood. But tension still lined her body.

"He's coming with us," I barked. I let the first water stairs I created drop when the water kept trying to grab Erin's ankles. "But he's going to be quiet and stay out of our way."

My second set of stairs were much less angry. After we descended, the stairs collapsed, and the water filtered back out to the harbor.

"Did you learn that in the castle?" Dana whispered.

"Bits and pieces. Being around other Wielders has given me lots of ideas. Does everyone have their stone?"

Everyone pulled theirs out except Aidric. Dana had one I'd helped her spell herself. I stood close to Aidric and threw the long leather cord I drilled through my stone over his head, too. Together we said the command and faded into shadows.

"Where did you learn to do this?" Aidric whispered.

"I got the idea from that day in the courtyard. I had to rewrite a couple of spells. Accidentally set a table on fire in my room, but it worked out."

"You never cease to amaze me."

"Hush, we're invisible, but people can still hear us."

Aidric put his arm around my waist so we could stick close while we followed Erin and Murphy to Berry Street. I knew I should protest his proximity, but I leaned in closer. No one could see us, anyway.

The crisp night meant more people were on the streets. Spring was still weeks away, but the mild weather was a welcome change. More people meant it was slow going to Berry Street, which lay on the far side of the city.

John waited for us at a secluded corner. He shifted his weight, glancing down both deserted alleyways as we approached. When we muttered the command to reveal, he jumped.

"Man! Give a guy a warning."

I ducked out from under the cord Aidric and I shared. I pulled three more viridite stones out of my purse and thrust them into John's hands. Erin explained how they worked.

"Nice, Lydia. These will come in handy. Thank you." His eyes shifted to Dana. Erin and Murphy took the cue and walked her out of earshot to explain where to go from here. Aidric frowned. Whatever John had to tell us tonight must not be good. John pulled a note from his pocket and handed it to the prince.

"There's been movement. Of supplies, of troops. There's

going to be an attack on Mountgarden in five days. The rebels have recruited members of the army, they're planning to take over Lord Bickson's estates."

Aidric slammed his fist against the building next to us. John's face set in a grim line. Aidric looked back at John.

"Any word on Reynard?"

"No." John shook his head. "Word is, he's still here in the city. But he hasn't contacted me. I'm low on the totem pole since the entire Palace Guard and army is looking for me."

"Okay. Just keep your head down. Your information is helpful, but you're better off alive."

"Thanks, Your Highness." John grinned. "Let's have some fun tonight."

We'd reached the part of the city where the houses seemed to be built on top of one another. We could move visibly now. John told us very few rebels congregated in this part of the city.

"We focus on surviving here," Dana said. She led our group down side streets, her pace increasing with each turn. "We don't have time for things like rebellions."

Aidric and I both kept our hoods up, just in case.

We turned a corner and the street we followed met a dead end. Three whitewashed houses sat in a row. The thatched roofing of each stood out in the dark, painted in various shades of yellow. Dana halted in the middle of the street. A young girl with the same flaxen hair as Dana came out of the middle house. When she caught sight of us, she squealed.

"Mama, Dada, Dana's here! Dana's here!" She ran straight for her sister and threw her arms around her waist. Soon, people streamed out of all three houses. They caught all of us up in a swirl of activity and before we knew it, Dana's family had ushered us inside their home.

"Mama, Dada, these are my friends from school," Dana said. Tears streamed down her face. Dana's mother wrapped her up in a hug.

"Dana, my dear, is everything okay? Why are you here so late?" She wiped a tear away from her daughter's face.

"Yes, Mama. We've been so busy this is the only time I had to visit. My friends came so I wouldn't have to walk alone."

"Welcome, welcome." Dana's mother went down the line, hugging our necks.

All three houses connected on the inside. Dana introduced us to her parents, her grandparents, and the rest of the family that shared the three homes. Children raced underfoot as the family moved a pile of straw pallets to the room. Someone threw a sheet over them, and they insisted we all sit in the main room.

Over by the stove, Dana's aunt went through the cupboards until she pulled out half a loaf of bread. She cut it into tiny chunks and brewed a pot of tea from a small scoop of tea bags. Even though I could see the walls were cracked and food was scarce, Dana's smile never left her face. As her mom served us tea, I glimpsed a brand on the inside of her arm. Dana saw me looking. She leaned over to me.

"My parents are both Wielders. They got caught up in the old laws. Thirty years ago, Wielders had all of their rights and property stripped. Most cities didn't enforce the new laws right away, but Windburn did. When King Bleddyn took the throne, he changed the laws, but it was too late for our family's home and bakery. The forgotten families like us banded together and built the houses on this block to live in. We don't have much, but it's home. And they need me here to help them."

Hearing Dana's story brought tears to my eyes. I scooted back against the wall. Erin and Murphy were speaking to Dana's uncle. He regaled them with a step-by-step demonstration—using a kitchen knife and a child's doll—of how he'd lost an eye in the civil war. John held a toddler on one hip and helped Dana's grandmother dislodge a leather ball stuck in the rafters.

Dana told her parents about school. She talked about her lessons and the people she'd met. She even showed them the trick with the stone she spelled. Pointing me out as the one who had taught her. Watching Dana bloom in the presence of her family delighted me. But memories of spending time with my family made me ache with homesickness.

Aidric scooted back to join me against the wall. He pressed his arm against mine.

"You okay?"

I nodded, unable to speak through the lump in my throat.

"It's moments like these I miss my mom the most," he whispered. I grabbed his hand.

We sat in silence and watched everyone for some time.

"I'm glad no one here recognizes us," I said.

"They do," Aidric guessed. "But they don't mind."

John caught my eye when it was time to go. Dana said her goodbyes, promising to visit again soon. My heart sank. She knew it wouldn't be possible. Outside in the dark, the wind chilled me to my bones. Everyone stood huddled together. They all had their stones in their hand, except me.

"Dana, stay here. Stay home if you want to."

"Lydia." Aidric turned me to face him. "You know she can't do that."

I leaned past him to see Dana.

"Dana, I mean it. I'll do whatever it takes. Talking the king around, hiding your family, I don' care. I'll figure out a way."

"I'll help," John said. "I can get you and your family out of the city."

Dana shook her head, resolve lining her features.

"No. I need to learn more about my magic. And I can learn other things too. I'll stay with the Scholars."

"Thank you, Dana," Aidric told her. "I'll see to it you return home as soon as you're done. And, with your help, I want to look into how we can make it right for the families who lost their property during my grandfather's time."

John hung back with Aidric and I.

"Are you being sent to Mountgarden?" Aidric asked. My heart jumped. I hadn't even considered that possibility.

"I don't know," John admitted. "My orders only come when I need them."

The hard glint in his eye returned, and I wondered what orders he'd already carried out. Aidric clasped him on the shoulder.

"Stay safe."

e made it back just before dawn and separated at the watchtower. Dana left to sneak back into the Scholars' level of the castle through a side door she'd found while Erin and Murphy returned to their quarters.

Aidric and I entered the front doors of the castle. Music poured out of the open throne room doors. Aidric froze.

"The Dawn Ball."

"What?"

"I forgot. The Dawn Ball. To welcome spring. It was tonight."

"No kidding!"

It was too late to turn invisible now as people started noticing us. How could we have been so stupid? I'd been receiving dance card invitations and gifts for weeks. Gabrielle had even put the light blue and orange ball gown on the stand yesterday. Our absence at a grand ball was conspicuous.

More and more people stopped to stare at us. The song ended, and the musicians didn't start another. My mind raced for an explanation. The truth wasn't an option. I tried to come up with any explanation that made sense for Aidric and me to be out all night by ourselves.

"This is bad," was Aidric's only contribution to our problem.

Jaclyn moved to the front of the crowd. Aidric was right, this was bad.

"Aidric, what's going on?" I'd never heard that tone from Jaclyn before. "Where have you been?"

"Jaclyn, now's not the time—"

"Don't put me off, Aidric. You miss the biggest ball of the season and then I catch you sneaking in with *her*. I want an explanation."

It was too bad I'd never learned how to make the ground swallow me whole.

"Lydia and I..." he trailed off.

"Aidric at a loss for words, I never thought I'd see the day." Jaclyn's tone dripped with contempt. Her cheerful demeanor had crumpled and unleashed all her pent-up emotions. "My father warned me when I accepted your proposal. He told me what I wanted would never matter. The royal family would always come first. You're just like your father, running with another girl. I'm your betrothed Aidric! You owe your loyalty to me."

"It's not like that!" I wouldn't let her drag Aidric's name through the mud. "There's nothing going on."

Jaclyn ignored me like I didn't even exist.

"I bring Fenwood to the table, Aidric. But now, you're willing to risk everyone on someone who doesn't even belong here. Gatebreaker or not, you know just as well as I do that she's leaving! She's not here to help us, she's catching the first horse back home."

The crowd gasped. Conversations erupted all over.

"Lydia leaving—"

"Gatebreaker going—"

"Lydia, is that true?" Annistyn looked at me like I was a stranger. "Are you really leaving?"

I opened my mouth, but no words came out. Denying it would be the smart thing to do. I knew that. I just couldn't make myself do it.

The crowd parted, and King Bleddyn appeared. He looked resplendent in a robe that sparkled with gemstones of blue, orange, red, and yellow. The sunrise personified. Three times he banged his glittering staff on the floor before everyone fell silent.

"Amid this distraction, the sun has risen. This ball is at a close." His soft words somehow echoed through the deathly quiet hall, raising the hair on my arms. "I suggest everyone return to their rooms to get ready for the day."

I dashed away from the crowd, leaving Aidric, Jaclyn, Annistyn, and everyone else behind. Gabrielle waited for me in my rooms.

"Well, it seems you're in a spot of trouble."

"How did you know? It just happened."

She gave me a smirk over her shoulder as she tended the fire.

"Word travels fast in the castle." She sat down on the arm of the couch. Movement under her hair caught my eyes. A small green sprite stuck its head out to look down at me.

"I'm sorry, Gabrielle. I should have told you my plans. You never would have let me leave the night of a ball."

"No, Miss Lydia. It's not my place to know your business. I know your path is different." She patted my arm. "I say this delicately, but it's best I don't know about it. However, it might be best if you ask about your social calendar then next time."

While I thought about her words, she stood back up and fluffed the pillows on a chair.

"I've drawn you a bath and put out an outfit. You better hurry. I have a feeling someone will summon you to an emergency council meeting soon."

Gabrielle's words came true. I bathed and changed into the sky-blue dress she laid out. Just as she finished wrapping my braid around my head, there was a knock at the door. A young messenger awaited.

"I am here to escort Lady Lydia to a council meeting in the king's chambers."

"Very official," Gabrielle noted. She gave him a cookie and sent me on my way.

The boy remained rigid and silent as he led me through the halls. I realized that since Aidric started talking to me again, no official messengers had come for me. He escorted me everywhere.

Faces were grim when I entered the king's study. Aidric sat against the far wall. I picked a chair at the opposite end of the room, unable to look at him. Smoldering rage pulsed off the king, making the room seem much tinier than it was.

"Where were you two?" he whispered.

"We went for walk—"

"Just talking—"

We answered at the same time.

"We were walking and talking and lost track of time,"

Aidric said lamely. Sitting behind the king, Nadine covered a smile with her hand.

"I suggest you two get your stories straight. You've created this mess. We have to find a way out of it."

"Why are people so upset?" I cringed when the king looked my way. "I'm just one person. Why does it matter if I'm here or not?"

King Bleddyn rubbed his head.

"I realize the concept is hard for you to grasp, but people cling to their symbols of hope. That's what royalty is—something my son knows all too well." Aidric dropped his head. "You, my dear, are a symbol of hope. Hope for magic to be restored and integrated. If people know you are leaving, many will take it as a sign that Wielders will never be accepted."

"Oh..." I let my voice trail off. I had no response that didn't seem silly.

"There's only one option here. We announce to everyone that Lydia isn't leaving." He paced while he brainstormed. "We tell them we broke off the betrothal with the daughter of Fenwood because of her unfitness, or behavior, or something. We say we were going to end it quietly, but she got mad and lied. Simple."

I looked around at the advisors. They all nodded as if they liked the idea.

"But I am leaving."

"Then lie," he snapped.

"I don't want Jaclyn's name dragged through the mud." It was the first time Aidric had spoken.

"You should have thought about that before you two spent the night together."

My cheeks blushed crimson, but neither I nor Aidric disputed the claim. If we did, they would insist on knowing where we were instead. Other people would get into trouble if we did, and I knew he wouldn't do that to Dana or her family.

"Jaclyn knows that kind of public behavior is unacceptable. She's here to represent her family. No matter how much I desire the alliance with Fenwood, for that alone, I would end this betrothal. She will leave by the end of the day."

"Father, you can't ruin her reputation. She won't get another proposal." Aidric jumped to his feet.

"How is that my problem?" the king demanded.

No one else in the room mattered as father and son argued.

"We promised a lot of things when we made the proposal. She has her whole life ahead of her. We can't pull the rug out from under her like that."

"Then how do you suggest I explain this?!" King Bleddyn slammed his fists on his desk, making me jump. "How are we supposed to make this right?"

"It's simple." The words came from Mirela. I hadn't even noticed her in the shadows of the room. "We announce a new royal betrothal."

The room fell silent. Everyone nodded as they considered Mirela's suggestion. Aidric flopped back down in the chair and covered his face with his hands. There was something I was missing.

"A new royal betrothal with whom?"

Nadine gave me a sympathetic glance, and it clicked.

"Oh no. No. That's a bad idea."

"A royal marriage." King Bleddyn nodded his head,

frowning thoughtfully. He seemed unperturbed by my protests.

"That could work."

"You could offer to pay her father double the dowry, so there are no hurt feelings—"

Nadine put in. "We can put out a vague statement about doing what's best for the country. The original betrothal happened before we knew Lydia was the Gatebreaker, after all."

"And we can add that the lady lied because losing the position of queen to Lydia upset her," Barwick added.

"Queen?" I squeaked.

"Father!" Aidric looked up, his word a warning. The council continued to ignore us.

"We will make the announcement soon," Olma said. "That way there's no time for the speculation to get out of hand."

"We have it taken care of by tomorrow," King Bleddyn noted.

"I'm too young to get married," I stated. Everyone but Aidric chuckled.

"My girl," Mirela said. "You'll be eighteen in a year and a half. Aidric sooner. That's the perfect age to get married. And if you're gone by then, it won't matter, will it? We can always stage your exit from this world as a sacrificial death."

Her words stunned me speechless.

"Father," Aidric said through clenched teeth. "We should discuss this in private."

"There's nothing to discuss." The king leaned back and shrugged. "It's a brilliant solution to a problem you created, my son. This gives the kingdom confidence that the Gatebreaker and the crown are working together. I'm surprised I didn't think of it myself."

"Bow to the wisdom of your elders, boy," Mirela barked, startling a laugh out of the king.

"Are you upset about this?" King Bleddyn asked me. "Given that you and my son were caught sneaking in this morning, I thought you were friendly. The law is clear, we can't move forward until you accept."

Speech still evaded me. There was no way I could decline the proposal without it being an insult. But this wasn't what I signed up for. I swallowed. Hard.

"I'm shocked," I admitted, honestly. "Real proposal or not, back home people don't get married until their twenties or thirties. Getting engaged at sixteen is just..." I trailed off again. No words existed to describe everything I felt.

Aidric stepped between me and the king.

"Lydia, you don't have to agree to this if you don't want to. Don't jump in with both feet. We'll figure out another solution."

"If you've got one, son, I'm all ears," the king said demurely behind him.

"I accept," I croaked. Clearing my throat, I tried again. "I accept. Your father's right, Aidric. This solution gets us out of this mess."

Aidric stared for a moment, then turned his head and returned to his seat. King Bleddyn clapped his hands.

"Well, that's that."

Just like that, I was engaged.

"Wait," I said as everyone got up. "I have news from John, you won't like it."

CHAPTER TWENTY-ONE

*A*fter the council meeting, the king ordered me to stay sequestered in my rooms. King Bleddyn needed a day to prepare the festivities before he announced our engagement. He would present us to the nobles in the morning, then in the evening we'd be presented to the county and dance at a ball in our honor.

"You're required to be at this ball," he'd admonished before I left.

The day after the announcement, Aidric and a small contingent of soldiers disguised as merchants would make the ride to Mountgarden to head off the rebels.

Since I wasn't allowed to leave, I convinced Gabrielle to find Murphy and Erin and tell them about the announcement tomorrow and that I would explain everything later. I spent the rest of my morning pacing. Gabrielle returned and outlined everything that would take place the following day, but I only half listened.

I knew Aidric was busy with preparations for Mountgarden. That didn't stop me from hoping he'd appear at my door.

In these daydreams, he told me he convinced his father to change his mind, or that he came up with a solution that didn't involve us faking a proposal. Occasionally, they involved Aidric down on one knee, a diamond ring in his hands. But those I didn't entertain for long.

In the late afternoon, I noticed the gate to the castle wall open. A carriage left, followed by a contingent of riders and packhorses. Lady Jaclyn pressed her face against the window as she and her father departed the castle.

Just after dark, someone knocked on my door. My heart leaped.

"Pst, Lydia. Let us in!" Annistyn's frantic whisper sounded in the crack of the door. I hid my disappointment and admitted Maren and Annistyn.

"You're not the only one who can sneak around at night," Maren quipped. I smiled and offered them some leftover puff pastries from my dinner.

"So, Lady Jaclyn left the castle today."

"Oh, did she say why?" I feigned innocence as I poured the tea.

"We were told an urgent matter had come up at Fenwood and she and her father were needed immediately."

"Well, I hope everything is okay."

Maren and Annistyn erupted into giggles. They laughed so hard I wondered if they'd gotten into Maren's father's stores of wine again.

"Lydia, where did you and the prince sneak off to last night??" Here was the question I knew they'd been waiting to ask.

"Sorry to disappoint you, but it was nowhere romantic, I promise."

Maren sighed, but Annistyn's eyes only gleamed brighter.

"Do you wish it was somewhere romantic?"

A side-eye glance was my only response. They erupted into giggles again.

"Really Lydia. You're not leaving us, are you?" Annistyn's disappointment seemed genuine.

"Neither of you are magic Wielders. Why does it matter to you if I leave or stay?" I tucked my feet under me and sat in between them on the couch.

"Well, for one you're our friend," Annistyn pointed out.

"But it's more than that, Lydia," Maren added. "Magic it's exciting. It's new. You give people hope. Hope that the last few years—all the trials and troubles we've been dealing with—aren't in vain. If you leave, then why does any of it matter?"

I nodded. She had given me a lot to think about. But it was too late to consider such things.

"Well, stick around for the festivities tomorrow and see what happens?"

The girls clapped in excitement.

"So, update me." I looked at Annistyn, changing the subject. "What's going on with you and Tristan?"

She blew a raspberry, startling a laugh out of me.

"Absolutely nothing. He's always excited to see me. Neither of us wants to say anything because our parents haven't officially started negotiations. But I'm hoping any uh —announcements—that happen soon will convince my father to get on with it."

"Annistyn, it's late." Maren stood abruptly. "We should leave Lydia to get some rest. Sounds like she's going to have a busy day."

The girls picked up their stuff and left. Annistyn gave me a wink on the way out the door.

A KNOT SETTLED in my chest overnight, and morning didn't relieve it. Aidric never came. As the day dawned and Gabrielle prepared me for my first audience, the knot grew tighter. Another messenger arrived to escort me downstairs. My chest heaved in quick breaths that had nothing to do with my corset. As we passed the throne room, voices from the already gathered crowd drifted through the wall. I didn't want to attend a party to pretend to be someone I'd never be.

Aidric waited for me outside the entrance. He brushed my fingertips against his lips when I arrived. His hands were clammy, too. I studied him closer. There was no mistaking the tightness in his shoulders, despite the charming smile he wore for the nobles.

More than anything, I wanted a moment alone with Aidric. But moments alone were what got us into this mess. We descended the staircase. The king announced our engagement with us center stage. As I felt the stiffness of Aidric's hand in mine, I wondered if he even wanted a moment alone with me. He seemed almost relieved when, after shaking hands and speaking to most of the nobles, we were separated and ushered back to our rooms until the next announcement at twilight.

My heart clinched as Gabrielle led me to the balcony above the entrance hall. I'd never seen the balcony used before. But as I peered through the window, I could see almost all of Windburn gathered in the castle courtyard.

"This is where the royal family does all of its announcements. It's where both my father and I were presented to the country as newborns."

Aidric's quiet voice in my ear sent shivers down my spine. His black and silver outfit paired well with my gray lace gown. For the first time since last night, we had a moment alone.

"How are you feeling?" Aidric asked.

Like I was standing on the edge of a cliff. If I took another step forward, I'd never be able to climb back up. And it scared me and exhilarated me all at once. I wanted to tell him that. Tell him that no matter how hard I tried to fix things, everything kept falling apart. That my biggest fear was starting this journey with him, and not being able to say goodbye.

Instead, I smiled.

"I'm good."

His pleasant expression faltered for a second, but then it was back again. King Bleddyn arrived.

"It's time."

"People have been gathering since morning," Aidric whispered as the Master of Ceremonies announced the king's name and titles. King Bleddyn stepped onto the balcony to tumultuous applause. My knees quivered at the amount of people waiting for Aidric and me.

I couldn't dwell on it. The Master of Ceremonies had already started announcing our names.

"Crown Prince Aidric, the wolf-hearted, heir to the throne of Thavell, Commander of the King's Armies and his betrothed, Lady Lydia, the Gatebreaker."

Someone pushed us forward, and the crowd erupted in

cheers. The glare of the sunset blocked the crowd from my vision. Aidric grabbed my hand and lifted our arms. The cheers became deafening. I could hear chants in the crowd.

"Long live King Bleddyn!"

"Long live Prince Aidric!"

The spots in my vision faded, and I saw the crowd stretched out all the way down the hill that led to the city. They chanted for the king and the prince. But they chanted something else too.

"Long live Lady Lydia!"

"Long live the Gatebreaker!"

My shock melted. I waved at the people chanting my name. Beside me, Aidric noticed my response and smiled.

As soon as finished on the balcony, the ball began. Once again, someone ushered Aidric and I to the throne room. One of the king's council members stayed close to us at all times. They directed us to dine and dance until my feet hurt and my head wouldn't stop spinning.

Aidric noticed my weariness. He had to be weary, too. With the distraction of everyone congratulating us, we never had a moment to speak to one another. The tension never left his shoulders, and each touch of his hand, whether in a dance or when we were side-by-side, was so rigid I was afraid he would shatter.

At some point it occurred to me this was the chance I'd been wishing for. Aidric and I could be together in public now. We didn't have to steal sleepless nights or longing touches. My mood soured with each reluctant touch.

"This isn't how I expected my engagement party to go," I said. Aidric didn't respond.

The ball lasted until deep into the night. But eventually,

even the hardiest nobles went to bed. Once the crowd thinned, the council quit babysitting us. We'd satisfied them that we'd behave and get through this change of plans.

With no eyes on us for the first time today, Aidric took my hand and led me from the throne room. He towed me down the stairs and through hallways. We left the building and entered the gardens. In the fresh night air, I caught my breath for the first time. Aidric didn't stop until we made it to the bench next to the pond. We stopped beneath the willow trees.

"Do you remember the first time we came down here?" he asked.

"Of course."

"Where did you go today?" He rubbed both of my arms. "You seem distant."

"I'm overwhelmed. This is all just so much. I feel like I'm being pulled in two different directions."

"Would it be that terrible to marry me?"

"No. Aidric, that's not what I meant."

I looked over to catch him grinning. I laughed.

"That was really mean."

He escorted me to the bench, and then dropped to one knee. My laugh stopped in a whoosh.

"Aidric, what—"

"I spent some time with Erin and Murphy today. I hope I'm doing this right."

"I don't understand."

"Lydia Catherine, you delight me. I never thought we'd get this chance. I knew I shouldn't, but I never could stay away from you. This is our chance."

"Aidric," I interrupted, panicking. "I don't care what your father says, I'm too young to be engaged."

Aidric just smiled.

"Lydia, will you be my... girlfriend?"

I giggled.

"This is a very dramatic way to ask me out."

"I'd fly to the sky and catch a star if you wanted me to."

His words hit me in the chest. Everything he said made my heart yearn for him.

"Aidric... I can't."

My voice caught. Aidric's face fell. He lowered the ring to the ground.

"I thought this is what you wanted."

I slid off the bench and onto my knees in front of him.

"It is, Aidric. But I'm—"

"I know," he said. "I know you're leaving. This isn't your home. But, Lydia, it could be. You could stay here. We could be together."

I didn't respond. He touched a knuckle to my cheek, wiping a tear away.

"I love you, Lydia."

There it was. The three words we'd danced around for so long. He said them with such frank earnestness. No fear clouded his eyes, no worry stopped his words. There in the garden under the stars, I decided I didn't need to be afraid either.

"I love you too, Aidric."

His sparkling eyes and joyous smile were more beautiful than any painting I'd ever seen.

"Don't you owe yourself the chance to make this work?

All we have is now. We'll worry about the future when we get there."

Nothing ever felt clearer to me. I nodded.

"Yes, Aidric. I will be your girlfriend."

His joyous laugh warmed my heart. He leaned, a hand caressing the side of my face.

"Now, I get to do something I've been dying to do for months."

I closed my eyes and sank into his kiss.

CHAPTER TWENTY-TWO

My sweet time with Aidric was short-lived. We parted for the night, and he rode for Mountgarden before dawn. I spent the morning studying spells in my room before giving up and going to find Erin and Murphy. I wasn't a love-sick damsel, waiting for her knight to return.

Both Murphy and Erin were on duty. I rifled through the information on the realms we'd gathered so far. We'd found stories about each realm from before and after the fall of magic. The only one we struggled to find information about was Abrexar. Two old books we'd found mentioned Abrexar in the first age of magic, but there were zero mentions of dragons in any stories we'd come across once magic had disappeared.

I added the names of the eight gemstones to my drawing of the eight affinities.

"Eight realms, eight affinities, six realms." Even saying the words out loud didn't help me make sense of it.

Giving up, I found Tristan in the stables and cajoled him into giving me another lesson with the daggers. I managed to hit a strip of leather he nailed to the wall of the stable. Of course, I'd been aiming for the circle he drew to the right of the strip, but that wasn't important. I yanked the daggers from the wood and returned them to their sheaths. I picked at the small gashes where my knife had pierced the wood.

Without saying goodbye to Tristan, I rushed from the stables. No one worked in the throne rooms, or in Lord Barwick's office, so I went to the next place I could think of, the king's office. Olma and Barwick were both there.

"Ah, Lydia, to what do we owe this pleasure?" Olma asked. From his furrowed brow, it didn't seem like Olma thought it was a pleasure at all. But I ignored that. He and Barwick had the best grasp of magic, so I needed to speak with him.

"I have a theory. It might be nothing, but I wanted to run it by someone."

"Of course," Barwick told me. "Come in."

I approached the tapestry of Thavell and held up the parchment I'd scratched on. I shoved a knife through both, pinning them together.

"We know the realms exist elsewhere, correct? They aren't like walking from this room into the next. We have old stories that talk about gateways, and now those are locked."

"I'm with you," Olma said. "Go on."

"If the realms exist side-by-side, maybe we're thinking about it the wrong way. What if we don't need to unlock the gate? What if we need to create a new entrance? And if the realms that belong to this world exist like that, then another world should, too. If we can find out what point to stick our knife in"—I pulled on the tapestry, my knife pinned it to the wall—"we can pierce three layers at once—and walk through the tear to get home."

Olma looked positively feral with delight. Even Barwick let go of his usually cerebral disposition and smiled.

"Lydia, I think you're onto something here."

"Assuming this works, how do we decide where to pierce through?" Olma asked.

I pointed to the four areas on the map Barwick had marked at my first meeting.

"A place where there's a higher concentration of latent magic seems like a good place to start."

I stepped aside so both Olma and Barwick could study the map.

"We could go to each of these areas and scry," Barwick mused.

"Some are more dangerous than others. We don't want to risk our strongest Wielders."

"What if we took the Scholars on a trip? We do in the spring, anyway. We could just move it up a few weeks. Hit at least the two spots in the north. Once we have some data, we will know what next step to take."

"I'll take it to the king," Olma said. He patted me on the head. I did my best not to cringe away.

"Good work, Lydia. Keep brainstorming and you'll be home before spring."

His words didn't make me as happy as I expected.

A HAND CLASPED over my mouth, stopping my breath. I jerked out of a deep sleep, my hands erupting into fireballs. John barely dodged my hand. It burned through the covers, setting my quilt on fire. I rolled out of the bed as John doused the fire with my wash basin.

"John, what are you doing here?"

"Shhh, shhhh," John warned me. "Lydia, Reynard is in the castle. He's here to capture you and kill the Scholars."

Everything froze as fear took over my body. John grabbed me by both arms and shook.

"You don't have time to be afraid, Lydia. Get some clothes on, we have to get you out of here."

His words broke me out of my stupor. Like a lightning bolt, I struck my closet, pulling on my pants and tunic from my army days. At the last minute, I grabbed my leather vest. John handed me the throwing knives I kept on my bedside table.

"We need to find a place to hide," John said.

"No," I told him. "If they're going after the Scholars, we have to warn them and alert the rest of the castle."

"Lydia, there isn't time. Mountgarden was never the target. The small force they sent there was only a distraction. This is the big time. If we don't go now, we might not make it out alive."

"Then go," I told him.

While he gaped at my words, I whispered into the fireplace.

"Ash? Anyone? Are you there?" I didn't know if this would work, but the sprite had found my location once. Something small and soot covered tumbled out of the chimney and hovered in front of me on small black wings.

"The Howling Moon has a colony of ash sprites. I wondered how they found you," John murmured. I barely heard him. "I didn't think the dreams were true."

"Ash, is there any way you can alert someone here in the castle to sound the alarm? If someone rings the bell and blows the horn, people will know there's an attack and will barricade themselves in their rooms or go to the throne room."

She hovered for another second, then dove into the fire and vanished.

"How did you get in here?" I asked John.

"There's a secret network of tunnels throughout the castle. Reynard has a map."

"Can you get me to the Scholars?"

"Lydia—"

"John, I'm going there one way or another." I lifted my chin. "I've faced Reynard once. You think I'm scared to do it again?"

Something in my eyes must have told John I wouldn't be swayed. He nodded.

"Let's go."

When we entered the Scholars' wing through a trapdoor in the library's ceiling, everything was still quiet. No one moved in the dormitory wing. John and I split up, going door to door and waking everyone as quietly as we could. As soon as we explained the situation, we sent them towards the throne room. We had three doors left when something exploded at the end of the hall, covering all of us in inky blackness.

"What's the meaning of this?" I heard Simon yell. There was a strangled cry and then the darkness evaporated. Light flooded the hall. Simon stood in a nightshirt and slippers. He spotted me and John, and the students racing for the other hall.

"We're under attack," I yelled, the time for caution gone. "We need to get to the throne room."

As if in answer, the bell rang raucously, rousing anyone in the castle from their sleep. Someone else blew the horn, calling the Palace Guard to protect everyone. I sent good thoughts to Erin and Murphy, knowing they would be in battle soon.

Simon nodded. Jamie emerged from the room across the hall. With everyone on their way, we brought up the rear, watching for another attack. We raced up the stairs to find the students already engaged in battle with another rebel.

"Wielders loyal to the crown must die!" he screamed. A student tried to hold him back with a torch, but the rebel clapped his hands and the flame exploded, engulfing the students and burning him to ash in seconds. Students screamed as more rebels emerged from nearby doorways.

Simon and Jamine raced to the front. John drew his sword and followed them. We were too far from the rest of the castle for help to reach us before the rebels slaughtered every scholar. Most Wielders didn't use their magic for battle, we didn't stand a chance. I had to make sure we made it to the throne room.

My magic erupted around me the moment I thought of it. My blast of wind sent the rebels tumbling. When they came back again, they met a solid dome of air. I laced the air with aether to absorb spells and the strength of metal.

"Everyone, group in the middle. The smaller the dome is, the longer I can hold it." I ground out the last sentence through clenched teeth as a rebel regained his footing and began hacking at the invisible dome with a sword.

The students listened and soon I was in the middle of the group. Simon and Jamine blasted the remaining rebels in the hall until they were unconscious or dead. I didn't pay enough attention to find out which.

"John, lead us to the throne room."

We ascended hall after hall. We met two more small groups of rebels. But something didn't feel right. The rebels had breached the castle, which was huge. But if they wanted to kill the scholars, why weren't there more people?

"I have a bad feeling about this," I whispered to John.

"Me too," he said. But we had no alternative.

My dome wavered each time someone hit it, but with John, the teachers, and the few students who caught on enough to help, I held it until we made it to the top level of the castle.

The throne room was in chaos. Nobles and servants alike rushed in from all doors, congregating in the middle while King Bleddyn stood by his throne, roaring orders. His axe gleamed in the torchlight. We burst through a side door, and I let my protection flicker and die. I steadied myself on a nearby table. Dana pressed a manalase stone into my hand.

"It's mine, but I have a few now. Replenish your power with it."

"Thank you."

Giving me her power was like giving me her essence. A devious mage could do terrible things with that. I tapped into the power of the stone. Raw magic filled my veins, stinging as it worked its way through me. Dana's magic felt different from my own. It was stalwart and strategic, not like mine, which thrummed with everything I felt. But then the magic merged and settled, becoming my power.

"Why didn't we know about this attack sooner?" Nadine yelled at John as she ushered a group of guard members to barricade a far door.

"I didn't know about it until we were already here!" John called back.

I glanced around the throne room, Murphy and Erin barricaded doors. Annistyn and Maren stood with a group of other nobles in the middle of the throne room. They huddled together, wary eyes on the doors.

"The stables are on fire," a student cried out. She stood over a bowl of water, scrying the castle grounds.

"So are the northern townhouses," another scryer said.

Deep in the castle, something exploded. The doors to the throne room blew open, knocking back the guard members who held them open. Through every door poured rebels.

And then shadows swallowed us.

Just like in Scholar's wing, the darkness overtook everything. It blotted out my vision and muffled all sound. I turned in every direction. Screams and clanging metal sounded miles away. My shallow breaths came quicker. Wrapped in darkness, it felt like any step I took would send me spiraling into the void.

Near me, a ball of light appeared and illuminated Dana. Sweat rolled down her forehead as she fought the shadows. Her light extinguished. More pinpricks of light appeared as other students fought back against the dark.

I used fire to punch through the darkness. But for every

shadow my flame burned, another took its place. Each time I tried to spot what was happening, but the blizzard of darkness blotted out everything except a few steps in front of me. I watched as, once again, it extinguished my flame and blotted out the hand in front of my face.

Words I hadn't thought about in ages came to mind.

Beware, the time is drawing near
If she is defeated by fear
The darkness will forever be revered.

"Not on my watch," I growled.

Eyes weren't the only way for me to see.

I blinked, and the room was no longer dark, but filled with threads of blinding light. If magic formed these shadows, it could lead me back to the Wielder who created them. The shadows still wrapped around me, but now I saw they were laced with strands of ashen gray. The threads tangled in each thread in every thread in the room, snuffing out the other magic when it bloomed.

I reached out a hand and touched the nearest strand of gray magic. It recoiled at my touch. I gripped it harder.

Fear wouldn't stop me now. No, fear was the furthest thing from my mind as I searched for the Wielder behind these tethers of darkness. Icy rage filled my veins instead. Rage at the fighting. Rage at the threat to my friends. Rage that someone would threaten this place and these people when I felt safe—and happy.

I used that rage and sent crystal shards of ice along the path of shadow. The Wielder's essence filled his magic, and I knew where to direct them. The magic resisted, holding my ice back. But my rage was stronger. And so was my magic.

The golden light of my magic pulsed around me, shooting the ice into every portion of shadow in the room. In the distance, someone screamed. Then the shadows froze. I pressed a finger to the darkness.

The shadows shattered.

They exploded in every corner, flooding the room with light.

Now everyone could see the mayhem evolving.

Under the cover of darkness, rebels had infiltrated the throne room. All of them dressed in black, and out to kill. The king battled three fighters from the top of the dais, cutting them down as they made a mistake. The Palace Guard was here in full force. Now that everyone could see again, Nadine was screaming out orders, forming them into positions to stop the oncoming tide of the enemy.

Forgotten in the middle of the room, the Scholars stood back to back. Rebel Wielders had found them. Simon lay injured on the floor. Dana, Jamine, and other students stood, keeping the rebels at bay. But one by one, the scholars were falling.

John still stood at my side. I grabbed his sword, whispering a spell under my breath. The metal ignited, sending a shower of blue sparks to the ground.

"We have to help the Scholars," I yelled. John's predatory grin as we eyed the advancing rebels fueled my own desire for revenge.

This fight wasn't like the clearing, or the Battle of the Forest. I wasn't reacting to my fear. My goal wasn't just to make this stop. No, I wanted these people to hurt. I wanted them to know what it felt like to have everything they hoped for destroyed.

I grabbed a dagger from my belt, setting it on fire like I had John's. A black-cloaked rebel faced off with a young student. The student's hands shook so badly, he could barely keep the rebel back with the back of a broken chair he used as a shield. He wasn't even trying to use his magic.

My dagger hit the rebel in the side and set his cloak on fire. As he went down in the flames, his dying screams melded with the racket of the battle raging. A familiar voice caught my attention. One that haunted my nightmares.

Reynard stood in the middle of the rebels. They held the outside of the throne room, forcing us all back toward the king. In a moment where the battle ebbed, he turned and locked eyes with me.

"There she is!" He pointed. "The Gatebreaker. She has betrayed her own kind and sided with the king."

I stepped back as more and more rebels turned their eyes my way.

"Just like the students who willingly let the king guide them. They've sold themselves to the great extortioner. He devours his subjects for his own gain. But he can't stop us any longer. The true Wielders will rise, and we shall be the ones in charge."

Reynard's eyes never left mine. My heart pounded against my ribcage.

"Capture the Gatebreaker. We will bend her magic to our will. Kill anyone who tries to protect her."

John tackled me as arrows carried by magic descended on me. He grunted as one hit him in the shoulder. I reached to take it out, but he shook his head. He shielded me as we crawled under the broken tables to the dais. Guard members rallied the scholars and sent them to the middle, too.

Three circles of protection now circled me, but it wasn't enough. John yelled as he yanked the arrow from his shoulder. Someone handed him a wad of bandages and I helped him wrap them around the wound. When I went to lay my hand to heal him, John grabbed my wrist.

"No," he panted. "Save your magic. I have a feeling we're going to need it."

Arrows showered down on us. A guard member at the front of the line fell. A student next to me went down, a bolt in his chest.

This had to stop. I jumped onto the dais.

"Lydia, take cover!" someone yelled.

"They need to take cover from me."

I gathered my magic until it pulsed in the air. King Bleddyn took a step back, shielding his face. I clapped my hands over my head and the magic poured out, ballooning around the throne room in every direction. The wind knocked the first two rows of rebel fighters flat.

When I finished, a dome of protective air like the one I'd created earlier covered every noble, fighter, and student. Only this one was much, much larger. I lifted my hands over my head, straightening and moving the dome every time someone hit it.

Bolts of magic rained. The dome stopped most of them, but now and then one weaseled through. Another Scholar dropped.

"She can't hold this forever." That was Barwick's voice.

"He's not wrong," I ground out as shadows snaked through my dome and headed for me. Jamine struck it with a flash of light and it vanished. Every time a sliver of magic or an arrow pierced the dome, it felt like it tore into me. Soon I sweated from the exertion. There was no Golden Forest here to draw on.

"Lydia, if you drop the dome, would you be able to take out the rebel Wielders?"

"There are too many of them."

Almost every fighter glistened in my vision. Reynard and three other people huddled in the back of the throne room, no doubt coming up with a plan to break the dome. Every person in the ring protecting him shone brightly with magic.

"We need to take the Wielders out, or at least hold them off. They outnumber us and we can't get close to stopping this onslaught if we don't."

"We have plenty of Wielders here."

"Untrained ones. None of the Scholars know how to use magic in battle. And our best Wielders in the guard went with Aidric so they could stay hidden longer."

"What if Lydia protected the fighters? They could get close enough to kill the Wielders."

"Splitting her magic up that much will be even harder than what she's doing now."

King Bleddyn, Nadine, and Barwick continued to strategize below me. Half of me heard what they were saying, the other half directed toward holding the dome. More magic rained. Every time someone else's magic touched mine, I shuddered. It was like—just for that second—they were part of me.

Tristan approached me. He kept one eye trained on the rebels still gathered around the dome, all of them ready to attack again when I failed. Tristan reached out a hand. When

I grasped it, his magic poured into me, strengthening the dome.

"Tristan, what—"

"It's not a lot, but I'm an air Wielder, remember? Mom and I have shared magic before. I figured I could with you since you use all the affinities."

His magic twined around my bones. It *felt* like him, humorous and steady, with a strong protective streak.

"Tristan, I have an idea. Get every single Wielder under this dome to hold hands. Or touch elbows, or even a foot. They all need to be in physical contact. But don't make it obvious, the rebels can still see us."

"Yes, sir."

He knelt and crept through the ranks, whispering to Wielders as he went.

"Your Highness, I have an idea."

The king stopped mid-sentence. No one turned around to look at me, but I noticed the shift as they all turned their attention my way.

"I might be able to stop the Wielders. It's a gamble. If I can get enough power, I can follow their magic back to them. And hopefully stop them."

"For good?" Nadine asked. I gulped.

"Maybe, but at least for now. If I can do that, Nadine, would it give your guardsmen enough of a chance to rally and break their ranks?"

"We will take whatever you can give us."

Tristan made his way back to me. He looked at Barwick and Nadine.

"Lydia says she needs all the Wielders." Barwick shifted so he could touch Nadine's hip, his hand hidden under his robe. Nadine put her hand on the hilt of her sword, touching Tristan with her elbow. Tristan leaned propped his leg up on the dais, leaning forward he grazed my leg with his hand. I sent a drop of power through Tristan, it raced between each Wielder, all of us connected in a winding string around the dome.

Listen up. A student jumped. A guardsman nodded. They could hear me. I made sure my face showed nothing but my concentration as I looked up at the dome. *When I drop this dome, I'll have seconds to connect to all the other Wielders in this room. As soon as you feel another essence, as soon as you feel that magic trying to attack you, destroy them. I don't know you; I don't remember your affinities. But if we don't stop these Wielders now, they will kill you.*

Shoulders straightened and muscles flexed. My people were ready.

"Sire?"

"Yes, Lydia?"

"I have to drop the dome for this next part. I need you and every other fighter who's free to confuse the rebels. Throw things, charge the line, fill the room with arrows. I don't care how, just make it chaotic. They can't figure out what we are doing until it's too late."

"Count to ten, and then let's go."

King Bleddyn jumped off the dais.

One, I shouted in my head.

"Reynard!" he called. His roaring voice pulled me into the memories of the Battle of the Forest, but I didn't have time for that now. I shut them out.

Two. Three.

"My king, what can I do for you?"

Four.

At my feet, John hauled himself up and walked to the front of the line. He slipped in between Erin and Murphy. Murphy thumped him on the shoulder, never taking his eyes off the battle before him.

Five.

"Is this it? Is this the mighty rebellion? After last fall, I thought you'd learned your lesson."

Six. Seven.

Nadine used hand signals and people began shifting.

Eight.

"Bleddyn, dear friend. You better hope it ends here. What we have in store after this is much, much worse."

The door above the stairs burst open. My heart leaped. Aidric had arrived. He sat mounted on Midnight, framed by all the soldiers he'd taken to Mountgarden.

Now

It wasn't ten yet, but this was as confusing as anything that would happen. Aidric and King Bleddyn charged at the same time.

I let the dome drop. No one noticed as the rebels scrambled to fight from both sides. Reynard stood on a table, yelling above the melee. My Wielders stood firm. Instead of using magic with my body, I let it reach from my mind. I risked closing my eyes, losing myself in the magic. Tristan and the other Wielders held me like an anchor. I saw the magic threads of the rebel Wielders.

My magic made called for each of those strands, drawing them in like quicksand. It was me they were after—me they needed to capture. Nothing else mattered, so they all came.

Even Reynard's air magic streaked by me. My magic expanded, freezing the strands in place.

The essences of the magic crowded in my consciousness. Anger and destruction assaulted me, pushing me back to reality. The sounds of the battle warred for my attention. But I held on. Only seconds had passed. Time ticked down until the Wielders would sense what their magic touched. They could attack me while I connected with them.

I yanked the threads of magic from the Scholars and the other Wielders attached to me. My magic became the conduit through which they traveled. I directed them into the magic of the rebels. My body convulsed, and my nose bled as the cascade of power raced through me.

Like a slow wave, the attention of the rebel Wielders shifted my way. I couldn't do this alone. It was up to the other Wielders now.

Dropped from the stasis of my power, the Scholars attacked. I sent the remains of my power along the tracks, bolstering the power of the magic. The silent explosion rocked the foundations of the throne room.

Underneath me, the dais cracked, breaking the connection, and throwing me onto the floor. My wrist cracked as I landed. I bit my other arm to hold in the scream. Cheers went up behind me, mixing the clanging of metal and groans of pain.

Gripping the arm of the overturned throne, I hauled myself onto my knees. Spots clouded my vision. But across the room, rebel Wielders dropped like flies. One screamed as his skin boiled. Another caught on fire from the inside. Some rebel Wielders fought back, and a Scholar went down. Tristan doubled over in pain.

But my plan had worked. The rebel Wielders weren't using their magic. Even Reynard struggled to get his magic back under and fight the battle. Hammered between two forces, and without the use of their Wielders, the rebels scattered.

Not all of them went down easy. Stopping magic didn't stop the swords and knives. A scuff behind me was the only warning. I rolled and a battle axe came down where my head had been moments before. My legs gave out when I tried to stand. The woman dashed in again, swinging the axe. The reserves of my magic surged forward. I had enough to push her back a few feet, but then it sputtered out.

Grabbing another knife out of my belt, I threw it. Even with shaky arms, it caught her in the shoulder. She dropped the axe with a yell. She advanced on me again. Tristan swooped in, driving a sword through her belly.

"Nice throw," he told me. Throwing my arm over his shoulder, he hoisted me up. His skin's grayish pallor was the only sign anything was wrong.

"Are you okay?" I asked. He grinned.

"Better than you." We made it to the edge of the throne room. He drew another knife from his belt and handed it to me.

"The scholars are mixed in with the rest of the crowd. They can't tell one from the other. But anyone can spot you and your red hair for miles. Hide."

"Tristan I can't—"

"You've done enough," he pushed. "We've got them on the run. Reynard is already trying to retreat. You can barely stand. Hide. Don't come out. I'll send Aidric for you when things are okay here."

He shoved me out the door and closed it behind me. The quiet of the back hallway shocked me after the noise of battle. I swayed on my feet, holding onto the wall for support. I couldn't stay in the hallway forever. Anyone could find me, and I was in no shape to defend myself.

I knew just where I needed to hide.

CHAPTER TWENTY-THREE

y the time I made it up the winding stairs of the hidden tower, the dregs of magic threatened to pull me under. The door squeaked open, and I pulled myself in. I didn't have the strength to pull myself into a chair, so I sat on the floor and draped myself across a cushion.

"It's about time you made it here," a mild voice stated. Panic gifted me a rush of energy. I swung around; Tristan's knife grasped in my palm.

The woman haunted me. She leaned against one of the floor to ceiling windows, picking her nails with a dagger. Like it was any other day. My knife dropped. There was no way I could win. Not with my magic depleted and my wrist broken.

"You win," I told her. "If you're here to kidnap me, go ahead. I've got nothing left."

"That was an impressive trick in the throne room. Using the magical essence, we all leave behind to track the Wielder. You've got good instincts. You still need training, though. Letting yourself run dry in battle is a bad idea."

She waved a hand, and I flinched. Instead of attacking

me, the torches around the room came to life. The woman walked over and sat down in the chair across from me. I hauled myself up into the chair with one hand, wincing as I bumped my wrist.

"Let me see."

I raised an eyebrow. She really expected me to get closer to her? She sighed and extended her hand.

"No tricks, I promise."

Touching all the magic must have made me crazy. I gave her my wrist. She leaned forward, her long brown hair obscuring her face. Seconds ticked by. Just when I was about to ask what she was doing, the rich smell of dirt filled the room. Then my bones snapped back together.

"Ouch!" I yelled, yanking my arm back. "You said no tricks."

"Maybe one trick." She shrugged. "Does it feel better now?"

I rolled my wrist. It didn't throb anymore.

"How did you know about this room?" I asked.

"Who do you think found it?"

I frowned, the pieces of what I knew about this woman coming together.

"Who are you? And what do you want with me?"

"I go by many names. And I'm here to protect you."

"You've got a funny way of showing it."

I eyed her for another moment.

"I've been calling you Sarge."

She snorted.

"I like that. And really, I am trying to protect you Lydia, even if you don't believe me."

"Why? So, the rebels can use me?"

"No. I use the rebellion when it suits me. But killing other Wielders or assassinating a king won't help anything."

"You have experience with that, do you?"

"Yes."

I searched her face, looking for some answer that wasn't there. She was completely unreadable. I gripped my knife again, just in case.

"I'm trying to protect you because I hurt someone a long time ago."

She lowered her eyes, for once showing something that resembled an emotion.

"What does that have to do with me?"

"Have you ever wondered where your magic came from? You know where everyone else gets their magic. So why would you be any different?"

I groaned. My head pounded, and I teetered on the edge of unconsciousness. I was not in the mood for riddles.

"Why will no one ever give me a straight answer?"

She smiled, although it held nothing of joy. Part of me wondered if this woman had ever been happy.

"If you come with me, I'll tell you everything."

"Just tell me everything now," I whispered. "Then I can decide."

I turned her words over in my head. I was different from every other Magic Wielder. Did that mean the origins of my magic were different, too?

The woman pursed her lips. For a second, I thought she might tell me. Then she shook her head.

"It's too risky. If the king finds out who you are, he'll know what you mean to me. And he will stop at nothing to destroy me."

She paced to the window, her brown cloak flowing behind her.

"I'll keep you safe, Lydia. I promise. Come with me, and you'll have all the answers."

Maybe the battle fatigue made me lose my common sense. But I considered it. The woman watched as guardsmen searched the garden for any errant rebels. No more flames jumped from the roof of the stable. Smoke rose in the direction of the northern estates.

I stood. The woman sized me up as I took a step closer. Nothing could hide the hunger in my eyes. I wanted answers. And I wanted them all. Somehow, she'd nailed the one thing that had bothered me all along.

You know where everyone else gets their magic. So why would you be any different?

The answer to that question could change my life. Did she really know?

"Lydia?"

Aidric's voice echoed up the stairwell. He stomped toward the top. The woman watched me again with the hard determination in her eyes. The same look she'd had in the courtyard. I stepped back. For a fleeting moment, I thought she looked sad.

Then she changed.

As I watched as her body shifted into a hawk. It's plumage brown streaked with gold. She jumped straight through the window. I ran over, my hand met glass. In the sky above me, the hawk soared into the sunrise.

"Lydia!"

"I'm here!" I called, my voice catching.

I forgot about the mysterious woman when Aidric

appeared at the door to the tower. He swept me up into his arms. I clung to him with everything in me. Sitting down on a chair, he held me on his lap. I kissed him, savoring the taste of him. The scratch of his beard on my hands, the feel of his chest against mine. Every part of him felt like home after the trial of the night.

His eyes roved over my face and arms, inspecting me for wounds.

"I'm okay," I told him. "Tristan got me out of there before I got hurt."

"Remind me to make him a knight immediately."

I traced a finger down a long scratch on his arm. He held my fingertips and pressed them to his lips.

"I'm okay, too," he whispered.

I nestled into his chest, melting into his arms.

"How did you get back here?"

"Well," he started, but then stopped to kiss me again. "John was right. The rebels had recruited some of the army soldiers stationed at Mountgarden. They didn't account for the loyalty of Lord Bickson's people. A maid discovered their plan to kidnap the lord. It was simple work to scout the rebels after that, especially since they weren't prepared to attack. A messenger on his way to the castle to tell the king of the foiled plan met us on the road. We came straight back."

He kissed the end of my nose, and then my mouth again.

"I'm very glad we did."

"I'm glad too," I said. My heart mended with each kiss. Aidric hugged me tight and rested his head on my hair. We sat like that until the sun rose above the horizon.

Aidric sighed. I knew that meant our moment of peace

was over. He stood, cradling me. I wrapped my arms around his neck.

"We need to get you to bed soon. You're dead on your feet. But first, we need to stop by the throne room."

"Why?" I wasn't ready to see the damage in the light of day.

"Because, my love, you've saved us all once again. And my father wants to thank you."

A LARGE CRACK in the stone floor split the throne room in half. Tables and chairs lay in splinters and tapestries were shredded. Nobles and servants alike worked together to clean up the mess. King Bleddyn sat on a chair with half the back broken off. He rested his head on the top of his axe. This was the first time I'd ever seen him look weary.

"We have cleared the castle on all levels," Nadine reported as we approached. "Soldiers will arrive from the third army post soon. One of them is a Finder and will scour the castle for any other rebels that may be lurking."

"Thank you, Nadine." The king's voice cracked. "Once the soldiers get here, you and your guardsmen stand down and take a rest. You all deserve it."

Aidric sat me on my feet, holding my elbow to steady me as I swayed. Barwick sat on the corner of the crumbled dais, holding a cloth to a bleeding cut on his elbow. He stood when he saw us. His movement caught the eyes of others and soon almost everyone in the throne room stopped what they were doing to look at me.

King Bleddyn stood. He surveyed everyone in the room, then faced me.

"Lady Lydia, the Spirits blessed us the day you arrived. Long live Lady Lydia."

He lowered one knee to the ground and knelt in front of me. Like a wave, the entire room followed. At my side, even Aidric bowed, his hand still holding onto mine.

I had the sensation of the world tilting under my feet. To see everyone *bowing* to me. I took a shuddering breath. The last wall I'd kept around my heart cracked and turned to dust.

"Don't bow for me, my friends. Without all of you willing to defend Thavell, this night would have gone much worse. I couldn't have succeeded without you, or the Scholars. Everyone deserves a world where they are free to be themselves. A place where everyone, no matter their magic or abilities, can live and love in peace. And I will continue to fight and work beside you to build that world. Forever."

The room cheered. I squeezed Aidric's hand. His eyes widened.

"For real?" he whispered.

"Forever. For real."

His answering smile was the only thing I needed.

CHAPTER TWENTY-FOUR

*D*reams tugged me into their undertow every time I tried to wake. On a river of memories and visions, I floated. Merry smiles—silent screams—decades of hope—years of trials. All crowded together in my consciousness, sending me tumbling through the void. One image kept surfacing over and over. An auburn-haired girl, like the one in my vision at midwinter. And that boy with dancing eyes.

The light pulled me to reality. My nightgown scratched against my too sensitive skin. Turning my head proved pointless as it pounded with each movement. Sandpaper coated my mouth and tongue.

Coughs caught in my throat, begging for moisture. I sat up, my heavy eyelids finally responded and opened.

"Easy there, drink some water."

We were in my room. Noon sun poured through the curtains. Murphy sat at my bedside. I grabbed the water and chugged it, and then another cup. And another. After the fourth, I handed the empty cup back to Murphy and fell back against my pillows.

"How long have I been asleep?" I croaked.

"Three days."

There was no arguing with him because I certainly felt like it. My arms weighed nine hundred pounds. I flexed each of my fingers, making sure they all moved. Warmth flooded under my skin as my magic woke up. My well was full, not drained like the last time I'd used that much magic. Murphy watched me as I woke up.

"Where is everyone?" I asked, my voice smoother this time.

"Erin and John are in your sitting room. Aidric is helping with the clean-up down at the northern estates. He told us to send a messenger as soon as you woke up."

"Already done."

Erin and John appeared in the doorway with trays of food. My stomach growled in greeting.

My friends sat on the foot of my bed and ate lunch with me. How many months had it been since the four of us shared the same room, alone together, without having to run or hide? Erin gripped John's hand so hard it turned red. Murphy kept stopping and staring at each of us.

Finally, Murphy cleared his throat.

"It's good to be back together," he said. John nodded.

His words broke the tension in the room, and I had questions I needed answered.

"What happened at the end?"

"The rebels scattered." Murphy shrugged.

"Reynard?"

"He escaped—again," John growled.

"At least half their Wielders were dead," Murphy

explained. "The other half were injured or incapacitated. Your trick worked well."

"Maybe too well," I whispered. "I didn't want anyone to die."

"Hey," John said. "If you hadn't fought back, they would have killed most of your friends in the Scholars. Probably us too. And I don't need to tell you to avoid being captured by them. You did what you had to do."

I nodded, thankful for the words that kept me from spiraling.

"It's so weird, between my dreams and now, all these feelings are inside me and as strange as it sounds, it's like some of them aren't even mine."

Murphy smirked.

"What?" I asked.

"Well, Barwick came a few times with a healer to check you over. He warned us something like this may happen. I think his exact words were, 'playing with other people's magic is not for the faint of heart.'"

"Well, I hope I never have to do it again." I shuddered.

"So." Erin crossed her arms, a wary look on her face. "What is this about you agreeing to stay here forever?"

I dropped my head, staring at the threads on my quilt.

"You heard that, huh?"

"Of course we heard it, Lydia." Erin tapped my knuckle. I looked back up at her. "You and Aidric told us the betrothal stuff was just made up. But after the battle—what you said. That didn't sound made up."

"It wasn't." My throat caught again, making it hard to speak. "I meant what I said. I'm staying."

My vision shimmered as tears blocked my eyes. I hadn't

thought it would be this hard to tell them. Erin bit her lip and leaned on John. Murphy had gone quiet and stiff as steel.

"But what about us, Lydia?" Erin's voice was thick. "What about home?"

"Home?" Flashes of my dreams race through my memory. "What if this is my home?"

My friends fell silent as I spoke about the thought I'd been considering for months now.

"What are you talking about?" John finally asked.

"Think about it." I stared at each of them, begging them to consider what I said. "The only way someone can be a Wielder is if their parent was a Wielder."

They stared at me blankly.

"We know my mom isn't a Wielder. And we know magic doesn't exist in our world. But what if someone slipped through a crack in the world before? We got stuck here. What if it happened in the opposite direction? I think my dad was a Magic Wielder."

Again, there was silence. Erin's brow furrowed as she considered my words. I didn't mention my conversation with Sarge in the tower. Part of me wondered if that had really happened, or if it was just one of the lost memories floating in my head. Besides, her words only confirmed what I'd already been thinking.

"Mom never talks about him. What if he got stuck, and they met and had me before he died? Maybe she doesn't even know."

"But Lydia," Murphy insisted, "home is where you were born, it's where you belong. With your mom, with us."

I fought the tears that threatened to overflow at the

thought of never seeing my mom again. Of never seeing my friends again.

"You know I love all of you. But there are people here who are relying on me. 'Magic will restore, balance will renew.' I'm the only one who can restore magic. If I leave, what's going to happen here?"

"Lydia, you can't take this entire world's problems on your own shoulders."

"I know that," I told Erin. "I know I can't fix everything that's wrong here. But... I like it here. I love using magic. And I still have all these unanswered questions. If my dad was from here, and a Wielder, where was he from? Do I have any other family? What about the realms? If I leave, will they ever open? Being here... it's the first I've felt like I can do something that matters."

"You can do something that matters at home."

At the tide of battle when I stayed here, I never thought of how Murphy and Erin would take it. My heart split in two. Part of me knew this was a shock, and not something they'd prepared for. But the other part of me wanted them to be happy for me. John was the only one who didn't look angry. He listened to us talk, his eyes thoughtful.

"I know I can. But it's not what I want. I want to do something more. Something bigger. This is where I need to be. This is where I belong."

The words came out in a rush. I realized it was the first time I had admitted them to myself. I belonged here. The feeling settled into my bones.

"My priority is still getting you guys back home. That won't change."

"Well." Erin dusted off her clothes as she stood. "You've made your decision. I guess that's all that matters."

I opened my mouth to protest, to tell Erin I cared about her opinion too, when a knock on my bedroom door interrupted us. Olma stuck his head through.

"Oh good, you're awake. I hate to put you to work so soon after you've risen, but I have something I need to show you."

He glanced at my friends.

"All of you should come."

Erin helped me get out of bed and get dressed. After three days of not using my body, it didn't want to cooperate.

Olma led us all the way downstairs to the Scholars' wing. He led us into the stone theater. I'd only peeked my head in here once. As we descended the stairs to the circular stage, I noticed the massive chandelier overhead. What looked like hundreds of candles were lit, giving the room a cheery glow.

King Bleddyn and Lord Barwick awaited us at the bottom of the stairs.

"It's good to see you, Lydia. How are you feeling?"

"Perfectly restored, Your Majesty."

"That's wonderful. You hear that, Barwick? She recovers faster after every battle."

"Well," Barwick said. "Let's hope there won't be a need for that again in the future."

As much as I wanted to believe what Barwick said would come true, a part of me knew if Reynard hadn't been caught, another battle would come eventually.

"So why are we here?" Murphy asked.

"Well, the day before the battle, Lydia came to us with an idea. A way to locate where the realms touched and find a way through them. Lydia suggested a place with a higher concentration of power would work. After she left, Barwick and I continued to research. The obvious answer is the Golden Forest. However, the forest is—temperamental. We couldn't guarantee she'd allow us to access the things we need."

I always got a chill when Olma spoke about the forest like she was a person.

"And after last night, traveling to the forest would be too dangerous for you." Barwick took over the explanation. I nodded; he had a point.

"So that led us here. We've identified Windburn as a place of higher-than-normal latent magic. I've been wondering why that was. The legends say the magic pulled the castle out of the mountain. And, you don't know this, but Windburn castle used to be the location of the Palace Scholars of the past. That's why they're down here on this level. This room we are standing in has been used for the greatest act of magic this world has ever seen."

We all looked around. I stepped around the podium in the middle and placed my hand on the wall. This place certainly felt ancient. I wasn't sure if it was because of magic, or because it was always dark and damp down here.

I spun back around.

"But how do we know we can access the realms from here?"

"That's where you come in," Barwick said. He handed me a slip of parchment.

Strength of the ancients.
Power of the mighty.
Pierce the veil with my vision.

Give me sight to see beyond.

"What is this?"

"It's a spell of my invention," he smiled like an eager child. "You gave us the idea for it. After you channeled other people's magic, Olma recalled something from the old spell books. They would often call the ancients, or spirits. We think it's a reference to latent magic, the magic that's been left behind by others. If we are correct, you can call on the magic in the room to help you."

He held his hands up in caution.

"But this is an untested spell. This one is crafted so you will just be able to see. Scrying doesn't take that much power, and to the best of our knowledge, you should be able to take a peek through to another realm without it affecting you too much. We are still working on the spell to actually pierce a realm."

I bit my lip. My magic thrummed within me, but my body still carried fatigue from the battle.

"You don't have to try this right now if you don't want to. We can wait."

I looked over at Erin, Murphy, and John. All three of them watched me intently. I could do this. For them.

"I'll look. That way, we will know. Where should I stand?"

"Here at the wall is fine," Olma said. His instructions seemed almost eager. "It brings you close to the magic."

I looked over my shoulder. All three of my friends held hands now. I smiled, hoping their faith would give me enough encouragement.

Placing both hands on the wall, I let my magic drift out

into the stone.

"Strength of the ancients.
Power of the mighty.
Pierce the veil with my vision.
Give me sight to see beyond."

The words were tough to get out, but I did it. As soon as the last one echoed in the theater, my body went rigid. Power poured into the wall. A spot of light appeared in the stone. It grew larger and larger until it shimmered like water before my eyes. Behind me, someone gasped.

The shimmering stilled, and the image cleared. We all stared into a forest. The green trees stretched into the sky. A squirrel jumped from one to another. I could almost smell the mountain air. Someone approached my shoulder. Nothing could tear my eyes from what I was seeing.

"Is it?" Murphy asked.

"Yes!" Erin squealed. She pointed, her hand grazing my chin. "Look, right there! It's the entrance to the cave! That's it, that's home!"

Murphy laughed and swept her up into a hug. John pounded on my shoulder. I released the magic, and the image faded. Barwick clapped his hands, celebrating with my friends.

"Excellent, excellent," he chanted.

"So, when do we do it?" I asked. "When do I pierce the barrier?"

"Latent magic is strongest during a full moon," Olma whispered. His eyes had taken on a far-off look. "The next one is in two weeks' time."

CHAPTER TWENTY-FIVE

"Just one more day, and my friends will go home."

Willow didn't answer. Instead, he snuffed in my pockets for sugar cubes. I fished one out and let him munch on it.

"I don't know how I feel. Sad, certainly."

Again, Willow munched on the sugar cube, ignoring me.

"You're a lot of help," I playfully punched him in the neck, and he swished his tail at me.

"So, you can talk to horses now, too?"

I looked up at John, sticking his head through the hayloft.

"Just one of my many skills," I teased. "The problem is, horses only talk when they want."

John laughed and lowered himself down to my level. After the rebel attack, there had been no talk of imprisoning him. And John hadn't mentioned running. The day I'd scried for home, John had attended a council meeting and told King Bleddyn and everyone else everything he knew about the rebels. Who they were, what their plans were, where they might attack next.

After the meeting, King Bleddyn told him he was glad he'd come to his senses. And that was that. John bunked with Murphy and offered to help in the stables since they were short handed after the fires.

"And I'm tired of fighting," he'd told us at dinner that night. True to his word, the only weapon John had touched since was the knife he kept in his boot to use in the stables. Murphy and Erin still did their duties as guardsmen to keep up appearances, but Nadine gave them fewer tasks every day.

Instead, we'd spent most of our time the last week wandering the castle or talking about home. It was an unspoken contract that none of us mentioned the fact that I wouldn't be going home with them.

In the unseasonably warm weather, John wore a top with the sleeves hacked off. He reached by me to grab a curry comb for Willow. Scars littered the back of his shoulders and down his arms. He never mentioned his time on the run with rebels. And I never asked. I hoped he confided in Erin, at least. Keeping things bottled up never worked out.

Silently, we groomed my horse. Willow nickered and let us know which spots he wanted brushed next. After months of being worried about it and unsure if he was even alive, it still amazed me to look over and see him standing here with me.

Eventually, Willow's bay coat shone like a garnet. John leaned against the stall door.

"I understand."

I froze, afraid to believe what he was talking about.

"I understand why you want to stay."

John was the first of my friends to mention it.

"Erin, Murphy, me. None of us can understand what it's

like for you. We've stood out in this world since the moment we arrived. But you're right, Lydia. You fit here. You slipped this place on like a glove. It suits you."

"I have some unfinished business here I wouldn't mind taking care of." He cleared his throat. "But no way will I let Erin out of my sight again."

The hardness I'd noticed before returned to John's eyes. He glanced down at the stable floor and then back up to me.

"You're responsible for your own happiness, Lydia. Erin and Murphy understand, too—I think. Even if they don't want to admit it, yet. And we will all miss you. Terribly. But never be afraid to do what's right."

That evening, Aidric and I sat together on the balcony that overlooked the castle courtyard. The rebel attack put a sudden stop to the social season. Many of the nobles stayed to help clean up the castle and the city. A curfew was back in effect in Windburn, and two more army battalions had arrived to secure the castle and city.

Aidric had been so busy helping with arrangements for the city and the army in other places I'd barely seen him for the past two weeks. Only for lunch, or a walk here and there. He sent fresh flowers to my room every morning. And I found I didn't mind his absence, because I knew we'd get all the time in the world together.

The past couple of days, with better weather on the horizon, many of the noble families were leaving the castle to secure their own homes. No one thought we'd defeated the rebels yet. We watched Annistyn depart the castle gates with her father and the rest of their household. Her father's fief sat along the river between Windburn and Fenwood. She turned to look back at the castle. I waved.

"I'll miss her," I sighed. Aidric smiled.

"What?" I asked. "Missing someone isn't happy."

"Of course, but now you'll get to see her again. Her home is only a bit more than a day's ride from here. Maybe we'll go on a progress this summer and introduce the kingdom to their new queen-to-be." He looked out past Windburn as if imagining the journey.

All the breath whooshed out of my lungs. *Queen-to-be.* Aidric noticed my change in mood.

"What?"

"Queen-to-be," I repeated. The phrase spun over and over in my head. "Our betrothal—it wasn't real. I wasn't staying."

His brow furrowed.

"Are you saying you don't want it to be real?"

"No, no. I just thought that... maybe there was someone better than me. I don't know if I'll make a good queen."

He leaned in and kissed me.

"You will always belong at my side."

My toes curled as he pulled me closer to him. I sat up, so I was half kneeling, tucked close into his chest. Aidric reached into his pocket and pulled out a small ring of twisted gold.

"I want you to have this." He pressed it into my hand when I opened my mouth to protest. "We rarely exchange rings as a sign of commitment here, but Erin and Murphy told me that's what you do back home. This was my mother's ring. It's not much, but it holds a lot of sentimental value for me. It's a sign of my commitment to you. I love you, Lydia. My heart is yours, Lydia. I want you to have it and wear it when you're ready."

I gripped the ring in my hand but moved it to my pocket

when Aidric pulled both my arms around his waist. He leaned in to kiss me again.

"Someone will see us," I whispered.

"I don't care."

A dropped plate clanged in the hall behind us. We jumped apart. At the look of surprise on Aidric's face, I devolved into giggles. He pulled me toward him again. Someone behind us cleared their throat. We froze, Aidric's hand still on the back of my head.

A young soldier with a beet-red face stood in the doorway, looking at anything but us. Aidric sighed and stood. I smoothed my skirt and sipped my cup of tea.

"What can I do for you, soldier?"

"Your Highness, Nunse has requested emergency help. They are having problems with a rampaging bull."

Aidric crossed his arms.

"A bull? Why do they need help with a bull?"

"Well, sir." The soldier glanced at the message he held in his hands. "It says here the bull has wings."

Aidric sighed and ran a hand through his hair.

"Okay, soldier. Find my squire and tell him to bring my lance. Then tell Commander Nadine I'm taking the Heron Squad with me."

The soldier bowed and left to take Aidric's messages. Aidric wrapped me in a hug when I stood.

"Do you need my help?" I asked.

"No, the herons have an earth Wielder who's good with animals. And you don't need to be distracted. Nunse is only a couple hours' ride from here. I'll be back by morning."

"Just be careful," I told him. "If it's magical, we don't know what this bull can do."

"Yes, my love."

I smiled as he pulled me in for one more kiss.

"Get some rest tonight," he called on his way down the stairs. "Big day tomorrow."

Rest wasn't what I had in mind. I waited on the balcony until Aidric left at the head of the squad. He saluted me before they galloped out of the gate. The sight of him in his plate armor made me nervous, but I pushed my worry to the side. Aidric could handle himself.

Instead of going to my room for the night, I headed to the library. Harman had already gathered the spell books I'd requested from the Scholar's library. He'd spread them out for me on a table. I flipped through a couple. I'd have to thank him later.

With a ball of light over my head, I flipped through the books. When I found a word or phrase I was looking for, I scribbled it on a piece of parchment. I considered bringing my friends in to help—or at least to spend time with them, but I didn't want to give them any reason to worry about tomorrow. Not that I was worried about it.

But we were dealing with intense magic. I wanted to be prepared. At least that's what I told myself as I copied down spell after spell that might help. I crossed out lines and added new words. Trust my instincts. Trust my magic. That's what I needed to do. And right now, my instincts were telling me to have a backup plan.

It was close to midnight when a flash of fire startled me from concentration. Ash stood on a book in front of me.

"Hey, there." I extended my finger for her to stand on. "Is this a social visit or do you have a message for me?"

She fluttered to my shoulder and nestled against my

neck. I laughed.

"Social visit it is, then."

I showed her the parchment I'd been writing on.

"You don't know anything about spells, do you?"

From the corner of my eye, I watched her tap her chin as if thinking. She shrugged.

"Well, it was worth a shot."

I copied down the spells I'd created on a neater sheet of parchment while I talked to Ash.

"Tomorrow I'm sending my friends home." I stifled a yawn. "This is bigger magic than I've done before. But Barwick has assured me he and Olma have taken proper precautions. Whatever that means. I hope so, but I still feel like I don't what I'm doing. I guess I'm not used to preparing for big magic, usually when a situation calls for it, I just go for it."

My next yawn was so big my eyes watered.

"I think that means it's time for bed. Are you going with me, or do you have somewhere else to be?"

Ash fluttered down onto the table and picked up my quill. She pointed to my hands and then the table. I spread my fingers palms down on the wood. Even with a quill almost as tall as she was, Ash used practiced strokes to write words in a showy script on my hands. When she finished, the ink faded into my skin. Before I could ask what she'd done, Ash dove into the flame of the nearest candle and vanished.

Erin laid on a pile of rugs in front of the fire in my room. I shed my stiff overcoat and laid down next to her.

"Do you remember that time, in kindergarten, when that mean first grade boy was picking on me, and you pushed him so hard he fell out of the sandbox?"

"I do. John sure has come a long way since then."

We erupted into giggles, burying our heads in the pillows.

"I always thought we'd go to the same college, get married, and live right next door to each other."

"Me, too."

"You'd marry Murphy, of course. Because you'd finally be my sister."

I propped myself on my elbow so I could see her better.

"I love Murphy, you know that. But it never worked out between us. But it doesn't matter, you'll always be my sister."

"It's hard to believe there are worlds out there like this. I mean magic, unicorns—"

"Flying bulls," I added.

"That sounds terrifying."

"But really"—Erin turned over to look at me—"if Adylra exists, are there any other worlds out there? How many? Or on other planets?"

My eyes widened.

"You're right. If Adylra's here, maybe there are more."

We both stared into the fire for long minutes.

"It's too much to think about," I said. "I've got enough problems with Thavell."

"That's true. Lydia, are you going to be okay here on your own?"

"I won't be alone. I have Aidric. And Willow." Erin understood a horse was just as much company as a human. "And neither Annistyn nor Maren are my besties like you, but they have my back when I need it."

Erin hummed, clearly unimpressed with any friend that wasn't her.

"John and I had a long talk today. He feels bad about leaving you here. Me too. But I'm afraid if we don't leave now, we're going to get swept up in whatever's happening here and won't be able to leave. And all of us have already almost died—multiple times."

"Oh, Erin." I grabbed her hand. "Don't feel guilty. This is my choice. Go home. That's where you want to be."

"You feel it, though, don't you? This place, it's on the brink of something. I don't know what, but it'll be messy. Do you know what you're getting yourself into?"

"No," I told her honestly. "I don't have a clue."

We both chuckled.

"But I know I need to be here to see it through."

"Yeah. I get that. I'll miss you, though."

"I'll miss you too."

We both sat up when my door squeaked again. Murphy and John stood in the doorway.

"We thought we might find you guys here."

"Lydia and I were just talking about when she beat you up in kindergarten."

Erin and I scooted to the middle so Murphy and John could squeeze in under the blanket.

"Yeah, she set me on the straight and narrow, that's for sure."

"That's almost as good as the time we found that stray dog and tried to hide it from Lydia's mom for a week."

"We thought we were so smart. And she was feeding it the whole time."

The night passed as we shared stories about growing up and home. As dawn arrived on my friends' last day in Thavell, we finally drifted off to sleep.

CHAPTER TWENTY-SIX

Nerves ate away at me like hungry wolves when I awoke the next morning. They harried me as I extracted myself from between Erin and Murphy. Pulling on the same overcoat from last night, I marveled at how these clothes looked common to me now. I wasn't even sure what normal clothes looked like on me anymore. Something hard in my pocket caught my attention. Aidric's ring.

Unable to take the swirling chaos of my head any longer, I ventured down to one of the Scholar libraries underneath the castle. Once Erin, Murphy, and John returned home, it would be up to me to find out the truth of the realms and set magic to rights. And maybe find the truth about myself while I was at it.

I waved my hand and the torches on the wall lit one by one, flooding the empty library with flickering light. My footsteps echoed on the stone floor, again reminding of the stark contrast between this place and home.

Pulling the ring from my pocket, I ran my hand over the

twisted side. I slipped it on my finger. It fit perfectly. I'd made my choice. This is where I needed to be.

I hoped.

For the next hour, I worked my way through the stilted text of a recent book. It claimed to be a treatise on the harmony of the magical affinities, but it was mostly a wandering memoir of the author and had little to do with harmony or magic.

Another set of footsteps echoed through the hall. I whirled to find Aidric trotting toward me. Raindrops fell off his coat, making puddles on the ground. I stood up from my table once he was close. Instead of hugging me, he shook his head like a dog, showering me with the rest of the rain coming off his clothes and hair. I giggled and brought my hands up, stopping the raindrops in the air with half a thought. With a flick, I sent them all pelting back into his face.

He laughed and grabbed me up to kiss me, despite how wet he was. I let his embrace melt all the nerves from my body. This wasn't where I needed to be, it's where I wanted to be. Erin, John, and Murphy could finally go home. And I would get to stay here with Aidric.

"We just got back. The bull put up more of a fight than we thought."

"Did you catch it?"

"No." Aidric scowled. "It got away."

"Well, I'm sure there will be more winged bulls for you to chase." I paused. "Well, maybe not."

Aidric laughed and guided me up the staircase towards the kitchens.

"I'm guessing you haven't had lunch yet?" He asked. I shook my head, nerves fluttering in my stomach again.

"You need your strength."

He laced his fingers through mine, pausing when he felt the metal of the ring. His fingers brushed over it. With speed that made me gasp, Aidric swept me into a shadowy corner of the landing and kissed me.

"Is this supposed to give me strength?" I teased between kisses.

"Yes," he stated, kissing me again.

We grabbed food from the kitchen and found Erin, John, and Murphy crowded in Erin's room. They stared at a pile of clothes on the bed.

"Lydia," she said as Aidric and I ducked in and squished together on the top of the desk, "can't you just magic these clothes to look like something we'd wear at home?"

"Sorry," I shrugged. "I haven't had my tailoring lesson yet."

Murphy's mouth twitched, but Erin glared at me. She fluffed a pair of plain linen pants with such force it surprised me they didn't break.

"These will have to do. And just plain shirts, I guess."

"But just think"—John held up an outlandish tailored coat he'd worn to the ball when we first arrived—"if we pack a bunch of these clothes we'll kill it at the next renaissance fair."

"You're welcome to raid my closet before you leave," Aidric offered.

"Excellent."

Murphy rolled his eyes at his friend. From his place on the floor, he grabbed the scrolls John held. He passed them to me after rolling them and tying them with a ribbon.

I lifted an eyebrow and Erin explained.

"They're from us. Don't read them until after tonight, okay?"

Heartache tightened my chest. I nodded and stuffed them in my pocket before tears escaped my eyes. Erin wiped a hand across her glassy eyes and returned to her clothes. Finally, she threw her hands up at them.

"Oh, forget it. I'm feeling restless. Let's go for a ride."

We saddled our horses and went for a ride along the bay. The edge of the bay extended for miles along the foothills of the mountain Windburn castle was built into. Aidric led us to a secluded mountain pond where we didn't have to worry about prying eyes or ears.

Murphy and John taught Aidric to skip rocks. Then all three guys competed to skip them the furthest. Erin joined at the last minute and beat them all. Then, Aidric led us down the path used by King Alec when he took the castle from his evil brother Neiryn.

"Do you think any of the legends are true?" Murphy asked.

Aidric rubbed the back of his neck and the gold flecks in his eyes seemed to glow in the setting sun as he looked out over the bay. "Yes, but I think they're only part of the truth. And I wonder if the history books will speak about this age as the time when our legends came back to life. Hopefully that will be a good thing."

Far too soon, the sun dropped toward the horizon. We headed back to the castle.

"What are you going to tell everyone when you get back?"

Erin and I had raced ahead of the boys on the beach. It was the first time we'd mentioned what was happening tonight. She took a minute to settle her horse, who pranced away from the water with each wave.

"I don't know." She sighed. "We've talked through a few different scenarios. We're hoping getting lost in the woods will be enough. But we don't know how long we've been gone, do we? It's been over six months here, but does time pass the same way? What if it's been years?"

And what were they going to say to explain my absence? The question went unasked between us. They could tell people I'd run away, but then my mom and stepdad would search for me. I didn't want to think about the alternative.

The boys had reached us.

"Different world or not, I expect a wedding invitation." She twisted in her saddle to glare at Aidric. "But not for at least six or seven years. You got that?"

"Yes ma'am," Aidric laughed.

I nudged Willow closer to Erin's horse so I could grip her arm.

"I'll miss you, too."

CHAPTER TWENTY-SEVEN

*T*ime has a way of speeding up as we approach turning points. It was like I blinked, and it was moon rise. Even though I knew a full moon hung in the sky outside, no outside light made it down this far in the castle. Back down on the Scholars' level of the castle, there was nothing but the crackle of the torches and the scratch of Olma's robe against the stone as Aidric and I followed King Bleddyn and Olma down to the stone theater. Erin, Murphy, and John walked behind us. I shivered and pulled my coat tighter around me. Only the dungeons were farther below the castle than this. I shivered as goosebumps covered my arms.

The chandelier in the theater was dark when we arrived. The combination of torches along the walls and gray stones gave the room an eerie glow.

"Where are the Scholars?" I asked.

"Barwick took them on a trip to Alvale to look for magical artifacts," King Bleddyn said. His eyes surveyed the entire room. He moved like a seasoned warrior, ready to react to anything. "He thought it best there was no one down here when we attempted our—experiments."

Considering the magic I was attempting, that was probably a smart move.

There was no denying the stone theater felt different at night than it did when we came down here two weeks ago. Even the air felt stale and ancient. Behind me, my friends stood shoulder to shoulder. For support or warmth, I wasn't sure.

The round stone podium sat in the middle of the stage. I'd barely noticed it the other times I'd been down here. It, too, glowed in the torchlight. Inspecting it, it looked like it had magically appeared from the floor. Which, given the history of this room, it probably had. Erin came up beside me and gave me a thin-lipped smile. I squeezed her arm. Murphy and John still hung back, watching the king and his steward with hooded eyes.

I attempted to swallow, but all the moisture had fled from my mouth. I cleared my throat instead. The sound echoed through the chamber and everyone's eyes turned to me. I squared my shoulders and willed some confidence into my voice.

"What do I need to do?"

"Stand near the dais," Olma instructed. I'd never heard him so sure of himself. He seemed almost energized as he motioned me toward the center of the stage. I walked over, but didn't stand close enough to touch it.

"This place is full of magic," I whispered. "I couldn't feel it before, but I can now."

"Can you tell why?" The room subdued even the king's booming voice.

I studied the dais and the walls above the seats.

"It's the stones." I pointed to a spot where the gray stone at my feet swirled in different shades. "It's been disguised to look the same, but this room is made of different stones. Magic stones. How many are here?"

"All the magic stones that exist in Thavell. Manalase, indoro, adenite, viridite, ochrodite, cryoase, daltelian," King Bleddyn recited.

"All of them except galcian," Olma added.

"It would null all the stones, right?" The question came from Aidric.

Olma nodded.

"Galcian only helps the holder."

I wondered how many other secrets this castle held.

"Now Lydia," King Bleddyn approached the other side of the dais. "You looked through the gateway the last time we were down here. Olma and I have been studying how to make sure you can access as much latent magic as possible."

"You will need to approach the dais and place your hands on the top," Olma said. "From there, you can call on your magic. Call on each of your eight affinities at once, focus on the dais and attempt to draw the gateway out of the stone."

"Once you can see the gateway, say these words:

Spirit of the night, pierce the barrier
Power of the ancients, call forth the way
Bringer of balance, show me the way home."

Magic bubbled in my veins as Olma recited the words.

"Tell me again why I need to use these words?"

A muscle in Olma's jaw twitched.

"Magic leaves a residue. An essence of the person it came from. You used that essence last fall to connect to the magic of the Golden Forest. And again in the throne room to trap the rebel Wielders. We believe you can connect to the essence in this room and from there call the gateway back to your home. From there you can create a hole in the barrier long enough for your friends to walk through."

My gaze flitted from Olma to my friends and back to the dais looming before me. I pressed something into Erin's hand. She opened the cloth to see small figurines, a horse, a crow, and a panther.

"For you, Murphy, and John," I whispered. "To remember me by."

All three pulled me into a hug.

When we broke apart, Aidric spun me to face him. He caressed both sides of my face and titled my head, so I looked into his eyes. The intensity in his gaze made my heart flutter. Everyone else in the room faded.

"Do you trust me?" he asked.

"Of course," I said. It wasn't even a question.

He kissed me on the forehead.

"I love you, Lydia."

"I love you too, Aidric."

Reluctantly, Aidric let me go. King Bleddyn motioned for everyone to retreat to the first bench. I took the moment to look at each of my friends one more time, memorizing their faces. This wouldn't be the last time I saw them. It couldn't be.

I faced the dais.

"Let's get started."

CHAPTER TWENTY-EIGHT

Closing my eyes, I turned inward. My magic rushed forward with barely a thought.

A smirk played on my lips. Power flooded my body and my limbs. Nothing would ever compare to this feeling.

I placed my hands on the dais.

As soon as my magic touched the stone, power flashed through my mind. My magic retreated with a jump. I opened my eyes and brushed the hair out of my face. My forehead was already slick with sweat. That power. It felt—familiar, somehow.

"Everything okay, Lydia?" King Bleddyn called.

"Yes, Your Majesty. Getting started is the hardest part."

"Take your time."

Something rustled in their direction, but I paid it no mind as I returned my hands to the dais. This time, I forced my magic into the dais.

Again, there was that flash of power. I let my magic intertwine with it. As my magic wrapped around the strands of yellow, black, and teal, I noticed the sense of familiarity again. My magic snaked around it and kept going. It made the most sense to push through the dais and into the floor to pull the gateway up.

The further I sunk in the dais, the harder it became. My magic slowed and stuck as I pushed it further, like traveling through a swamp. I was close now. As I neared the floor, more magic rubbed against mine. Something felt off.

Without opening my eyes, I slowed my push. My magic expanded, letting the other powers wash over me. I slowed my push without moving my body and let the other powers wash through me. They didn't feel like remnants of magic that were stagnant for hundreds of years. The magic stuck to every inch of the stone, like someone had infused magic into its very pores.

Again, I studied the first strands of power. Yellow, light. Black, aether. Teal, water. Dana's face flashed through my head. My magic stilled. With the puzzle solved, more and more faces rushed through my mind. Barwick. Simon. Jamine. Arete. The more I pushed my magic through the stone, the more it all made sense.

I knew the essence of this magic. I'd connected with it before. And I knew every person who carried it within them.

My stomach revolted as the realization hit me in the gut. The quiet hall. The field trips. I had the last piece of the puzzle and it all clicked. My magic felt it before I did. It had warned me not to push too far. Because there was nothing residual about this power.

And there was only one way to sever the connection between a Wielder and their magic.

My eyes popped open.

"The Scholars didn't go on a trip, did they?"

"Would you believe me if I told you they lent us some of their magic before they left?"

No remorse colored King Bleddyn's expression.

"No." Rage for my fellow Wielders consumed me.

Murphy, Erin, John, and Aidric exchanged glances. Only King Bleddyn and Olma looked unruffled.

"What's going on?" Aidric asked.

"Would you like to tell him, Your Majesty? Or should I?"

My rage and heartache boiled beneath my skin.

"I think you should continue the spell, Lydia."

"Where are the Scholars?"

Aidric asked, more insistent this time.

"They're dead."

My pronouncement echoed through the chamber. Erin gasped. John and Murphy both reached for weapons that were no longer sheathed at their waists. Aidric's face crumpled. He looked at his father with the question written across his face. King Bleddyn ignored him. He rubbed his brow, looking more annoyed than regretful.

"We should thank you, Lydia. Without the demonstration of your powers during the attack, I never would have learned how to do this," Olma whispered.

Cold shame doused the rage that was building. My racing mind settled on one thought as Olma stepped forward.

This was my fault.

I accepted the Scholars.

I let Dana come back to the castle.

I'd taught them how to connect magic.

Now the Scholars were dead.

"Continue the spell, Lydia."

The demand came from Olma. He stood directly in front of me.

His eyes were nothing but swirling black voids.

But this time I wasn't afraid.

"No."

I tried to yank my hands from the dais. They didn't budge. Panic streamed through my body.

"I can't move my hands."

My friends and Aidric raced to me.

"I don't think so," Olma whispered.

He spun and punched the flat of his hand through the air.

Aidric dove to the side.

Erin, Murphy, and John were thrown back against the stone seats.

"Let us go!" John roared.

I tried to yank my hands again as my friends fought against their invisible bonds.

"I'll need you to be quiet, too." Olma waved his hand again. Even though John's mouth opened and closed, no words came out.

Aidric crawled to me. He grabbed my arm to pull me from the dais. As soon as he touched me, he yelped and let go. The palm of his hand was red from the touch.

Aidric stepped between me and Olma.

"Move, before you force my hand, Aidric," Olma said.

Even though his voice was still a whisper, it carried through the stone theater.

"You're not a Wielder. I would have seen it," I said.

"Let's just say you're not the only one who can borrow magic."

His voice slithered over my skin, and I shivered.

"Father, this was not supposed to happen!" Aidric yelled. "Let Lydia go."

"You know, Olma, we also need to thank my son. Without his help, we wouldn't have known how to get you exactly what you want."

"Aidric?" I whispered.

"Don't listen to him, Lydia, this was not the plan."

King Bleddyn talked over his son.

"My son befriended you because I asked him to. People from Barr don't come to the castle willingly. When you and your friends rode in last fall, I knew something was going on. After my son told me about your adventures on the road—including your magic—I thought he would have a better chance of getting to know you than I would. I was right."

Something in my chest crumpled.

"It's not like that, Lydia—"

"We don't have time for this," Olma interrupted. "Sire, this needs to happen now."

"Aidric, move. Remember what we are fighting. Lydia will not be harmed if she listens."

"Aidric, please."

With one pained look in my direction, Aidric stepped aside.

Any fire I had left snuffed out.

King Bleddyn stepped up beside Olma.

"Lydia, continue. If you don't, there will be consequences."

"I'm not opening the gateway to my world, am I?" My voice was hollow.

"No," Olma replied. "You are opening the gateway to my home—Eidoran."

The phantom realm.

"During the war between Neiryn and Alec, it imploded on itself. Now, only raw power exists behind the gateway. Once you open it, the king and I can siphon the power into ourselves. We will become the most powerful beings this world has ever seen."

"Nothing will stand in our way," King Bleddyn added. "Not men. Not magic. Not even death."

Frustrated tears pricked at my eyes. I screamed in anger. The king laughed.

Suddenly, Aidric leaped for Olma, a dagger in his hand. Faster than I'd ever seen him move, Olma twisted. He blasted Aidric to the side, but Aidric's fingers grasped a corner of Olma's robe, pulling it off.

The fabric peeled off Olma like a second skin. A foul stench hit me. It took all my willpower not to vomit. I looked at Olma and blanched. Even the king's dark skin had paled. I couldn't look away.

Underneath the robe, Olma's body had rotted away. Pieces of skin clung to his arms. Organs fell from his torso. Only rotting bone and tendons held his legs together. Olma looked down at his body with mild curiosity.

"Many years ago, a spell went awry. Now, I am neither phantom nor human, but a cursed hybrid of both. My life doesn't end. Yet, I can't exist without a body. However, my power isn't enough to keep the ones I use alive."

He glanced at Aidric, who knelt on the floor, unable to move. The dagger skittered across the stone floor, out of his reach. "Not what you were expecting, was it, boy?"

Olma pointed a skeletal finger at me. I flinched.

"Now open the gateway, girl."

"No."

Olma chanted under his breath. Something drew my magic through the dais. Underneath my skin, gold veins glowed as my magic drained from my body. I hauled back on it as hard as I could, willing my magic to stay with me. The strange pull paused. My body shook from the exertion. There was no way I was going to help Olma or the king gain unlimited power.

"Lydia—" The king's eyes glowed with desire. "Do what we ask, or your friends will die."

Murphy wrenched against his invisible bonds. John and Erin both shook their heads.

King Bleddyn smiled.

He had me, and he knew it. I wouldn't let my friends die.

To emphasize his point, King Bleddyn snapped his fingers and soldiers marched through every door of the auditorium. I recognized none of the black clad warriors. They grabbed Erin, Murphy, John, and Aidric. As one, they pulled them back by the hair and pressed knives to their throats. With a nod from the king, they did the same with Aidric.

"Don't think I won't give the order, Lydia. Please continue."

I stared into the eyes of a tornado, and I was powerless to stop it. Unending shame consumed me. I dropped my head and quit fighting the pull on my magic.

Now untethered, my magic pulled me and my consciousness through the dais and deep into the stone floor. I didn't know what was going to happen when I opened the door to Eidoran, but I had a feeling I wouldn't like it.

The floor rumbled. I leaned into the power. Pushing it to obey me wasn't difficult this time. One with me, my magic knew this was the only choice we had. Imperceptibly, a stone archway drew itself up from the floor. Olma opened his arms like he greeted an old friend. With each chant, my magic pulled further and further away from me.

I hesitated, and the gateway stopped halfway through the floor.

"Don't make me show you how serious I am," King Bleddyn growled.

"I'm running out of magic," I gritted through my teeth. I needed to delay this. Time to figure out how to stop this madness.

"Then you better use all of it."

The king wasn't buying my excuses. I let my magic go again and the gold veins beneath my skin glowed again. My reflection showed my gold eyes staring back at me.

The rumbling became louder and louder as the archway rose from the floor. I was close to the dregs of my magic. I didn't know how to save it. If I didn't keep some of it back, I wouldn't be able to help my friends. And if I kept pushing, I would die. Sweat dripped from my forehead.

"Now say the words, Lydia."

Eagerness dripped from King Bleddyn's voice.

"*Spirit of the night, pierce the barrier,*" Olma said the words with me. Our voices melded and took on new life. As the first words of the spell echoed in the dark, the gateway cracked on one side.

"*Power of the ancients, call forth the way.*" With each word, more magic poured out. The magic in the dais came forward to fill the void. Dana's face filled my mind again. She was scared the day she came in. I called her out anyway.

When I ignored Sarge and the others who tried to warn me, I sealed their fates.

Instead, I'd trusted the king.

I'd trusted Aidric. Fallen in love with him.

"Bringer of balance," I recited the lines as slowly as I could manage. The magic of the dais bypassed mine and streamed into the gateway. Could magic act on its own even after the death of its Wielder? I had a reserve of my magic. We needed a way out. Once King Bleddyn and Olma had their power, there was no way they'd let us walk out of this.

Olma pressed his palms against the crumbling stone of the gateway. My dress and hair flailed, caught in the wind coming from the sides of the gateway.

"Show me the way home!" The dais released me, flinging me onto the floor. The stone in the gateway crumbled.

No buildings or forest greeted us on the other side. A formless mass of darkness lay beyond.

Only small pinpricks of light broke up the swirling void.

"Yes!" Olma yelled. "I feel the power!"

During the spell, Olma had captured my magic. Even though I no longer touched the dais, he still drained me.

Something in the phantom realm called to me. My feet drew me toward the gateway of their own accord. A rush of wind poured out of the gateway, blowing my hair back. I put up an arm to block it. Behind me there was noise, but the wind carried the sound away from me.

"Do you feel it, Lydia?" Olma called. Tendrils of the darkness extended from the doorway. Olma reached a hand forward. "Join and feel the power forever."

The call was irresistible. The tendrils reached for us. I

took another step forward. If I had this power, I could save my friends. I could save everyone.

"Lydia, no!" Aidric fought against the guards holding him. King Bleddyn pushed past his son and grabbed the tendrils that were coming through the gateway. They wrapped around his hands and sparkled.

"I feel it coursing through me."

Olma connected with the darkness as well. A scream ripped through him as his body knitted together before my eyes. I dropped to my knees as pain wracked me. My magic sustained the gateway and was rapidly depleting. More tendrils of aether drifted through. I reached for one.

King Bleddyn kicked my arm away.

If I didn't do something soon, I was going to die. And my friends wouldn't be far behind.

Leaning against the dais, I recited another spell.

"Righter of balance, lend me strength.
Ancient spirits, I call on the eight.
Restore the power. Bring forth the way."

The theater quaked. Chunks of rock fell from the ceiling. Guards jumped out of the way. My friends took the opportunity to grab for their weapons and fight back. I hauled myself to my knees. Ancient residual magic, the kind Olma told me was here, rose from the floor and into my veins.

Olma saw what was happening and ran for me, but the quaking room stopped him.

Five more gateways appeared in the room. Silver, wrought-iron, gilded. Spots flashed in my vision. My power was giving out too fast. I fought for consciousness. I needed to remember the last spell I wrote.

"Magic of the ancients,
I call on eight.
Reverse the curse.
Break the gates."

My last words were a whisper. With a crack like thunder, each gate cracked from top to bottom. I fell onto my hands and knees. More guards streamed through the doors. All the hurt and pain of my failure flooded back to me. But if the magic carried me to death, I could restore power and stop the king and Olma first.

"Lydia!" Aidric screamed.

He sounded so far away. Time seemed to slow. I didn't even hurt anymore. I watched the room quake and the gates crack from a distance. If this was death, it wasn't so bad.

"Stop the magic. It's going to kill you. Lydia—please."

Aidric wrenched one arm from his captors' hold. He punched the other man in the face and grabbed something from around his neck. A red stone.

Aidric was right. I had to stop the spell. I couldn't help my friends if I was dead.

He threw the galcian to me. There was another crack in the gates and the floor tilted again. The leather slid through my fingers. Another jolt of the floor sent me flailing. But the crack revealed a piece of manalase.

A drink of ancient magic cleared my head. I reached for the leather cord again.

"What is that?!" Olma screeched. He jumped across the

room, knocking me away. The leather cord skittered across the floor. But magic doesn't like to be separated from its Wielder. As soon as Olma's hands touched me, strength flooded me. I grabbed him in the face and set fire to his healing skin.

He threw me to the floor, his screams filling the room. Aidric's dagger glinted in the corner of my eye. I grabbed it and thrust it deep into Olma's stomach as he advanced on me again. Putrid blood sprayed me in the face.

I leaped forward. My fingers grasped the leather cord. I pulled the stone into my chest.

CHAPTER TWENTY-NINE

As soon as the stone touched my skin, the spell broke.

A blast of power rocked through the chamber, knocking everyone off their feet. Aidric broke free and threw himself on top of me as chunks of rock fell from the ceiling. I looked through Aidric's arms as each gateway melted back into the stone.

As soon as the portal vanished, my magic returned. It was weak, but it was back. Before I could blink, guards grabbed me and Aidric. They yanked us apart and bound my hands behind my back.

Soldiers dragged Erin, Murphy, and John up the stairs. I couldn't stop them.

King Bleddyn advanced on me.

"Make. It. Come. Back."

"She can't." Olma's voice cracked. He was on his knees clutching his still bleeding wound.

The king roared. The sound echoed in the chamber, causing more rock to fall from the wall and the ceiling. He jerked his crown from his head and threw it at me. With my hands bound, I had no way to block it. My cheek tore, and the blood dripped onto the stone floor. I sagged in the guard's hold, almost too weak to stand. All I could do was watch.

King Bleddyn drew his sword.

"Father, don't!"

One guard hit Aidric on the back of his head. He dropped forward, unconscious.

"Bleddyn, stop."

The king whipped his head toward his steward.

"We still need her. We must wait for another full moon."

Olma tried to stand, but he stumbled forward. With the bits of magic that remained in me, I saw the black aether leaking from him.

"I will not wait as a specter!" he screamed.

A figure made of nothing but black aether fled the body and sped toward the only person nearby.

Murphy screamed.

Then he dropped to the floor.

John and Erin stopped fighting. The guards dragged them from the room.

Someone else was screaming. It might have been me. I sagged in the guard's hold. Everything around me disappeared except for Murphy's body, unmoving on the floor.

His arm twitched. Then a leg.

Before my eyes, Murphy stood up and dusted himself off. He turned to me.

His eyes were black.

"Now this is better." The voice sounded like Murphy. But every nerve in my body tensed. Something was very, very wrong.

A guard reached for Murphy's arm, but recoiled when Murphy glared.

"Get your hands off me, you oaf."

The guard glanced at the king, who nodded.

Murphy approached me, his eyes as black as night. He reached out and dragged a hand across the cut on my cheek. Then he licked his finger.

I stumbled backward.

"Don't you recognize me?"

"Olma?"

Olma—now in Murphy's body—grinned. My blood stained his teeth.

"Smart girl, aren't you? Using galcian like that. Tonight was a setback. But this body is much better. So young and fit, I should have lots of years to use this one."

"Where's Murphy? What have you done with him?"

My voice sounded hoarse with the rage and grief that washed over me.

"Murphy. Strong young man, that one. He put up a good fight. But he's not here anymore. If only you'd listened, sweet Lydia. Maybe you would have saved your friend." He shrugged. "But we probably would've killed him, anyway."

King Bleddyn picked up his crown and placed it back on his head. He nodded to the guard holding me.

"You know what to do."

Before I could scream, a hood covered my head.

Unable to see and too weak to walk, the guards dragged me up the stairs of the theater, bumping my knees with each step on the way up. The black fabric over my head blocked my vision and hearing. I didn't know where they'd taken my friends. And now I didn't know where they were taking me.

The guards dragged me down two spinning staircases and through another hall. They slammed me down on a table so hard I lost my breath. Before I could find it again, they tied my arms and legs to the table.

I jerked, trying to free myself. Someone removed the hood and revealed the metal cuffs circling my legs and feet. I was no match. My head dropped back onto the table. Magic was only a mist inside me.

One soldier held a torch directly above my face, making it impossible to see anyone around me. I squinted against the glare of the flame.

"Good," a deep voice said. "She's awake. She'll be able to feel everything."

Something sizzled. A man lifted a red-hot rod from a roaring fire. A circular design at the end glowed with the heat. My cries echoed through the room as two men came over and held my right arm still.

"Please, no!"

I was no longer in control of my body, of my mind. I writhed and jerked against the restraints as hard as I could. They dug into my skin but didn't give.

"Don't do this!"

Tears streamed down my face.

The man stuck the rod against my skin.

Searing pain hit me like a bludgeon. The smell of burnt skin filled the room. My screams echoed in the room. The overwhelming pain consumed me. Soldiers continued to hold my arm, no matter how much I screamed and begged. The pain continued.

Time stretched into an eternity. This pain was going to last forever.

The edges of my vision went black.

Honeyed leaves crunched under my feet. Ethereal mist clung to my arms and body, casting everything in the forest in eerie shadow. A forgotten dream slipped into the corner of my mind. I'd been here before.

But no wrought-iron gateway greeted me this time. Before me, the mist parted and revealed twisted branches, knotted bark, and trunk and leaves twined together to the top of the gold crowned tree.

Two pine-colored eyes appeared from the bark. The trunk shivered. Out of the tree stepped a being with deep brown skin and hair made of golden leaves. A shiver worked its way down my spine as the dryad fully emerged.

Even though I knew this was a dream, when her gilded eyes pointed my way, I took a step back. Roots emerged from the forest floor and wrapped around my ankles.

The dryad stepped closer until she towered over me. She grinned, revealing black teeth made of thorns.

"You're weak." Her voice suggested the crack of too close lightning and rainfall on leaves. "Too weak. The forest is ready to take back what is hers."

She reached for me.

I threw my hand in front of me, and gold light flared from my palms. Something hit me in the chest, shoving me backward onto the forest floor. But instead of hitting the leaves, the ground opened and darkness swallowed me. A rainfall of laughter followed me into the abyss.

My breath fled from my lungs as I landed on stone. Stars

appeared beneath my eyelids. Equilibrium found me again, and I realized I wasn't falling. I sucked in air. Sandpaper grated my mouth and throat. All I could get out was raucous coughs.

"Lydia?"

That voice. Something thumped near my head. I reached up to feel the cool side of a waterskin. I pulled the skin to my mouth and drank deeply. Too many gulps in, I realized I wasn't drinking water.

The memory of the last time I drank tea like this flashed through my addled head. I chucked the water skin back the way it had come.

"Lydia, you need to drink something."

That voice threatened to pull me back into the darkness. Maybe it was better than this.

Through nothing but strength of will, I opened my eyes.

My mind fought with the fog that clung to its edges as I took in my surroundings. Dark, damp walls greeted me. To my left was a rough wood bench. Part of my skirt still clung to the splintered board. As I pushed myself up on my hands and knees, the skirt ripped and fell to the ground.

My right arm stung as I reached for the fabric.

I sucked my breath through my teeth and flipped my arm over. Red, mottled skin greeted me. The fresh wound was still swollen, but the design of the brand was clear. A star with a perfect, filled triangle above each of the eight points. A Wielder brand. My Wielder brand.

Now I was the Gatebreaker for all to see.

"Here, I brought this for you—it will help."

My gaze shot to the front of my cell. Iron bars criss-crossed from the low ceiling to the floor and across to each wall. Less than a foot of space existed between each bar. And on the other side, with his hand pushed through the middle with ointment and a strip of linen in his grip, stood Aidric.

He tilted his head. I looked away from his gaze. That gaze that always felt like he was looking past all my insecurities and seeing right into my soul. And those eyes that shone when I'd told him I loved him—no. I couldn't—wouldn't—think about that. Not when the weight of everything that had happened threatened to swallow me whole.

"She was right all along." My voice escaped me in a deep croak.

"Who?"

"Sarge. Morghan. Whoever she is. She told me not to trust the king. Told me not to trust you. She probably already knows what happened. I bet she's sitting in a tavern somewhere laughing at my misery."

I sat back on my knees and swiped at the traitorous tears leaking down my face. Grime and soot from the falling stones in the theater coated my face. The flickering shadows of the torchlight hid Aidric's expression. Some part of me wondered what he thought of me now—covered in dirt, marked, and thrown in a dungeon.

I scoffed at myself.

It must have been so easy for him to convince me of his feelings. How could I have been so naïve? How could I have let this happen?

"Lydia, please. Put this on your wound. If you don't, it could get infected."

I made no move to get closer. Everything that led up to this raced through my mind. From the moment we arrived in Adylra, every choice laid out in front of me on a winding path. But it was too late. The king and Olma laid their trap. And I'd walked right into it.

Nothing would be the same again.

"Lydia—"

I made no move to stand. The thought of getting closer to Aidric right now was reviling. And I didn't want him to see my weakness. Because only weakness existed in the pool that used to be my magic. And without it, my body felt close to falling apart.

"Unless you're giving me a key, Aidric, I don't want to hear it."

Aidric sighed and pulled his arm back through the bars. I thought that was it. That he'd leave my mess and despair behind in the dark. I closed my eyes and leaned my head against the wall. Stretched out in front of me, my feet almost touched the bars.

"I'm sorry—"

"Don't." My eyes snapped open. Aidric still stood on the other side of the bars. "Don't you dare apologize."

"Lydia, you have to believe—"

"I don't have to believe anything that comes out of your mouth, Aidric. I was stupid for believing anything you had to say."

Aidric covered his face with his hand. I didn't care. I was so beyond caring about how anyone else felt.

"Where are John and Erin?"

Aidric shifted his shoulders and stood up straighter.

"Come and put this on your wound and I'll tell you."

A scream of frustration threatened to break loose from me. With my back pressed against the wall, I stood, gritting my teeth against the aches in my body. Imagining reaching through the bars and ripping out Aidric's throat with my bare hands was the only thing that propelled me forward. I yanked the ointment and linen out of his hand and plopped down on the rickety bench.

Aidric tried to reach through to help. I jerked my arm away.

"Don't touch me," I growled.

He stepped back, and I struggled with the ointment alone. I hissed as it touched the raw wound and more tears leaked from the corner of my eyes, blurring my vision. Why couldn't my eyes leak burning arrows of flame instead of this pitiful mess of tears?

"Where are John and Erin?" I asked again as I finished tying the bandage.

"They're safe."

"Why should I take your word for it?"

"You don't have any other choice."

I shot up and walked until my body touched the bars. I forgot about my shaking legs as I held his gaze.

"And whose fault is that? Did you know what was going to happen down there? Did you know what your father and Olma were trying to get me to do?"

Rage blossomed in my heart, and I clung to the feeling like a long-lost friend.

Aidric stepped back into the shadows. The flickering of the torchlight across his face made him seem older than his eighteen years.

"Are you scared of me, Aidric?" I purred. I didn't feel scary right now. Even as anger warmed me, there were no threads of magic to grasp within. And even if I'd wanted to knock Aidric's head off his shoulders, I was weak as a kitten.

But a small part of me enjoyed the fear that momentarily flickered in his eyes.

"No—" he lied.

"You didn't answer my question. Did you know?"

Aidric opened his mouth, but no words came out. I doubted he was ever going to answer.

Then—a whisper.

"Yes."

His voice was a knife through my heart.

Whoever said words couldn't hurt was a fool. I thought my heart had already been damaged beyond repair, but Aidric's confirmation of my darkest fear sent the rest of it shattering into oblivion. Even though I'd already known the answer, hearing him confirm it broke something inside me I wasn't sure would ever mend.

I slid down the wall until I sat on the damp floor. Any physical strength my rage had lent me eked out of my body like drops of water off a petal. Despair enveloped me.

"Why?"

It didn't matter. And I hated myself for asking. Like I was still some lovesick girl who believed her boyfriend cared. But I had to know.

Aidric didn't move. And from my angle on the floor, his face was lost in shadow. Maybe it was better this way.

"There are far bigger things happening than you and me, Lydia."

"Like what?" I didn't even recognize the hollow sound that emerged from me, pretending to be my voice.

Aidric ran his hands up and down his arms. Was he cold? The chill leaked into my body as I paid attention to it for the first time. Of course it was cold deep in the dungeons.

"Just say it, Aidric. It's not like I have anyone to tell."

"There's going to be war soon. Losing magic didn't just set Thavell back. Its loss was felt throughout Adylra, even across the sea. And those countries blame us. And now they're coming to get it back."

"What are you talking about?"

"My father has information from across the Everlasting Sea. Lithune has allied with the Raskon further across the ocean. They are superior to us in strength—in fighting power. In everything. With magic gone and the realms closed, Thavell stagnated. We've had ample resources, but even those run dry. The countries across the sea haven't fared so well. Now they're coming for us."

I pulled my knees in and cupped my head with my hands. None of this made sense.

"How do you know this?"

"My father led a quest across the sea when he was young. He witnessed their technology for himself. And he laid down a plan for information from there. He knows they're getting ready to move."

"And you believe him?"

"He's my father. Of course, I believe him."

I stood again, unable to listen to Aidric talk without moving. Restless energy threatened to consume me. I paced back and forth in the cell. Five paces one way, five paces back. I finally faced Aidric again, my arms thrown wide.

"And that's how you justify all this? That's how you justify lying to me from the start? How you justify the death of the Scholars, putting my friends in danger, Murphy—"

My voice cracked. Murphy. I couldn't even think about what happened to him. What I let happen to him.

"I didn't know any of that was going to happen, Lydia. Not at the start. My father only told me I needed to earn your trust. He wanted to know if I could convince you to open the phantom realm on your own. But I knew you wouldn't."

"What about Barwick, Aidric? Or Dana? You knew them. You met Dana's family for crying out loud! You were there when she came back here, to be part of something bigger. And now—" My voice cut out.

"I didn't know! I didn't know about the Scholars. Olma convinced my father it was the only way. And I never would have let him do that to Murphy."

"What about now? You're out of excuses. You know exactly how far Bleddyn and Olma are going to go to get what they want. Why do any of it? Why is the phantom realm so important?"

"We need the power. If we have any hope of saving this kingdom, we need magic. Magic that we can control."

I huffed a humorless laugh and ran a finger lightly over the bandage that now covered my brand.

"When will you learn that magic can't be controlled? Not by me, not by anyone? All this death, all of this fear and destruction. There's no point in any of it."

"How am I supposed to save my people? How can I be a good leader?"

He stepped forward and met my eyes. His fear and struggle were clear now. But still missed the bigger picture.

"You're supposed to be a good person, Aidric."

He shook his head and ran another hand through his hair.

"It's not that easy."

Any scrap of empathy I left for him dried up.

"You can't tell me that Nadine and Tristan and all of your

friends told you this was a good idea. Your father and Olma are wrong. This is not how you win the war. It is that easy, Aidric. Be a good man."

"And how am I supposed to do that?"

I placed my hands on the bars, so they framed his face on the other side.

"For starters, let me out so I can try to fix this mess we made. And if you can't do that—the least you can do is bring me some water, so I have a chance of holding my own when your father and Olma come back for me."

Aidric let his hands drop to his side. He made no move to do either of those things.

I chuckled.

"Of course you won't."

"We still need you to open the phantom realm, Lydia. We must channel that magic. If we don't, we won't win this war."

I turned and faced the back wall of my prison.

"Unless you agree to help us, you'll stay down here for a month until the full moon comes out again. One way or another, you'll open Eidoran for us."

I didn't respond. Eventually, the torchlight and his footsteps faded into darkness.

CHAPTER THIRTY

ime slid by in silence. My stomach and muscles cramped, calling out for sustenance. I resisted drinking the tea for as long as I could. But the cries of my body won out. I downed the skin Aidric left me. Once it was gone, I fell into a drugged sleep full of lights and music. None of it made sense. When I awoke, a tray of bread and gruel waited for me. Another skin of tea and clean bandages sat next to it.

So that was their plan, keep me powerless and drugged until they needed to use me again.

Even though hunger gnawed on me, I only ate the gruel. Then, I used half the bandages to wrap the bread and stuffed it into the dark pocket of space in the corner of the cell. I only took a sip of tea each time I felt close to my breaking point. Dizziness overtook me with each sip, but it didn't knock me out. To find a way out of here, I needed to stay awake.

No one else visited. No footsteps rang down the hall. Torchlight didn't dance on the walls. My world shrunk to only the stone and the dark. Everything else ceased to exist.

Did King Bleddyn have no other prisoners in the dungeon? I found that hard to believe. Maybe he'd saved the deepest, darkest corner for me.

Somewhere in this castle, King Bleddyn and Olma were waiting for me to break.

I wouldn't give them the satisfaction.

Music became the only thing that could keep my shattered heart from unraveling. When the hunger and thirst became unbearable, or the brand on my arm itched so much I wanted to rip the skin off, I belted every song I'd ever learned. Songs from preschool, from the radio, my high school spirit song. They ran through my brain and out of my mouth and crowded out the despair. I even threw in some ballads I'd learned since coming to Thavell.

Just as I began the third verse of a particularly bawdy song Tristan taught me, the crackling of fire tickled my ears. The song died in my throat. I raced to the bars. Nothing but darkness greeted me. No light from a torch. No footsteps. I started singing again, softer this time.

In the corner of my cell, I heard bells. Was the brick moving? I rubbed my eyes. The darkness was playing tricks on me. As I approached the spot, a glimmer of magic twisted and revealed Ash sticking her head out from a gap between two bricks. My dry lips cracked as my face broke into a grin. She found me.

I sat on the bench and Ash hopped from the brick to the nape of my neck, tangling her hands in my hair as she made her way to my shoulder.

"Ash, what are you doing here?" I whispered. She put her finger against my lips and pointed to the bench. As I laid flat, Ash began her song that reminded me of a warm crackling fire, apple cider, and wolves howling at the moon. Before I knew it, I was asleep.

When I opened my eyes, I was standing on a black plain. This was not a drug-induced dream. A lady stood on the outer edge of the plain, shrouded in shadow.

"Where are we?"

"Fire can show you many things, if you know where to look."

I squinted and stepped closer. It couldn't be.

"Ash?"

The shadows around the sprite shifted, and her dark skin and black curls became recognizable. Her translucent black wings fluttered in an invisible wind. Here, in this place, Ash stood as tall as me. Or was I as small as her?

"I can understand, you know."

"You can always understand me, Lydia. Magic doesn't just control the elements. It can help you know them. Your magic is how it's all connected."

"What's connected?"

Ash's wings fluttered again.

"It doesn't matter right now. We don't have much time. Your magic is only strong enough for a moment. How can I help you?"

Ash's kindness sent me over the edge. I dropped to my knees, grief consuming me. I cradled my face in my hands even though I was too dehydrated for tears.

"I don't deserve help."

I needed to just drink my tea and wait until the king retrieved me. If I helped him, maybe he would let John and Erin go, at least. I no longer held hope for myself. I deserved this pain. I deserved this prison.

Ash lifted my chin.

"You do not deserve this, Lydia. And you cannot do what the king is asking. If you give the king and his steward untapped power to Eidoran, the consequences will be devastating. You must look beyond the power."

Something rocked my consciousness. I was waking up.

"What can I do?"

"Water, and food." My answer came immediately. "But mostly water. If I can stop drinking this tea, I can get my power back. Then, maybe I'll have a chance."

Ash nodded and then vanished into smoke.

I wasn't alone. I didn't need to open my eyes to know it.

Ash was gone, the place on my shoulder cold. Still, I felt eyes on me.

My body tensed in anticipation as I opened my eyes to reveal King Bleddyn and Murphy—Olma—standing on the other side of my bars.

I didn't bother standing as both peered down at me.

"It's a pity it had to be this way, Lydia."

King Bleddyn's voice was as grand and as solid as always. But far from comforting, it sounded like nothing more than gravel grating in my ears.

"Stuff it, Your Majesty."

"Is that any way to talk to the king?"

My gut clenched as Murphy's voice filled the dungeon. Because it was his voice. It was his body. But nothing of Murphy spoke to me through the swirling darkness of Olma's eyes.

"I'm going to kill you one day."

I knew it with more certainty than anything I had ever

known. Olma wouldn't get away with taking Murphy from me.

"Oh dear, if that's what keeps you going, then go ahead and believe it."

I kept the roar threatening to escape my chest inside as I stood to face my adversaries. Lifting my gaze to stare at Murphy was harder than I ever imagined. Nothing could have prepared me for this.

"Lydia, it's been three weeks," the king stated. I started, realizing how long I'd been here.

"If you've enjoyed the dungeons by all means, continue to stay here. But if you'd like to comply with us, we will reinstate you to your rooms. Under guard, of course. And when the full moon rises, you will complete the mission we gave to you."

"And if I do, what happens then? Do I get to go home?"

"Aidric told you of the coming war," the king answered. "And we need all the power we can muster. It would be a travesty to let you leave."

"I'd ask if my friends could go home, but then why would you miss out on the opportunity to control me?"

"You learn fast," Olma said.

"I do learn fast." I inched closer until the only thing separating me from those swirling black eyes were the bars of my cage. "And I've had a few weeks down here to think. I know you're not Murphy. And I know you're not Olma."

"Who am I then?"

"Neiryn."

King Bleddyn paled. But Olma only sneered.

"I haven't heard that name in a long time. Even King Bleddyn here didn't suspect something was amiss when I met him all those years ago. He never figured it out. I had to tell him who I really was, and what price I paid for my magic."

King Bleddyn's face darkened as Olma revealed their history.

"So, you think you've got everything figured out? You might have been a formidable opponent if our enemy had gotten hold of you. Don't you think I know who tried to capture you in the courtyard? Who tried to convince you to go with her in the tower? I find sweet solace in knowing that when she had you in her grips, you ran back to us. Twice."

I looked away; the shame of my ignorance unbearable.

"Aidric believes in you, you know," I told the king. "He thinks you're a great king and that your only goal is to help your people."

The king grunted, clearly not impressed with my loose tongue.

"He's a dutiful son."

Anger burned through my body. My eyes glowed, and even without my magic, the king took a step back.

"He's a good man. And you've corrupted him. Why don't you tell him the truth, Your Majesty? Why don't you tell him what you're really after?"

My hands balled into fists.

"The threat is real."

"But that's not what you really care about, is it? All you care about is the power."

I nodded my head toward Olma.

"Is this what you want for your future? A half-life with corrupted power you have to steal, bodies you have to seize?"

King Bleddyn stepped forward. His simmering rage met my own. I didn't care. They'd already done everything they could to destroy me. But they still needed me, so I was going to say what I wanted.

"Once we open the door to Eidoran, Olma can purify his power and I can have enough for ages. I can be the most powerful king Thavell has ever had."

I glanced between them both and snorted. From the surprise coloring their faces, it wasn't the reaction they expected.

"Both of you are delusional. Down here or in my rooms, it doesn't matter. Wherever I am is prison. I will never help you willingly."

King Bleddyn glowered and stormed off. Olma stuck his hand through the bars and tossed me another skin of tea. I reached to catch it and as it touched my hand, it heated for an instant and cooled just as suddenly. I kept my eyes trained on Olma, trying not to reveal my surprise.

"Drink your tea, Lydia."

I snarled and lifted the skin to my lips. Crisp, clear water poured down my throat. I grimaced to hide my surprise.

"We can't have you getting your powers back before we're ready. Drink your tea and be good. We will be back. Maybe we'll wait another month just to make sure you've learned your lesson."

I couldn't stop my look of fear as I considered being stuck down here for another month. Olma grabbed the torch from the bracket behind him and laughed.

As the sound of Olma's footsteps disappeared and left me alone in the dark once again, I smiled.

CHAPTER THIRTY-ONE

J had to get out of this cell.

If three weeks had passed already, I only had one to come up with a plan. And I wouldn't put it past the king and Olma to lie about how long I'd been here. The full moon could be any time.

The clean water and food helped clear my head. New food and tea appeared each time I slept. And with each touch, it heated and purified. I still tried to ration what I had. The last thing I wanted was to tip Olma off that something had changed.

Taking stock of myself, the picture was grim. After weeks of surviving on bites of food and snatches of drinks, my dress hung off my frame. Without the tea constantly in my system, I could sense the spark of my magic once more. But if I was too weak to use it, having my magic back meant very little.

Each time I woke up, I ran my hands along every inch of the rough walls of my cell. My eyes had adjusted enough to the dark that I could make out the gray outline of the bricks of my prison as I felt for any loose stone. If I could work just a piece of one out of the wall, then I would have something to use as a weapon.

Three times I ran my hand over every nook and cranny. Nothing. I growled and kicked the bench. The chains rattled against the old piece of wood and my toe throbbed. A pinprick of rage rose to the surface above the despair lodged in my chest. There had to be a way.

A plan borne from the obsessive darkness played out on the edges of my mind.

There had to be an antidote to the tea. I could play along, get the antidote, and then open Eidoran for King Bleddyn and Olma. Part of me wanted to risk it. What would I find behind the force of aether at the gate? Is that what Ash had meant about pushing 'past the power'? There was something there, something called to me. I knew it in my bones. Did I dare try?

But would I be able to fight Olma's pull on my magic a second time? I'd barely made it out the first time. And Murphy hadn't made it out at all. Guilt threatened to consume me.

Another darker plan formed in my swirling thoughts. When they came to get me out of my cell, I could fight. Except King Bleddyn was much stronger than me, especially in my weakened state. He was a trained warrior. And for all the training I had gone through to be a soldier, at the end of the day, I was just a teenage girl. And he would bring help to retrieve me.

But none of that mattered. If I attacked him and kept fighting, the soldiers he brought with him would have no choice but to kill me. If I died, Erin and John would never get back home.

But they would be safe. I knew enough about the king to know if they were no use to him as bargaining chips, he'd forget about them. Bleddyn couldn't use them if I wasn't in the picture. The thought of dying scared me. But I would do it. It was the only way to make sure my friends were safe and couldn't be used as pawns anymore.

I started running my hands along the walls for a fifth time. As they drifted underneath the chain that held the plank to the wall, something shifted.

I paused. My breath caught in my chest as I tried again. This time, the brick definitely wiggled. I wiped my sweaty palms on my now tattered clothing and pulled at the stone again. Slowly—so slowly I wanted to scream—the stone came loose. I hefted it in my hand.

The brick was hollow, and not as heavy as I expected. I could even grind down one side and make a knife. Something fell from the hollow stone and clunked on the floor. I held my breath as the sound echoed in the silent dungeon.

When I was sure no one was coming to inspect, I knelt and felt along the floor. Something sliced into my finger.

"Ouch."

I brought my hand to my body, holding my bleeding finger. With shaky hands I opened my palm. Sweat gathered on my brow as I used what little strength I had to conjure the tiniest flame. As I lowered it to the floor, the flames illuminated the black hilt of a dagger.

I bit my lip to stop myself from crying. The hilt and blade were the deepest black. A small piece of black paint had chipped, revealing the jade green stone underneath. Manalase. A piece of parchment was wrapped at the end. I unfollowed it and made out the fading writing.

May this blade give you strength and an advantage when you desperately need it.

"Give you strength?"

I repeated the words to myself as I let the parchment burn in my dying flame. Could it be?

I sat on the bench and prodded the blade with my magic. Stale magic touched my own. I sighed as I pulled the magic from the blade into me. A Wielder with fire and earth affinities had filled this blade with their own magic and left it.

Whoever it was, I hoped I could thank them one day.

I ripped the bandage off my brand and stared at the eight filled triangles above each point of the star.

Fire and earth magic may have filled this blade, but I was the Gatebreaker.

I could use it for whatever I wanted.

he time for thinking was over. I needed to move.

I listened to the silence at my door. Nothing moved in the hall. I pressed my palm to my cell door. The lock popped, and the door swung open.

My heart beat rapid fire in my chest as I left my cell for the first time in a month. If anyone found out I'd escaped, it would be over. I needed to get into the castle, find where they were keeping Erin and John, and get them out of here. I didn't know where we'd go after that. But once my friends were safe, I could figure out how to stop King Bleddyn and kill Olma.

I kept my back to the wall as I crept forward, each step surer than the last. I made it to the end of the hall without seeing a single person. Every other cell was empty. That was good. I unlocked the door and waited for a moment as my head swam. The magic within me wanted out. But I knew my physical weakness would limit what I could do. I needed to pace myself.

The door opened into an empty antechamber. Doors

surrounded the circular room. Most of them led to more halls of cells. I stuck to the shadows and listened at each door. There were other prisoners in each of the other halls. I crunched in a shadowy corner and bit my lip. What would happen if I searched for Erin and John here and one of the other prisoners saw me? What if King Bleddyn had imprisoned more Wielders? I shook out my palms. I didn't have enough strength to unlock all the prison doors.

I cursed under my breath as a door to my left opened. A guard dressed in the king's livery stepped through. His back was to me. Using all the strength I could muster, I wrapped my arms around him, holding my dagger to his throat. He tried to scream, but I used my magic to carry his voice away on the wind.

His eyes widened when he realized he couldn't make a sound. Sweat poured down my face from holding the magic, but I didn't have time to be weak right now.

"Do you know who I am?" I asked. The guard nodded. "Then you know I can do much worse to you." My voice came out thin and raspy from lack of use.

"I'm going to give you your voice so you can answer my questions. If you try to scream, I will stop your heart."

He nodded again. I let go of the magic.

"Are my friends here?"

"No," the guard whispered. "I know all the prisoners. They aren't down here."

"Then where are they?" I growled.

"I don't know." I let the dagger draw blood. He sucked his breath through his teeth. "I swear I don't. Can't your magic tell if I'm lying? I'm just a prison guard. I don't know what happens in the rest of the castle."

I didn't need magic to know he was telling the truth. The quake in his voice told me enough. I loosened my grip slightly.

The guard swung his head back, bashing me in the nose. I cried out and stumbled against the wall. The dagger sailed through the air. Blood coated my mouth and throat. Before I could cough it up, the guard landed a punch in my stomach. I doubled over and brought up the little food I'd eaten. As soon as my back hit the ground, I kicked out with both legs, nailing the guard in the side of the face. I rolled to my knees as the guard's head snapped to the side and he backed away.

My chest heaved as I sucked in air past my bloodied nose.

"I'm sorry," the guard said. "But if I let you escape, the king will have my head."

The guard advanced across the antechamber.

I extended my hand, and the dagger flew to it. I flicked my wrist and launched it at the guard. It hit him in the thigh. His leg collapsed under him. Before he could recover, I extended my hands and ropes of flame wrapped themselves around him. One gagged him. I kicked him over and yanked my dagger out of his leg. I'd have to thank Tristan for the training next time I saw him again.

"If I don't escape, things will be much worse for all of us."

I knew the guard didn't understand. He stared at the dagger in my hand. Spots swam in my vision, and I knew I couldn't keep him tied up with magic for much longer.

A rope of flame twisted around his neck. I increased the pressure until he was grunting and flailing. I looked away until he went still. When I looked back, his eyes were closed. The flames disappeared.

Kneeling, I pressed my fingers against his neck. A faint

pulse fluttered against them. With my remaining strength, I rolled the guard back through the door I came out of and locked it with the keys I stole from him.

I used the keys to unlock the door to the stairwell and headed up. I couldn't think about leaving the guard there to face the king's wrath. He'd attacked me, and I couldn't risk him waking to follow me. I'd meant what I said, if the king got ahold of me again and got the power from Eidoran, we'd all be in trouble. I ripped fabric from the tattered hem of my dress and held it to my nose as I unlocked the last door between me and freedom.

Knowing my friends weren't in the dungeon was helpful, but this castle was huge. I didn't even know where to look. It took all my strength to stay upright and continue up the stair-case. I reached the top and opened the door. The dungeon came out in the long hallway. I peeked out the sliver of window. The cold breeze that greeted me sent tingles through my lungs and into my body. It was the first breath of fresh air I'd had in a month. I wanted to claw the window wider so I could get more of it.

I allowed myself to suck in two more breaths. From this vantage point, I could see I was in a hallway on the side of the sea. And it was night. Excellent. Fewer people to alert to my escape. I tucked myself in the corner of the hall where I could hear if someone ventured this way in either direction as I thought through my options.

Gabrielle would know where they were keeping Erin and John. But my rooms were all the way across the castle. Would I be able to make it there without being seen? Or before someone noticed I'd escaped? And I didn't even know if Gabrielle would be there. I didn't know what happened to her after they put me in the dungeons. I added her name to the growing list of innocent people whose lives I'd endangered because I existed.

The scuff of feet coming down the hall meant the time for thinking had ended. I took off in the opposite direction, holding the ripped fabric tighter to my nose so drops of blood didn't trail my escape. I turned left down two hallways and ran behind a piece of fabric. On this side of the castle, there was one place I could go.

Two hallways and one set of stairs later, I rapped on the door. Maren's heart-shaped face appeared in the crack as it opened. She squinted to see me in the dark hall.

"Maren? It's Lydia. I need your help."

"Lydia?" Maren's eyes lit with surprise. She pulled the door open fully, and I stepped inside.

My friend clutched her dressing gown to her neck as she looked me over.

"Oh Lydia! What happened to you?"

I shook my head and winced as the movement jostled my broken nose.

"It doesn't matter." I reached out to grip one of Maren's hands and stopped when the grime and blood on my own hands was illuminated by the moonlight. "Can you help me, Maren? Please. I need to find my friends Erin and John and get out of the castle."

Maren remained silent as she took me in. I could only imagine how crazy I looked. My hair hung over my shoulders in knots. My dress was in tatters and in the moonlight, my pale skin practically glowed. Not to mention my nose still dripped blood through the ripped fabric of the dress I held against it.

The silence dragged on. Shifting my weight, I readied drawing my magic. I really didn't want to have to knock Maren out, but I couldn't risk her alerting the guards to my presence. I let my hand drop when Maren finally nodded.

"You're safe with me, Lydia." She patted my arm on the least objectionable piece of fabric. "I've been so worried about you."

I sagged with relief as Maren pulled up a chair.

"Rest here while I figure out what to do." She disappeared into her dressing room.

My eyes shifted to the window as I waited. Even though the moonlight was dowsed by clouds, I still had to cover my eyes from the light. Even this late in winter, there was fresh snowfall on the ground. It gleamed across the courtyard and into the sea.

Maren returned to her sitting room with a basin of water and clean rags draped over her shoulder. She set the basin on a nearby table and then scooted the full-length mirror in front of me. I grimaced at my reflection. Before I could say anything, Maren shoved the basin in front of me and the rag into my hand.

"We need to get you cleaned up."

"Maren, I don't have time, I need to get out of here." I tried to stand, and she stopped me with her hands on my shoulders.

"It's almost dawn. If you have any hopes of getting out of this castle, you can't run around looking like this. We need to get you cleaned up and disguised. Now start cleaning your face and that nose." I grumbled my displeasure but obeyed. Soaking the rag in the warm water, I held it to my face.

I almost cried as the soothing warmth touched my skin. I would never take a bath for granted ever again.

"What happened to you?" Maren whispered. She wet a brush and started working on the knots in my hair. "You just disappeared. Aidric said you'd taken sick, but Tristan noticed your friends were gone too. And now Murphy is the king's right-hand man. Because of valor, the king said. But no one would say why."

I cleaned the blood off my nose and face. Thankfully, my nose wasn't too bad. Hopefully, it wouldn't heal crooked. I couldn't look at Maren's reflection in the mirror.

"Murphy's dead." Maren's hands paused on my head. "Olma is a Wielder. He and the king needed me to—do something. Something bad. I stopped them, but somehow Olma took over Murphy's body. They threw me in the dungeon and they're keeping Erin and John somewhere. I need to find them and get them out of the castle so King Bleddyn can't hurt them."

"You've been in the dungeon all this time?"

I nodded. Somehow, Maren tamed my hair. She braided it and pinned it around my head with precise hands. I'd finished cleaning my face and my arms. When I finished, Maren took the basin back to her bathroom. She wore a coat when she came back.

"There're leftovers from dinner on the table. Eat something. Then go into my dressing room and change."

"What are you doing?" I eyed her warily.

"I'm going to find out where they're keeping John and Erin. Whenever I can't sleep, a guard on night duty keeps me company." She winked. "Be ready to go when I get back and we will get your friends and get out of here."

Dirty dress or no, I hugged her.

"Thank you, Maren."

Tears lined Maren's eyes as she smoothed my hair.

"You're a true friend, Lydia. I've missed you. Now hurry."

CHAPTER THIRTY-THREE

Once Maren left, I headed toward her table. I pulled the sheet to reveal an assortment of meats, dried fruits, and bread. My stomach groaned with hunger. I stuffed a piece of sausage into my mouth. My jaw cramped with the taste. I needed to pace myself. If I ate too much, I would make myself sick. And I needed to be ready for anything. I grabbed a piece of bread and ate it as I made my way to the dressing room.

Maren's closet was smaller than mine, but her clothing was much more elaborate. It took me a few minutes to find a serviceable pair of green breeches and a top with embroidered foxes. Seeing the snow outside, I grabbed a coat and scarf. Thankfully, she had a pair of leather boots that fit me. I sighed at the thought of my purple cloak that Aidric had given me. I'd probably never see it again. But I couldn't dwell on sentimental things right now.

As I was lacing up the boots, I heard the main door to Maren's rooms open. I headed out of the dressing room into

Maren's bedroom. Hopefully, she'd found where Erin and Murphy were.

The sound of another voice stopped me in my tracks.

"There's no one here," Aidric announced.

"Lady Maren said the prisoner had escaped and came to her rooms. Lady Lydia was her friend. I have no reason to disbelieve her. Should we check the other rooms?"

My heart turned to ice. Maren had told the guards I was here. The betrayal hurt me in a way I didn't think was possible anymore. Would my spirit ever recover? Could I trust no one?

I didn't have time to think about it as multiple footsteps headed my way. I ran to the window, but Maren's room was four stories up. There was no way I could jump right now and not severely injure myself. And that wouldn't help John or Erin.

My time was up.

Aidric and four guards entered the bedroom.

My mind went blank as the men filed into the room. The lavish bedroom that had seemed so grand before shrunk. Aidric gripped his sword in one hand. He spotted me standing on the far side of the room and something like anguish dashed across his face.

"Maren was right!"

A guard stepped forward. Aidric threw his arm out to hold him back. The guard lifted an eyebrow at the prince. But Aidric never took his eyes off me.

"Gatebreaker, remember?" another guard muttered. "We don't know what she's capable of." They fanned out behind Aidric, cornering me like hounds around a doe.

"Lydia, come with us and no one needs to get hurt." Aidric stood in the middle of the guards. He extended his hand. It was a cruel twist of fate that even when he was trying to imprison me, the sound of his voice made something warm in me. "Come back to your cell before my father discovers you're gone."

I flinched away from Aidric's outstretched hand. My muscles tensed, readying for action. But nothing happened. No game plan came to mind, no way out of this. I needed to run. I needed to hide. But neither my body nor my magic listened to my internal pleas. Out of the corner of my eye, the guards gripped their weapons. My hands trembled at the thought of returning to that dark cell.

A guard lunged. This time, Aidric was too far away to stop him. He tackled me around the waist and sent me flying into the corner of the bed. I collapsed on the ground, my head spinning with the impact. The guard fell on top of me but then jumped up with a yelp, hands clapped over his eyes. Smoke poured from under his palms.

The world still spun as I looked at my hands. What had I done?

"Lydia!" Aidric's voice brought me back to attention as another guard advanced on me. I struggled to my feet. Everything was happening too fast. The guard lunged for me. I twisted out of his reach, and his hands gripped nothing but air. Now my back was to the wall. I had nowhere else to go.

Just as the other two guards reached me, the lantern above my head exploded.

The blast sent me to my knees. I squeezed my eyes shut and clapped my hands over my ringing ears. Someone grabbed my arm and tugged me with them. I attempted to yank out of their grip, but they were too strong.

Somewhere someone was screaming.

A hand covered my mouth, and the sound stopped.

I opened my eyes just as my captor carried me behind a tapestry into a hidden passageway. The darkness in the passageway smothered me and I struggled again. Whoever had a hold of me held both my hands in one of his and refused to let go. My breaths came in short, quick gasps. I couldn't go back to the darkness. I wouldn't.

There was a tug and grunt, then my captor dropped me onto the ground. I rolled to my feet. We were in a small room adorned with only a tiny window and a single chair.

Aidric pushed the door shut behind us, locking us in the room together.

"Aidric? Let me go."

My voice was half whisper, half plea.

Aidric only shook his head and put his finger to his lips. He knelt next to the short door and pressed his ear against the worn wood. I pulled my dagger from the borrowed sheath on my belt. Freezing up again wasn't an option.

What was he waiting for? Aidric kept his ear pressed to the door, and he didn't look at me. I glanced around the room for a potential escape. There was none. The door Aidric blocked was the only way in or out. Had he called his father? My heartbeat skipped with the thought.

Whatever he was waiting for was over. Aidric stood and whipped around to look at me. Even though my hands still trembled, I raised the dagger between us.

Aidric eyed the dagger with suspicion. He ran a hand through his hair and then grimaced.

"Lydia, what are you going to do with that?"

I lifted the dagger higher.

"I'm not going back to the dungeon."

The panic was clear in my voice.

"I'm not taking you back to the dungeon." He sheathed his sword. "I'm here to break you out."

Again, I had the sensation of the world stopping.

"I don't understand." My hand dropped to my side.

Aidric's arm twitched in my direction, but he stuck both of his hands in his pockets instead.

"You almost foiled my grand plan to come rescue you in two nights. I knew better than to doubt your abilities. I don't know how you broke out with no one noticing. But when Maren and Glen showed up at my door telling me you were in her rooms, I almost lost it on them." He paused; his eyes hooded. "I'm sorry she betrayed you."

She wasn't the only one who had betrayed me lately. I crossed my arms, my dagger still in my hand.

"Why should I trust you?"

Aidric sucked a breath between his teeth. I didn't move.

"Lydia." It was a lie to pretend the crack in his voice didn't thaw something in my core. "I am so sorry. The last time I saw you—everything you said—you were right."

He tapped his toe on the ground and looked up. I glanced in that direction to see a painting of thick green vines adorned the ceiling. An auburn-haired girl stood at the center.

"I grew up with my mother and father telling me how they were going to heal this country. Father always said he would undo the damage of his father's lifetime and put things right. He would give Wielders their rightful place."

Why was he telling me this? I shifted my weight,

glancing up at the painting again. Something about it bothered me.

"You know, just before you got here, I had a plan to contact the rebellion. His false promises got to me. I knew he was up to something. I didn't know what I was going to do, but I knew I had to do something."

"Then why didn't you?"

"Like I told you before." He finally turned his eyes back to me. "My father told me about the threat. Showed me what we were facing and tried to rationalize what he was doing."

"How do you know he isn't lying?"

The hollow laugh barked out of Aidric's throat and startled me.

"That's always the first question you should ask about my father. But he's not lying this time. He showed me what we were up against. I didn't know what else to do but go along with him to save my people."

He stopped talking. I looked away, but his gaze heated my cheeks.

"That's supposed to make me trust you?"

Aidric said nothing. Instead, he took three long strides across the room until we were face to face. An almost forgotten memory of his strong arms wrapped around me surfaced. And I hated myself because part of me knew I'd give anything to have that back again.

Aidric held his hand out between us. A spark lit in his palm. I glanced at his face. All his concentration was on that little flame. Sweat broke on his brow as he let it grow until it was a ball of fire bigger than his fist. The warmth of it covered my face. He released a breath, and it disappeared.

"I can't do much," he offered when I remained speechless. "And the explosion earlier used up most of my reserves."

"Who else knows?" I whispered.

"No one. I've kept it a secret since the day I turned sixteen."

"But... I thought—"

"That neither of my parents are Wielders?" he finished. "That's true."

The implication hung in the air between us. Unable to stop himself any longer, Aidric reached out and brushed a lock of hair that had fallen from my braid. I didn't stop him.

"I don't know who to trust anymore."

"I won't ask you to trust me, not after what I've done." Gently, he tucked his finger under my chin and lifted my head. "But I will spend the rest of my days making it up to you."

My throat constricted. All of this was too much. Too overwhelming.

"And I'm going to start by getting you out of here and to safety."

I turned and sat down in the chair, breaking the physical contact and the intensity of Aidric's words. I propped my arms on my knees and cradled my throbbing head.

"I'm not leaving without Erin and John."

"Nadine is sneaking them out as we speak. It didn't happen exactly the way I envisioned, but I alerted her to set the plan into motion early when the guards informed me you'd escaped. She's hiding them in the city. With John's contacts, they'll be okay."

I tried to stand, but the world spun underneath me, so I stayed in the chair. My weakness threatened to drag me down. I couldn't give in yet.

"I'm going with them."

Aidric stayed silent long enough that I looked up at him. He knelt in front of me.

"Lydia, you can't. You and I trying to stay hidden is going to be hard enough. If we add in John and Erin, they will find us within a day. My father won't look for them. His priority is going to be finding me and you."

He paused.

"They're safer if you're not with them."

The gentleness in his voice threatened to shatter me all over again. He was right. I knew that. But it didn't lessen the pain of being separated from them. I kept talking to shield myself from falling into the pit of my emotions.

"What do you mean we?"

"I'm not sending you alone."

"Aidric, you're the prince!"

"Don't you see? I don't care anymore." His voice rose, but he stopped himself. He spoke softer, but the passion of his words still infused his voice. "My only priority is getting you to safety. Once you're safe, I'm going to make good on my promise and join the rebellion."

"Aidric, if you join the rebellion and your father finds you, he will kill you."

"Let him try." His eyes glinted.

"So where are we supposed to be going?"

Aidric stood, his knees cracking as he pulled a map out of his pocket. He spread it on the floor. I slide from my chair to the ground for a closer look. He pointed at the Golden Forest.

"We go south. We have to find a woman named Taina. Word is she lives in the ruins of Old Galan."

"The castle the forest took back," I muttered. Aidric nodded.

"They say she helps Wielders disappear."

"They say? You don't even know? Then how are we supposed to find her?"

I wasn't sure if I wanted to leave my future in the hands of a woman who lived in a ruined castle.

Aidric pointed to a small, isolated town at the edge of the Golden Forest. Barr.

"We go to Barr and find the inn. Find the innkeeper and tell him we need a room, but we can't pay. We offer two days of work. After that, he'll get us in touch with her. That's all I know."

I sat back on my heels as Aidric folded the map and tucked it away. When I didn't say anything, Aidric stood and pressed his ear to the door once more.

"If they haven't come down the passageway yet, then they don't know about it. They'll try to sound the alarm about your escape. Tristan can stall them for a little, but not forever without raising suspicion. It's now or never, Lydia."

He reached out to help me off the ground. As soon as I was on my feet, I stepped away from his touch.

"Aidric, your father will send his whole army after us. Barr is days away. Weeks, maybe. How are we going to make it without him finding us?"

"The odds aren't good," he admitted. "But what other choice do we have?"

I drew my dagger from its sheath and nodded. Even though I was tired of being backed in a corner, I knew he was right.

"Then let's get on with it."

CHAPTER THIRTY-FOUR

e traveled down the passageway in tense silence. Aidric let me through the dark, using a conjured flame to light our way.

"Only we can see it," he told me in a rushed whisper. It did little to soothe my nerves. Every pop and crack of the castle had me jumping out of my skin. Around every corner, I expected to run into King Bleddyn and Olma.

Aidric led me deftly down hallways and hidden staircases. I thought I'd done a good job unearthing the castle's secrets these past months, but as Aidric tapped a loose stone and revealed another hidden passageway through the building, I realized just how little I knew.

After half an hour that felt like ten years, Aidric opened a door at the bottom of a twisted staircase and cool night air rushed to greet us. I breathed the air deep into my lungs. The cold bit angrily in my throat and on my skin, but I didn't care. The crunch of snow beneath my feet was the best sound in the world.

As we stepped into the courtyard, I couldn't stop myself

from bending down and plucking a small blade of grass. I never thought I'd be outside again. Aidric cleared his throat, and I realized he was waiting for me.

"Come on," he whispered.

His eyes looked watery, but he turned his head before I could get a good look. We were between the castle and the holding wall on the east side, as close to the mountain as we could get.

We stuck to the shadows, pausing anytime we had to cross a moonbeam or a shaft of light from a torch. I didn't have enough magic to wrap us in shadows, so Aidric made extra sure no one spotted us as we used the shadow of the mountain instead.

By the time we reached a door along the wall, my heart pounded so hard, I thought it would leap from my chest. With one more look over his shoulder, Aidric ushered me inside.

A smoldering fire warmed the cozy little room. A bookcase leaned against the far wall. Two full packs sat waiting on the bed.

"This is a room used by the watchmen. The captain made sure no one would be here for a couple of hours." He nodded to the packs. "I hope he packed enough."

I picked up a leather cuff that sat beside one of the packs. Aidric rubbed the back of his neck when he saw what I held.

"It was the best way I could think of to hide your brand."

I flipped my arm over and touched the scarred skin. In the rush to escape, I hadn't even thought about it. A lump formed in my throat as I pulled the leather cuff on and tightened it so it wouldn't slip.

"It's a good idea."

I couldn't name the restless emotion swirling in my chest.

"I need to go see where the watch is and make sure no one is following us."

Without thinking, I grabbed his hand that was on the doorknob.

"You can't leave me."

I heard the panic in my voice, but there was nothing I could do to hide it. I didn't know how to explain what I was feeling. All I knew was that every time I trusted someone, it blew up in my face. And the last time someone had left me alone in a room, they'd returned with guards. I couldn't handle that again.

I didn't have to explain. Aidric read everything I felt on my face. He moved his hand away from the door handle and pulled the map out of his pocket. With deft hands, he tucked it into a pack and then handed the pack to me.

"I will be back. But you have the map now. There's a tunnel behind the bookcase. It will lead you through the mountain, away from the castle. From there, you can double back to avoid Windburn and head south. After I leave this room, you can go without me. Or you can wait for me. It's up to you. But if I haven't returned in fifteen minutes, go."

When I remained silent, Aidric eased out the door.

I didn't even bother moving the bookcase. I wouldn't leave him. There was no way I could make this journey alone. At least that's what I told myself. I didn't want to consider the alternative. That—despite his betrayal—I still had feelings for him.

Now wasn't the time to think about it.

Bread, cheese, and coffee sat on the small table. My nerves made me jittery, and I was sick of bread. But I needed strength. I ate the cheese and washed it down with a glass of coffee, followed by a glass of water. The bread went into my pack for later.

I glanced at the cloak. Five minutes had passed. I fiddled with the stitches on my leather cuff. If I didn't know what it was hiding, I might think it was a decorative bracelet.

Restlessly, I raided the captain's wardrobe. I traded Maren's fancy leather coat and green breeches for sturdy guard pants and a fitted jacket. I kept the embroidered shirt. I'd grown fond of the foxes on it.

Ten minutes gone. I braided my hair again, pulling it up tighter. I grabbed a hat from the armoire to cover it. For extra warmth, I pulled on a pair of gloves and wrapped an extra scarf around my neck.

Thirteen minutes. Would Aidric come back? Had King Bleddyn found him? Had he told them where I was? My anxious thoughts spiraled. The door handle twisted and my heart leapt into my throat. Aidric reappeared.

He couldn't stop the relieved smile when he saw me.

"I thought you'd leave me."

"I couldn't," I told him honestly. My relief at his return was palpable.

"Tristan and I met at our rendezvous point. John and Erin made it safely into the city. Tristan caused a distraction and got them to search for us in the army barracks down by the sea. We planted a boat in the cove to make it look like our getaway plan. But we need to go now before they decide to search the rest of the castle."

We both pulled the packs onto our backs. Aidric pushed aside a bookcase and revealed the squat tunnel behind it. Aidric motioned for me to go first.

"I'll set the bookcase back in place behind us."

I made it to the edge of the tunnel and my feet refused to move forward. My breath hitched in my chest as I stared into the blackness before me.

"I'm scared."

My confession loosened something in Aidric. He pulled me into a tight embrace. His lips rested against my head.

"I know, my dear. I'm so sorry. But you can do this." He took me by the shoulders and pulled me back so he could look down into my eyes. "I know you can."

"I can't."

My eyes brimmed with tears, blurring my view of him.

"I'm not this person. I'm not brave. I don't want to do this anymore." I tucked my face against his coat to hide my shame. "It's too much. Every time I make a decision, someone gets hurt or killed."

His arms wrapped around me. His soothing presence calmed my panicked heart.

"Oh Lydia," the tenderness in the way he said my name made me tuck myself closer to him. "I wish I could make this all go away."

Reluctantly, he pulled back. He wiped a stray tear from my cheek, and I winced slightly when he jostled my nose.

"None of this is your fault."

I wanted to argue, but he held up his finger and continued.

"No, Lydia. It's not. This is not your fault. But my father made it your battle. And if we want to get out of his reach, we have to go now."

"But what then? Do I hide forever? Where do I go?"

"What do you want, Lydia?"

"I just want to go home."

The only problem was, I didn't know where home was anymore.

The words struck something within Aidric. Pain was written on his face.

"Then I will do everything in power to get you home," he choked out. "And the first step is getting you away from this castle."

Without another word, I stepped into the tunnel. The bookcase slid back against the wall with a bang. There was no going back now.

Aidric squeezed by me in the narrow passage. After a moment, light from the magic fire in his hand illuminated his face. With his other hand, he reached back and grabbed one of mine.

Together, we walked into the darkness.

FIREBRAND

michellereneewilson.com/gatebreaker3

ABOUT THE AUTHOR

Michelle Wilson writes stories filled with magic and wonder. She lives in a small town in the heart of the bluegrass state with her family and three dogs. An avid reader, Michelle enjoys reading and writing young adult fantasy. Michelle is a Kentucky girl, ballerina, and lover of all things magic.

Michelle is working on new novels in both of her current series. The Gatebreaker series is a portal fantasy series, and her Animage Academy series is an urban fantasy academy series. You can also find her short stories published in the volumes of the Hidden Worlds Anthology books.

Sign up for Michelle's newsletter for new release announcements at michellereneewilson.com/gatebreakernewsletter/ or sign up for her Patreon to get exclusive behind the scene information and early access to her books!

 patreon.com/michellewilson

ACKNOWLEDGMENTS

First, I'd like to give a shout-out to my very first Patreon member, K.D. Reid. Thank you for supporting me!

This book is my longest according to word count and the time it took me to finish it. It was a labor of love that wouldn't have been possible without my husband and my village for supporting me and helping me make it happen.

Thank you to everyone who has asked about my books, or encouraged me, and read an excerpt along the way. All of you are amazing.

None of my books would be complete with my amazing team that helps me get them ready for publishing consumption. Thank you to Cate Ryan of Cate Edits for her editing skills and helpful advice. Thank you to Elyssa for her amazing proofreading skills. And thank you to Kelley York of Sleepy Fox Studio for another beautiful book cover.

And last but not least, thank you to all of my readers. You make writing and publishing a joy. I hope you enjoy reading the next part of Lydia's story as much as I enjoyed writing it.